"Krista Montgomery. Please step away from the edge," Will said over the microphone.

Krista registered the drop behind her and stepped forward. She waved at him and grinned.

He felt a lift, that same lightness as when she'd hung his arm around her shoulders. "We need to deal with that drop. It's possible that there are other people here as oblivious to danger as my girlfriend."

He stopped. He'd just said Krista was his girlfriend to hundreds of people.

The crowd roared.

"Just finish the speech," Alyssa hissed.

But it was impossible now. He'd spent all day looking forward to seeing Krista. He'd fooled himself into thinking it was because he needed his fake girlfriend, but the truth was, he had just wanted her by his side. Had from the time he'd proposed the plan to her.

And now her as his fake girlfriend was just an excuse...until he found a way to convince her to be his real one.

Dear Reader,

The Montgomerys of Spirit Lake series continues with the youngest of the three sisters, Krista. I had a lot of fun creating this city girl/country boy story. I'm a country girl—I grew up on a farm with a cow-calf operation, which my brother still runs. All the bits about ornery cows and broken machinery are straight from my experience. For the parts about horses, I drove up the road from the family farm to my cousin's. Let me tell you, saddles are hea-vy!

The layout of the Claverley Ranch is based on my experience attending a local rodeo years ago run by a well-known ranching family. I was slinging jerky there, a vendor much like Krista with her speed pedicures, and got a few glimpses behind the scenes of the rodeo life.

I love hearing from my readers. You can contact me via my website, mkstelmackauthor.com, and on Facebook by searching M. K. Stelmack. I'm also on Goodreads, as is the group Harlequin Heartwarming. We Heartwarming authors also have a vibrant Facebook page with frequent guest appearances from the Heartwarming sisterhood.

Enjoy! Hope you all get the chance to have a warm, green country summer.

Best,

M. K.

HEARTWARMING

Her Rodeo Rancher

—

M. K. Stelmack

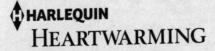

HARLEQUIN®
HEARTWARMING™

ISBN-13: 978-1-335-17989-0

Her Rodeo Rancher

M. K. Stelmack writes historical and contemporary fiction. She is the author of A True North Hero series with Harlequin Heartwarming, the third book of which was made into a movie. She lives in Alberta, Canada, close to a town the fictional Spirit Lake of her stories is patterned after.

Books by M. K. Stelmack

Harlequin Heartwarming

A True North Hero

A Roof Over Their Heads
Building a Family
Coming Home to You

The Montgomerys of Spirit Lake

All They Want for Christmas

Visit the Author Profile page
at Harlequin.com for more titles.

To Lionel and his farm

CHAPTER ONE

KRISTA MONTGOMERY GRIMACED behind her mask as Janet Claverley held up four fingers in serious need of cuticle care. "Spring snowstorm about to hit and four calves wandered off."

Krista tapped the towel encouragingly with her cuticle pusher. "Oh no. Did you find them?"

"They hadn't gone far, but it's all brush, thick as wool, and I wouldn't take Silver in there."

Silver? Oh, the horse. Janet floated her hand down and Krista resumed lifting off more cuticle tissue on one nail than she did on both hands of other clients.

"I went in myself without work gloves, that's why my hands are all scratched up. Laura was supposed to cover, but she was with the caterer. I'll be so glad when her wedding is over and done with."

And when Krista's run of luck would also be over and done with. She'd opened her private salon three months ago in February, and her old high school friend had been her first half-day spa customer. During the manicure, Krista had suggested bridal updos which excited Laura so much that she pleaded with Krista to do them for her and her bridesmaids on the day of the wedding. Up to her ankles in a footbath, Laura then decided what better thank-you gift to her loyal bridesmaids than their own pedicure.

One of those bridesmaids was looking for a hairstylist for her own bridal party. And that sister had a friend who booked massages for *her* bridesmaids. Three bridal bookings in a month. Not bad word-of-mouth business from one wedding.

Proof positive that her salon was her true calling, her rocky social media start aside. And even that online debacle with her ex had only toughened Krista for the challenges of running a business. She'd learned not to give up, focus on first steps, set doable goals, change obstacles into opportunities. She was her own walking motivational poster for determination. Nobody or nothing—including her own fears—would stop her from operating the best little spa around. One that had Janet Claverley, the well-to-do mother of her high school bestie, booking regular treatments after Krista wowed her with an awesome manicure.

She started innocuously. "Laura certainly came up with a great apology gift for leaving the calves to you."

Janet frowned at her nails. "I'm not sure why she thinks I need a manicure. I keep my nails trimmed and clean. And there's not much you can do about the cuts and scrapes."

Didn't she see the state of her cuticles? That she had two hangnails as a result? Lost on Janet was the healing potential of the pampered body. "It's nice to get something you wouldn't give yourself but still secretly want."

Laura's mom eyed the stylized heart on the bathrobe Krista had cajoled her into wearing.

"Why undress for a manicure?" she'd wondered. *"What kind of spa experience is it if someone walks in on us?"*

Janet read the lettering on the bathrobe. "'The heart wants what the heart wants'?"

Krista's motto also featured on her store sign and on her business card. Krista would display it on her social media platforms, too, if she ever got the courage to launch them again.

"We all need to indulge ourselves," Krista

said. There, done with that hand. She rubbed cuticle oil on the nail base.

"You make the heart sound like a tyrannical two-year-old. I told all my children, 'Lose your head, lose your heart.'"

Krista's motto was as much a warning as inspiration, but she couldn't resist teasing Janet. "Laura can barely get out a sentence without mentioning Ryan."

Janet sliced the air with her freshly moisturized hand. "That girl lucked out with him. He'd remembered her from her barrel-riding days, and he ranches, too, so they have loads in common."

Krista took Janet's other hand, every bit as weather-beaten as the first. She'd have to find a way to introduce Janet to her line of oil-based hand treatments. "Insta-love is how Laura describes it."

"Maybe to her, but to me those two simply see eye to eye on a number of very practical matters like money, career, kids, even the trees for their new orchard. Common interests make for lasting relationships."

Provided they really were common. Krista's last relationship had blown up because she'd pretended to like what he'd liked, and that had done them both a disservice.

"It was the same with my husband and me. Dave and I were friends long before we were—" Disgust twisted her mouth. "Goodness, what is all that?"

Krista wiped away tiny white flakes. "Cuticle overgrowth. The stickiest tissue in our body."

The toughened ranch matriarch looked alarmed. "Is it normal?"

"The amount depends on how often the nails are treated," Krista said delicately.

"I really don't have time for all this." Janet looked around at the room Krista had designed for tranquility and comfort. Was there an ever-so-faint note of regret in her voice?

"I'll also apply a layer of filler to smooth out your ridges."

"Ridges? Doesn't everyone have those?"

"Time and wear increase them."

Janet quietened, absorbed with Krista's work. When Krista had cleaned and smoothed the final nail, she wrapped each of Janet's hands in a thick washcloth.

Next, Krista's coup de grâce. She unhooked her mask for filtering out fine nail dust and rubbed her absolute favorite oil into her palms. Lavender—a warm, soothing scent. She unwrapped Janet's hand and laid it gently on her own left hand. Krista's regulars knew at this point to sink into their chair and let the magic happen. Janet stared, her eyes widening when Krista slipped her hand up the sleeve of Janet's roomy bathrobe to her dry, dry elbows. Krista massaged the radius muscle. Janet Claverley had serious tension there.

"I wish," Janet revealed, "that my son Keith had listened to me. He led with his heart and Macey stomped all over it."

Krista wasn't surprised by Janet's sudden confession. She'd discovered her touch unloosed many secrets or hidden desires and fears in her clients. In this case, a mother's anger.

"I can understand her deciding she's not cut out for ranch life. What I can't forgive is how she left him with their child. What kind of mother leaves their baby behind?"

Keith, Krista had learned from Laura, was a single dad to Austin, a year-old go-getter. Krista murmured her agreement and worked her way down to Janet's hand, gently rotating the wrist.

"But Keith always had a type. Leggy, blonde, girly—" Janet stopped, her scornful words lining up with Krista's general appearance. "Not that there's anything wrong with that, per se."

It wasn't the first time Krista had been typecast. When she'd moved to Toronto years ago, her looks had helped her nab a handful of bit parts in films. And it had helped when she'd dabbled in the fashion industry, sold department store perfume and even when she'd sold athletic socks door-to-door, because yes, she had done about everything and traveled about everywhere on the continent, trying on Life's outfits. Now that she'd found the perfect career fit for herself, she'd still take every advantage of her type, but it wouldn't define her. "I understand," she said soothingly. She applied gentle pressure to Janet's hand and her eyelids began to droop. Yes! "The only saving grace is that it's shown Will why it's important to choose your wife wisely."

Will Claverley. Laura's oldest brother. Rodeo star until his shoulder injury last year had sent him into retirement at the ripe age of twenty-nine. Number one ranked bachelor among the bridal party.

Krista knew Will from her high school days with Laura. He'd avoided all of Laura's friends, except for that one instance when Krista at sixteen had stepped in his way and humiliated herself. Ten years on and her face heated at the memory. Heated more from holding hands with his mother who, Krista suspected, had divined her crush on her first-born.

The older woman sighed. "At least I can count on Will. He won't let a girl take advantage of him."

Krista rubbed her thumb on the palm of Will's mother who blinked like a cat lounging in the sun. Another client on the verge of slipping into Krista's pool of sublime nirvana. "I'm hoping," Janet said, sounding drugged, "that he and Dana take their friendship to the next level."

Laura had a very different view of her brother and his childhood friend. *They'll never date*, she'd confided when the topic had arisen during the bridal party pedicure. *Dana is like a sister to him.*

Not for Krista to debate. Will Claverley was none of her business. Krista eased Janet's hand onto the table and wrapped it lightly in the washcloth. She warmed more oil on her palm and reached for Janet's left arm, which the older woman had already extended for her to take. "This is only a small part of what I do during my full massage."

Janet replied by leaning her head against the lavender-scented towel on the chair and closing her eyes. Krista conducted the rest of the massage in silence tampered only by the trickle of the fountain from the corner, the rush of tires through spring puddles outside and the occasional murmur from the afternoon crowd next door at her sister's restaurant.

Krista let herself sink into the experience, too. This, after all, was why she'd decided to open a spa. To use her gift of touch to create a connection with the people who came through her door.

As Krista rewrapped Janet's hand, her client's eyes flickered open. "That full massage… You wouldn't happen to have an opening right now for one, would you?"

I'll be another hour and a half. Can you wait?

HIS MOTHER'S TEXT came at the best possible moment for Will Claverley. He'd rushed through his errands and was now next door to Krista's Place, sharing bread and dip with Dana at Penny's, the restaurant owned by Krista's sister and her husband. He was trying to find a way to ask his lifelong friend out on a date. Again.

Yep. He texted his mother. Take your time.

"That was Mom," Will said. "She's going to be a while longer at the spa."

"Krista's?" Dana said, loading spinach dip onto her bread. "Laura goes on about her magic hands."

Wasn't that the truth? Ever since Krista had returned to Spirit Lake to stay last November her name had floated around the supper table with the same regularity as the salt and pepper shakers. "Laura has always thought Krista can do no wrong."

"No kidding." Dana bit down on her bread, greenish-white dip sticking to her chin. "Krista used to fly in from Toronto every year or so and spend a few hours with Laura, but now that she's home to stay they're best buddies again."

Will tapped his chin, and Dana scrubbed off the dip with her napkin. "Those two were always best buddies, didn't matter the distance."

"True."

A silence borne of a lifetime of friendship settled between them. Usually it was a comfortable one, but Will's self-imposed assignment kept him chewing on the bread like it was a cud. Dana spoke first. "I was wondering...do you know if Keith wants my help with Austin at Laura's wedding? I mean, he's groomsman, right?"

Will gave his brother a mental kick in the shin. Dana and Austin had taken to each other from the day she first smooched his week-old face, but Keith shouldn't take advantage of her love for Austin. "I'll have him give you a call."

"You don't have to," she said quickly. "If he wants to get in touch with me, he has my number. I mean, he and I are friends, right?"

Her voice held a note of doubt. That kick might become more than mental. "I'd say you're more of a friend to Keith than he is to you. I think he's counting on your help but what if you are busy that day?" If this meeting went well, he would keep her occupied, for sure.

"I'm going to the wedding anyway. And frankly, I'd rather be with Austin than mixing with that big crowd."

"Could be a dry run for your wedding."

"No way will my wedding be that big. It'll be quick and painless. Early afternoon service, luncheon, then done."

"No dance?"

"Pointless when there'll only be a couple

dozen people there. Most will be non-dancers like me."

"Couple dozen? Is that all?" That was how many Claverleys got together for Christmas dinner. He'd always pictured a wedding as big as possible without it taking too long to plan. But after watching Laura take nearly a year to plan her special day, maybe he could downsize. More economical, too.

"Yep, definitely keeping it small." Dana shoved another chunk of bread into her dip. "All I'm missing is the groom."

Here went nothing. "I might be able to fix that."

Dana popped bread into her mouth. "Don't tell me. You're going to introduce me to one of your rodeo buddies."

"Not exactly."

"Because you know how I feel about those so-called cowboys. Absolutely useless when it comes to roping a calf out of the ring."

"I was thinking more—"

"I'd like to see any one of them catch a calf that's got a quarter section and two hundred head to hide in."

Would she let him get a word in? "Me," Will said. "I meant me."

Dana swallowed. Maybe she had bread

stuck in her throat, because she swallowed again. "You're not serious," she hissed. "You and me? Married?"

"Not married," Will said, his voice dipping to her level. "I mean, maybe. I just thought that it was about time we notched our relationship up a level."

Dana's eyes narrowed. "Your mother said that. Last week at the shower. She talked about how she was glad Ryan and Laura took their relationship to the 'next level.'"

"I didn't hear her say that," Will said truthfully, dodging the other accusation, but Dana had it all figured out. That was the downside of their longtime friendship. She knew his thoughts before he did.

"You're taking your mother's advice about who you should date," Dana said.

"I'm not taking her advice but she does have a point." That sounded lame. He tried again. "She said what I was already considering."

"Right," Dana said. "Will, we've already talked about this. Remember?"

Of course, he remembered. It had been after his first championship five years ago. High on his victory and the attention of buckle bunnies, he'd asked Dana if she wanted to date him. In retrospect, he had made it sound as if he was doing her a favor. She told him that if he valued their friendship, he wouldn't bring up that stupid idea again.

But now he was no longer a rodeo star, which he figured upped his ranking in Dana's eyes. "I was thinking we could revisit that talk."

"Why would we ever revisit it? Nothing's changed."

Will shifted in his seat, the uncalculated motion catching his right shoulder in a white-hot vise grip. Time to book another never-ending physio appointment that lessened but never eliminated the pain.

Dana noticed. "Your shoulder."

"It's acting up some."

"Ah, that explains it. *We* haven't changed, but *you* have. Your injury bumped you off the circuit a couple of years before you intended and suddenly you want to settle down, get married, live happily ever after on the family ranch."

She made him sound dull and plodding. But he'd seen enough of the world to know he'd had the good fortune of being born exactly where he wanted to be. That he also wanted a good woman and a family to share his part of the world with—like every other Claverley firstborn—made him...traditional.

He searched for common ground with Dana. "You've got to admit we agree on a lot of things."

"No, we don't. We agree to disagree on a lot of things, which doesn't work well in a relationship. Especially marriage."

"We're not that far apart."

"Really? You prefer early or late calving?"

"Somewhere in between."

She looked peeved, like Keith when he'd shot off the same question.

"Where would we live? My place or yours?"

"My place."

Her lips thinned. He fumbled for an explanation. "My yard is bigger. We'd have more room to build our own house."

"And horses? How many?"

As many as he could fit. He wanted to go big on horses, since his rodeo days were over. "That," he said, "is nonnegotiable."

"My point. I threw a bunch of questions at you, and you and I didn't line up on any of them."

Will tried one last one. "Kids?"

"Yes."

"There you go. We agree."

"I want four."

"Uh…"

"Exactly."

"But you're already thirty. Don't you think that's a little unreasonable?"

"Don't I know it? Don't I know that with every ticking minute, I'm getting further away from where I want to be?"

Beneath her snappish anger, Will heard her pain. "I'm sorry, Dana. If you're so set against me, do you have anybody in mind?"

Dana sighed, not all dreamy-like, more exasperated. "Yeah, I do. But he doesn't notice me that way, and never has. And don't even ask me his name because I'd set myself on fire before I'd tell you."

"So what's his name?"

"I just said—" She stopped when she saw his grin, and reluctantly smiled.

Back on safer ground but uncertain where they stood, Will decided to ask about a different matter. "Since we're both single for now, are we still on for the rodeo?" Ever since Will had made it big, he'd collected points, trophies…and the attention of buckle bunnies. When he'd been on the circuit, he'd spent his downtime dodging them. And every year when the rodeo came to his family ranch for five days, Dana posed as his girlfriend to give him a break.

She tossed down her half-chewed chunk of bread. "You know what? You're right. I'm not getting any younger. And pretending to hook up with you for any amount of time will not get me where I want to be."

She stood. "Your turn to pick up the bill." She started to leave, then whipped back around. "Wait. Even that's changing. We go dutch. No. Even that implies we're in a relationship." She slapped a ten on the table. "You deal with the rest."

"Dana," he called after her. "We still friends?"

"Sure, Will, sure. But we both know that's not what either of us should be going after."

After she left, Will sat back. He grasped the what of the matter, but no longer the who. And truth be told, he was relieved that Dana had shot him down again. She'd make a good wife for someone else. But she was right—he needed someone he had more in common with.

FROM BEHIND THE steering wheel of his truck, Will watched his mother emerge from Krista's spa. She blinked and raised her face to the sun, then lowered it to take in the fresh blue expanse of the lake across the street, finally snow-free here at the end of April. She carried a mint green paper bag that she swung as she walked—no, strolled—her way to the truck, settling into the passenger seat like a hen onto her nest.

His mother moved to lift her hand, but as if made of cement, it fell to her lap. Her nails were painted a shade of pink he'd never seen before. Sort of orange, like a sunset. "I had a massage. It was…heavenly."

She never used that word to describe anything.

"Uh, good to hear, Mom. You deserve to put your feet up."

"I do," she murmured and smiled as if she'd received secret wisdom.

What had Krista done to his mother? The exterior of Krista's Place was all done up in light blues and greens. On the step was a giant vase filled with grasses and dried flowers. All innocent and friendly and inviting. Except inside was Krista with her magic hands turning sharp-tongued mothers into boneless dreamers.

They drove the seven miles home in silence. His mother didn't ask about the groceries she'd asked him to pick up, whether he'd bought the spaghetti that was on sale, or if he'd placed the order for binder twine. She didn't ask about his meetup with Dana, something he was grateful for. Instead, she leaned back and closed her eyes, and didn't open them until he pulled to a stop at the ranch house.

She stepped out, slow and easy. The house had the advantage of being sheltered by spruces planted there by his grandparents, but was set high enough on a hill to give a view of the barn, corrals and beyond that to the pastures. His mother contemplated the view, her head tilted, like she was admiring a painting.

Into the picture walked his father from the barn. He lifted his gaze to them, and Will's mother waved. A little finger waggle, her pinky raised. Weird. Will grabbed a couple bags of groceries and went inside the house. Normally, his mother would have picked up the last two, but today she had cooked noodles for arms.

When he returned for the rest, his father had his mother up against the passenger door— and they were kissing! His dad's cowboy hat obscured the exact particulars, but from the way their bodies were cinched together there was no mistaking the nature of things.

He'd never seen his parents kiss, other than the odd peck or two on special occasions. Nothing like this full-body engagement.

He tried to sneak the last two bags from the driver's side without a sound, but they broke apart. Whatever Krista had infected his mother with, his dad had caught it, because both of them had the same heavy-lidded, sun-warmed look.

"I suppose," his mother said, "I should go inside and fix us a bite to eat." Then she sauntered to the house, the little green bag swinging away.

His dad watched her as Will moved to follow with the grocery bags.

"Hey," his father said, "I'll take those."

He stepped in front of Will. "Do you know what's got into her?"

"She went for a manicure at Krista's Place. She stayed on for a massage, and she came out like this."

His father stripped the grocery bags from Will's hold. "You go back to Krista's and sign her up for more of where this came from."

"What? Now?"

His dad was already following his wife inside. "What are you still doing here?"

CHAPTER TWO

WILL PULLED UP to Krista's Place in time to see the "Open" sign with the front silhouette of a woman flipped to her curvy backside marked "Closed." He cleared the two steps in one leap, rattling the vase of grasses, and rapped on the door.

Common sense told him to leave it for another day, except his curiosity had got the better of him. He'd barely exchanged a dozen words with Krista in a decade, but between Laura and now his mother, he wanted to see what was happening for real.

The wooden blinds parted to reveal a cheek and blue eye. He called, "I'm sorry, could we talk a moment?" A family of four on the sidewalk looked at him, then at the sign with its crazy, illogical motto.

He must sound like some heartbroken guy begging for another chance. C'mon, Krista.

The lock snapped back and the door opened. There she was. Tall, blonde, blue-eyed. Hard to deny her beauty, even in her casual getup of white cargo pants and yellow top. Ten years on, and he still felt her pull.

Her hip jutted out. "Will. What can I do for you?"

"It's actually not me. It's my mom. She was here earlier."

A tiny V-frown appeared on her forehead. "Janet left not a half hour ago. Is she okay?"

"She's a lot okay. That's why I'm back here. My dad sent me. He'd like to get—" what did "more of where this came from" exactly constitute? "—book another appointment. Or session. Or whatever you call it."

Her lips twitched into a near smile. He didn't blame her. If he looked half as foolish as he felt, he could understand if she doubled over with laughter.

Her hip curved out a titch more. "Ever hear of a phone?"

Well now, he'd never thought of that. What did that say about how badly he wanted to see her? "I—I prefer to do this in person." It was the truth, although it came off as if they were about to undertake a shady transaction.

She straightened and opened her door wider. "I appreciate your honesty, Will."

He might as well have stepped into her

home. There was a light blue sofa piled with yellow cushions. Curtains, blue and yellow, hung on the large front window. Wood plank flooring in warm browns. A couple of deep armchairs angled to each other, an art book on the small table between them. A fountain took up another corner, the little terraces wet and dark from where water had probably spilled those irritating trickles like a tap not properly shut off. A scent hung in the air—half like freshly cut hay and half another kind of sweet cleansing smell.

He picked out details of her business. A coat stand of bathrobes. Shelving with thick towels, and lines of lotions and shampoos along with small dark blue or brown glass bottles. Likely one or two of them had ended up in his mother's little bag. On the wall was a large, antique mirror with an old-fashioned dresser in front covered with hair paraphernalia, and a swivel leather chair for cutting hair.

Krista stepped behind a table in the same blue as the sofa and sat at a matching wood chair, tapping on her phone. "When did your mother want to come back?"

"If it was up to my dad, later tonight."

This time, she didn't hold back her smile. She had a great one. Quick and so wide her eyes crinkled up. "I'm glad she enjoyed herself in the end."

"She didn't take to it right away?"

"She seemed to think it was an unnecessary expense on Laura's part."

"An expense my dad will happily pay."

"I do have a loyalty card, if you—or your dad—is interested." From a little basket she handed him her card. White with her business name in the same blue as the chair, underscored with "The heart wants what the heart wants."

He was tempted to find out what she meant by that roundabout motto, but then again, he'd taken on enough matters of the heart for one day without asking for more. He flipped the card over. Ten small squares with FREE filled in the last box and in smaller letters "Any service of your choice."

"What all did you do to her?"

"A manicure and then a full body massage. I also do wraps, pedicures, facials, full hair packages. I don't do extensions but that shouldn't matter in your mom's case."

Good, because he'd no idea what extensions were.

Krista seemed to sense his quandary. "Here. I have a Mother's Day package. It includes a massage, body wrap, facial and her choice of a manicure or pedicure. Plus, the purchaser also receives a complimentary service. I'll write it up as a gift card today, and then she can call me whenever to book her day."

"Day?"

She turned over the pamphlet and pointed to the price at the bottom. Holy. Then again, it was for a full day. And his dad would pay him back. Except it was a *Mother's* Day special, and he'd yet to find a way to thank his mother for being right there for him during his surgeries.

"All right. I'll take that, then."

"Sure. And what service would you like?"

Will couldn't imagine ever submitting to any of her services, especially when they'd be one-on-one in her half home. He hadn't been alone with Krista since she was sixteen, leaning against his truck, so close he could've pulled her into his arms and she would've let him. It had taken every shred of willpower to step away from her. Back then, Krista had dated many and stuck with none. She'd made no bones of the fact that she was leaving town as soon as she could, and he didn't think he had what it took to make her stay. After he'd set young Krista back on her heels, they'd dodged each other.Until now, when he'd entered her space. Still, he wasn't prepared for her magic hands on him. He'd seen what she'd done to his hard-as-nails mother. "How about I'll take it as a gift certificate and pass it on to someone else?"

"I'm sorry, the certificates are nontransferable."

"You made the rules. Can't you change them for male customers?"

"A lot of men enjoy my spa services, particularly the pedicures."

She was teasing him, he was sure of it. Her eyes were extra wide and her mouth pinched tight against laughter.

"How about I just decline the service?"

She set her elbows on the table and rested her chin on her hands. "Scared to bare your feet to me, Will Claverley?" She made soft chicken-clucking noises.

"Fine. I'll do it. How about now?" This far on in the day, she'd haggle for another time and he could say he was busy and save face.

Her mouth dropped open. Ha, she hadn't expected that. She glanced at her phone, probably scrambling for a way out. But then she raised her blue eyes, the same ones that had nearly ensnared him a decade ago. "Sure, let's do it."

Shoot.

From the coat rack, she unhooked a pair of men's pajama bottoms and pointed to a rear room. "Unless you can roll your pants up to your knees, time to change. Then meet me back here."

KRISTA HAD EXPECTED Will to reject her. Give her the same easy smile, same regretful head tilt, and tell her he had other plans. That's why she laid on the chicken noises, pushing him, because she trusted he'd push right back. Instead he'd countered with the perfect chance to reject *him* and she'd caved. He emerged from the changeroom. The slouchy pajama bottoms in blue plaid clashed with the bright red plaid of his shirt. He'd removed his hat and his thick, brown hair was a mess. He wore the slippers she also supplied to her clients, and he looked ready for a night at home watching movies with—with someone special.

Krista snapped her attention back to her clipboard. "I—uh, need you to fill out my Health History form since you're a first-time client. It's confidential, it makes me aware if there are any services I shouldn't perform."

He took the clipboard and his hazel eyes widened. "I filled in less when I went for surgery on my shoulder."

She already knew about his injury from Laura. He'd been kicked by a horse named Tosser. He'd undergone emergency surgery, followed by months of painful rehabilitation. He'd quit the circuit, his family relieved that his career hadn't ended more seriously. Krista was pretty sure Will wouldn't appreciate that his sister had divulged his personal information nor would Laura like her confidentiality with Krista breached. Better to pretend ignorance and disinterest. "See? Now that I know about that, I won't suggest a massage, or at least not there."

He raised his eyes from the checklist. "No way are you ever giving me a massage."

Krista's cheeks blazed. His tone was every bit as final as when he'd knocked back her advance in high school. Well, he wasn't the first one who'd made her feel stupid. She forced herself to give him a perky smile. "So I take it a makeover is out?"

He paused again. "I'd say. I'm allergic to most creams. Break out something horrible."

He didn't crack a smile, and she wondered if he was teasing or telling the truth. A lot more men now were using moisturizers as a matter of course and his rodeo champion status might have required some kind of beauty regime for the cameras.

He returned the clipboard and she scanned his responses. *Right shoulder. Right elbow. Right wrist.* A whole lot of hurt for one arm. One very muscled arm. *Left knee. Occasional pain.* She came to the comments: *leg spasms. Will kick without warning.*

"Ha. Duly noted." She gestured to her chair, her prize possession. She'd found it on Kijiji at a rock-bottom price, and unbelievably, in immaculate condition. But Will eased gingerly into the black leather with the mahogany tray and elevated foot rest, as if mounting one of his broncs.

"Relax. Enjoy." Once his back made contact with the chair, she switched on the Shiatsu massage. He squirmed as the kneading rods rolled upward along his spine. When they reached his shoulder area, his suspicion faded and he breathed out. "This isn't bad."

"Like a little heat?"

"Where?"

"With electrodes to your prefrontal cortex. On your back, silly. Here. I'll power it on, and you decide for yourself."

She knew the exact moment the heat hit him. He melted, his shoulders sinking down. The tension in his face disappeared. He must be in constant low-level pain. She hoped he was getting physio or massages from someone.

"I could get used to this," he said.

"So the chair can give you a massage, but not me?"

"I've seen what you did to my mother. I need to operate a vehicle to get home, so no thanks."

That was almost a compliment. She decided to take it.

"You relax while I prepare the basin. You can adjust with the remote."

While in the bathroom, she texted her sister to say she'd be late with a client.

You just said you were done for the day, Mara responded.

A walk-in. For a pedicure.

That needed doing right now?

If she so much as mentioned Will to Mara, the double whammy of psychologist and sister, there would be no extracting herself until a full analysis under the influence of wine and chocolates was completed. Her other sister, Bridget, might also be called in. A long story. I'll explain when I get home. Around 8. Then she ditched her phone and quickly carried the full basin to Will to avoid any more badgering texts.

She tossed in a handful of salts, and switched on the heat and vibration modes.

"Who knew a pedicure was so high-tech?" Will said as she pulled up to his soaking feet on her wheeled stool, also a black leather one. She felt a spurt of proprietary pride at how impressed he was with her setup. Not for nothing had she brought in the best of the best…at the cheapest of the cheapest.

"Don't worry. There'll be plenty of hands-on work." She'd made it sound as if he was looking forward to her touching him. Which they both knew wasn't the case. She patted the footrest. "Bring those puppies up here and we'll start."

Her work was cut out for her. Side calluses, rough heels, dryness, nail ridges, overgrown cuticles. She might have to send a second text to Mara, tacking on an extra half hour.

She thought her expression was neutral enough but then he said, "You don't need to go whole hog on them. We'll be here all night."

How insulting. "First, we won't be here all night. Second, your feet *deserve* my pedicure. These two babies might be the farthest body part from your head, but they've been with you every step of your life. The least you can do is treat them to my care."

They regarded each other down the long length of his legs, then his toes did a wiggly dance. "Well, then. Have at 'em."

Krista clipped 'em, nipped 'em, soaked 'em, and then she applied the paddle to remove the calluses. His foot jerked in her lap. He squirmed, grinning.

She gasped. "Oh, I'm sorry, I didn't mean that." How embarrassing. The last thing she wanted Will Claverley thinking was that she was deliberately tickling him.

She tried again with a firmer stroke. His foot twisted in her grasp like a caught fish. "You're doing it," he sputtered from laughter, "on purpose."

"I swear I'm not. It happens if I don't apply enough pressure. Here, I'll switch to a coarser grade. That might help."

It didn't. He giggled, tried to squelch it and

up it bubbled again. "Couldn't we skip this step?"

"Will, that would be like—I dunno—you in the rodeo, asking if you can skip the step of actually riding the horse."

"I can't keep laughing."

"No," she said, "that most certainly won't do."

He frowned. "You're not making fun of me, are you?"

It was hilarious actually, and with any other client, they'd both be giggling. But if what his heart wanted was not to laugh, then that's what she would deliver. "No," she said honestly, "I'm not."

He sat back. "Talk to me, then. Distract me. Tell me what's been going on in your life."

What about her life could possibly interest him? "Well, as you can see, I run my own little spa. I opened up in February and it's been going great. I could always do with more clients." She bit her lip. That was unprofessional of her to complain about lack of business to a client. Because really, that's all Will was. She gave a quick swipe of his foot and pressed his sole with her hand, as if she'd pulled off a wax strip. His grin faded. "Okay, I'm good. Continue."

"I, uh, offer a full range of spa treatments—manicures, pedicures, massages. I—uh—" swipe, apply pressure, wait for grin to pass "—also am a hairstylist."

Swipe and apply pressure. "So what made you decide to open this spa?" Will squeaked out.

She could tell him of her epiphany while giving an impromptu foot massage to a tired actress in Toronto but Will wanted a distraction, not a longwinded testimonial. Better to keep it simple. "Because I finally found something I was good at."

"Found? You never struck me as somebody who had to find a thing. More like you could take your pick."

Another almost compliment. She couldn't be sure if he meant it but Will Claverley had never held out on her before. Still, it was odd to hear him say nice things to her, to even confess that he wanted to see her in person. It felt too much like how she'd wanted him to be ten years ago.

"Look, why don't I charge through both feet as fast as possible and then you can relax and we won't need to talk about me anymore?"

He gripped the arms of his chair and gave her the go-ahead nod.

Two minutes later, he lay back in his chair, breathing heavily but free of giggles.

"I think it's over," she mock-whispered. She stroked the sensitive middle part of his foot. He didn't flinch. "Indeed, we're done here."

Their eyes met. They had created a new memory between them. Something else besides the decade-old humiliation. One of lightness and laughter and touch, though not one he'd want repeated or spoken of. She'd keep the secret of his ticklish feet, just as he'd kept silent about her asking him out. For which Krista was eternally grateful.

She cupped her hands around his feet. "This'll be our second little secret."

Will hesitated, then gave a brief nod.

"All right, then," she said quickly, "bath time." She lowered his feet into the basin, searching for something to say.

He seemed happy to stick to the subject of her, though. "So," he said. "you were saying business is going great."

"Thanks to your sister. She's brought a lot of business my way. Word of mouth is big in this line of work."

"That and giving a service people keep coming back for."

She didn't know if that was yet another compliment, so she went with a neutral "True." She lifted his dripping foot onto her lap and wrapped it in a towel. "I guess the key is to find enough mouths to put the word into."

"Who are your clients?"

"Women. All ages, really. Right now, I'm trying to cast out as wide a net as possible and then if I develop a niche, focus on expanding that." Finished with drying his foot, she applied lotion and began her foot massage. His eyes widened and he tensed. She said nothing, and he slowly relaxed. Twice in the same day, a Claverley had succumbed to her magic touch.

Instead of sinking into silence, however, Will seemed determined to fight it with talk. "Who have you been catching?"

This was where the truth came out. "To be honest, friends of Laura, married or getting married. Which means they either live on a ranch or are marrying into a ranch or cattle operation. So yeah, my niche so far is country, especially country weddings."

"I'm going to quite a few weddings myself. Which ones are you involved in?"

Krista hesitated, not sure if she ought to reveal the names of her clients. Then again, everybody knew everybody in Spirit Lake, and hadn't Will already proved he could be discreet? "There's Laura's and Ryan's. I'm a guest."

"Best man here."

"There's Laura's friend, Caris. I'm doing hair for the bridal party, and she also wants me there for the photographs."

"I'm a groomsman."

"Amanda's wedding?"

"Guest only."

"Me, too. High school friends. I'm also doing bridal makeup."

She set aside his freshly massaged foot and patted her lap. He obediently lifted his other foot for its turn. "I have an idea," he said, "that might help us both."

Us both. As if they were partners. Krista feigned disinterest. "Oh?"

"You remember Dana?"

Her excitement fizzled. Had Laura got it wrong about their sibling-like status and Will was about to spring for a bridal package? No, Laura would've said something. Anyway, it shouldn't matter either way. She began to massage his foot with the same professional care she gave to every client.

"I do," Krista said. "You two are buddies."

"We are, but the thing is she used to help me out when the rodeo came to the ranch." He hitched in his seat and looked as uncomfortable as when she'd been scraping at his feet. "We had an agreement. We've never dated, but during those few days, we'd pretend to because when I was in the rodeo, I—uh—got a lot of…unintended attention."

Krista knew those girls. "Buckle bunnies." Girls who hung around rodeos to hook up with a cowboy and if not, to steal his trophy buckle, or at least vie for bragging rights.

"Yeah. But when Dana was by my side, she kept them on the other side of the fence, so to speak."

Krista had no idea where he was going with this. Was he going to introduce Krista to the buckle bunnies as prospective clients?

"Only this year, Dana can't help. I don't want to get into her reasons.

"So, I'm kinda short my—uh, pretend girl-friend."

"But why do you need one? You won't be competing in this year's rodeo, right?"

"No, and I probably won't get as much interest because of that, but I was still planning to do a celebrity ride. It's a fundraiser for Alyssa's nephew."

Alyssa was Laura's maid of honor, and she'd told Krista about the event herself. Jacob had been in and out of the hospital for leukemia treatments since January. Alyssa and her family's fear must be constant. Krista would be devastated if either of her nieces, nine and six, got that diagnosis. Will's ride would raise money for the Alberta Children's Hospital in Calgary, a short two-hour drive away. "Why not ask Alyssa to be your fake girlfriend?"

Will hitched again. "Well, that's the thing. I get the feeling she's...more into me than I'm into her."

Krista sympathized with Alyssa. She knew exactly how it felt to get the big thumbs-down from Will. "And you don't want to send mixed signals."

"Right. So... I was thinking..." He looked at her long and hard.

No. He couldn't possibly— "You want *me* to be your fake girlfriend?"

"Only for those few days. You and I seem to get along well enough and we both agree we're not exactly suited."

"Yes," Krista said firmly, "definitely. Polar opposites. And opposites attract but then—"

"Blow apart," Will concluded.

He sounded like his mother. Krista cut to the point. "You want me to be your girlfriend because we mix like cake and cabbage. We both know that we don't want each other so we don't have to worry about hurt feelings. I get it. Sure."

He blinked. "Don't you want to know what you'll get out of it first?"

That would've been the obvious thing to ask. Instead she'd come off sounding no better than a buckle bunny. She set aside his freshly massaged foot. "You as my A-list client?" she joked.

He smiled, not a suppressed giggly kind, but a wide, open one for her and her alone. "Even better. How about five days of you schmoozing with the entire rodeo crowd from central Alberta, exposure to hundreds. Even if you picked up a half-dozen clients, wouldn't that be worth it?"

It would be. Every month was still touch-and-go. She couldn't fail. Not when she was finally where she was meant to be and doing what she was meant to do. "When's the rodeo?"

"Second weekend in June."

About six weeks away. "That'll work."

"We have a deal?"

"Deal."

Will leaned back and closed his eyes. Technically, she'd finished her massage but for the first time since entering, he appeared entirely relaxed. She wheeled her stool gently away. A few minutes more of making her latest client happy couldn't hurt.

CHAPTER THREE

"YOU?" BRIDGET SAID. "Will Claverley's fake girlfriend?"

"Didn't I just finish saying that?" Krista tapped her sister's empty wineglass. "How about I drive you home now?"

"No way. Girls' night out. The one night of the week I drink, even if it's a Thursday."

"Pick-on-Krista-night more like."

"You have to admit," said Mara, ever the diplomat, "that you have introduced a remarkable element into the evening."

The sisters were out on the deck, taking in the last rays of the setting sun from the upper balcony of the townhouse Krista and Mara rented. It was usually one of Krista's favorite times of the week, but not when she was in the hot seat. She had reasoned that by waiting a few days to casually inform her sisters of her deal with Will, she could pass it off as an incidental tidbit.

Instead, they were turning it into a full

meal. "It's not at all remarkable. We're together four, five days off and on."

Bridget filled her wineglass to the brim. "What's 'off and on'? How exactly does this arrangement work? Do you pretend to kiss but then don't?"

Krista wondered herself. She cut herself another slice of lemon meringue pie. Not only was Thursday her weekly dose of sisterhood but also of dessert. "I guess we'll figure it out when the time comes. He and Dana must've come up with a system. I'll do the same thing. Except I'll come with business cards."

"As long as it doesn't involve you and horses. You're terrified of them."

"Will is well aware I'm not a horsey or ranch-y kind of person. That's the point."

Mara perked up. "The point? Wouldn't the point be to have a fake girlfriend that could— well, fake it? Not somebody so obviously unsuited."

"No." Krista wrapped her mouth around her forkful of pie and pulled it slowly off. Heaven. "This way, there is zero danger we'll become a couple for real and complicate things."

Mara opened her mouth to speak but Bridget interrupted. "The Claverley Rodeo is a huge deal in this town. Jack and I have upped the restaurant's food orders and plan on three full breakfast sittings from Thursday to Sunday, and we're opening for dinner service, too. Every year the rodeo gets bigger. People come from Saskatchewan, Montana, you name it. And—" she pointed her finger at Krista "—the media gets bigger, too."

"But the focus is on the cowboys and the ranch and…those kinds of things. Not me."

"And did that matter when it came to Phillip?"

The tang of the pie soured in her mouth. The pain of her breakup with her Toronto boyfriend still chafed. In November, she'd flown back to Spirit Lake for her aunt's funeral, but she'd stayed longer than intended. Phillip had given her an ultimatum: come back to him now or stay put. When her Auntie Penny's will bequeathed her a commercial unit to launch any business her heart desired, her answer was clear. She'd called him to break things off. He'd barely uttered a dozen words during that conversation, apparently saving up all his fury for the days and weeks ahead.

It started with a post on Instagram showing a picture of her clothes inside a dumpster with the attached lines, "This is what happens

when my ex doesn't heed the move-out date."
His followers and even some of hers whom
she'd counted as friends joined in with their
own hyena-like nasty comments.

Except it hadn't stopped there. Next he
posted photos of his new girlfriend with innuendoes about how she could be trusted—
unlike some. Krista posted a pic of Krista's
Place with its boarded-up windows and crum-
bling steps before the renovations. She'd wanted
to share her own excitement and, yeah, maybe
let everyone out there know she was about
more than appearances, that she was willing
to put in the hard work. She'd prettied up the
image with the lettering "The heart wants what
the heart wants."

Her one-time friends had a field day with
backhanded comments. "Congratulations!
Hope you get everything you deserve." "This
a picture of your heart?" "No, the guy's after
she's done." After a few attempts at lighthearted replies which only spurred more
snarkiness, she stopped responding alto-
gether.

Meanwhile Phillip and his pack tagged her
in photos with the hashtag #becausekrista-
wants. Next a picture of a freakish blonde
plucking hundred-dollar bills from a guy's

back pocket. The same blonde stabbing a heart, and then an image of her roundhouse kicking a guy.

Phillip had been able to stage the photos because he freelanced as a set photographer. The hashtag trended for an incredible three weeks. *Krista* became an Instagram meme for any chick who crushes hearts in pursuit of shallow dreams.

Krista had closed her Instagram account with her seven thousand followers and, because Instagram was connected to Facebook, she'd shut off her four thousand followers there, too. She didn't have a profile on Twitter and didn't dare open one, dead certain she'd be hunted down and trolled. She had retained her website which she could control and had deleted one nasty comment after another from her contact page.

"All that stuff with Phillip has died down," she said. "I haven't had any action for the past two weeks or so."

Bridget scrolled through her phone. "Things are already coming up for the Claverley Rodeo on Facebook and Instagram. It's going to be hard to avoid."

Flutters of panic rose up in Krista but her bossy, well-meaning sister was not going to fluster her. "It's not like that crowd in Toronto is searching up a rodeo, anyway."

Bridget pulled a face. "No, but they will hunt you up."

"I'm not on social media, so there's no linking back to me. Anyway, Will shies away from the media spotlight. That's the reason he wants me to run interference. So he can sneak away from it all." He actually hadn't said that, but it was a safe assumption.

"You might not be on social media, but Laura and Alyssa are," Bridget reminded her. "Krista, I'm worried that one wrong photo will bust it wide open for you again, except this time your Spirit Lake rodeo friends will be dragged into it."

"Laura will be on her honeymoon, and Alyssa and I aren't all that close. I will talk to Will and explain the situation, if I have to. Okay?"

Bridget didn't seem convinced, but Krista had quieted her for the moment. She enjoyed a breath. "Can I now enjoy the rest of the evening with my two favorite sisters?"

Bridget snuggled down into the patio cushions, but Mara stayed upright. Her eyes were thoughtful and penetrating when she turned them to Krista. Uh-oh.

"Wasn't Will Claverley the one you once asked out and he refused?"

Bridget shot to full alert. "What's this?"

Mara gestured to Krista to take the stage, which she grudgingly did. "It was a lifetime ago. I was sixteen. He was twenty."

Bridget gasped. "You asked out a twenty-year-old when you were only sixteen? Did Mom know?"

And this was exactly why she'd sworn Mara to secrecy. "No! Anyway, considering I was old enough to have a driver's license, I was old enough to date a guy four years older than me."

Bridget snorted her disagreement but circled her hand for Krista to continue. "It was over at Laura's place. I'd had a couple of drinks, and he was older and good-looking, and so I went for it. He said, 'I appreciate you thinking of me that way, but I don't see us going anywhere, thank you.' And that was that."

"Is that what he said?" Bridget asked.

"Word for word."

"Ten years later and you remember it verbatim," Mara remarked, licking her lips after her last bite of pie.

Except her remarks weren't ever just remarks. They went soul deep. That probably accounted for her small but very dedicated client base. She was like a wise oracle that people pilgrimaged to. It didn't help that she also dispensed her wisdom to Krista when it wasn't asked for.

"What can I say? It was classic."

"And," Bridget said, "it was probably the only rejection you ever got."

She was right. Krista had never had to ask for a date. More to the point, she'd never felt as compelled to ask a guy out as much as she had with Will. And that seemed to be the point Mara was driving at.

"Are you saying that I'm doing this so I can finally date the guy who rejected me? Strike him from my bucket list?"

Mara tilted her head, a small gesture that made both sisters suck in their breath. It was her signature "gotcha" move—quiet but deadly.

"It's not true," Krista said. "No way. Because we already hashed it out. We both agreed that opposites might attract but never last. And if there were ever two opposites, it's him and me."

Bridget turned to Mara. "I do believe our little sister has her head screwed on straight."

"Yes," Mara said, "but even Krista knows that the heart wants what the heart wants."

"All *this* enterprising little heart wants," Krista emphasized, "is more clients. That's it." She paused. "And for Will to raise a ton of money for the children's charity." She gave it more thought. "And the rodeo's general success because it'll be good for Penny's. Right, Bridget?"

She pretended not to notice the exchange of raised eyebrows between her sisters. "See? Everyone's hearts are perfectly aligned."

WILL WOKE TO sunlight busting through the east window of Harry's House, the name the Claverleys gave to the modified double garage their old hired man had fashioned for himself. When he'd moved into Spirit Lake a few years ago, it had stood idle until Keith had moved in temporarily with his bride. Very temporarily. She'd been pregnant when they married and was gone six months after Austin was born.

Keith and Austin had moved into the main house with their parents. So Harry's had become Will's. It would do until he'd reason to expand. He rubbed his bare feet together. Four days since the pedicure and his feet were still as soft as little Austin's. He didn't know a grown-up's feet could feel so good. Figured once a man had calluses you kept them, like lines on your face.

He also didn't think his feet had ever been touched as much, even by himself. When Krista had squirted hay-smelling lotion on her hands and begun massaging his feet, it was all he could do not to pass out from pleasure. She'd pressed her thumbs down the arches, tugged on his toes, rotated his ankle joints.

I usually go up to the knee, she'd said, *but I can stick to your feet if that makes you more comfortable.*

What made him *un*comfortable was how *comfortable* her hands on his feet felt.

They would never be the same again.

Dana knocked on the side door. He could tell it was her from the soft, quick pattern. He swung out of bed and his feet hit the laminate. "Get used to it," he ordered them. He called "Come in" as he headed to the bathroom in his pajama shorts.

"Why aren't you up and at it?" she barked as he closed the bathroom door. "I'm the one who had to load the posts and drive over.

You just had to get dressed, maybe get some eggs in you."

"Good morning to you, too. I had to pull a calf at two this morning."

"That's what you get for late calving. Cuts into time for fencing and seeding."

Will flushed the toilet in answer. As he stepped out of the bathroom, he smelled coffee. He spotted the red container on his nightstand. "By Tim Hortons already?"

"Up at the crack of dawn."

"Should've slept longer and then you wouldn't have needed the coffee," Will said and crossed past her to his chest of drawers. Harry's, actually, but he'd had no room for it at the seniors' lodge. Passed from one bachelor to the next. Depressing.

Dana shifted from one booted foot to the other. "I got the coffee because I kinda overreacted about the rodeo gig the other day. I feel bad, I can do it."

He couldn't remember the last time Dana had ever felt bad about anything she'd done to him. It always fell into the for-your-own-good category. He dug out a pair of underwear and socks, located his jeans on the back of the lone chair.

Will tossed his clothes on the bed and

whirled his finger around to indicate she ought to turn away. She complied with an eye roll.

"Actually, don't worry about it. I figured something out." Will noticed his socks had a hole in the right heel and the big toe of his left wouldn't make it through the day. His pampered skin would rub on the sole of his boot, and he'd have blisters and blood by day's end. With Krista's reprimand about his feet deserving care still ringing in his ears, he rooted through his drawer for a brand-new pair he'd been saving for a special occasion. "I found someone else."

"To be your fake girlfriend? Who?"

It wasn't a secret. Krista had probably told her family already. Will had put off telling his. Krista Montomgery had a way of riling up the Claverleys. Typically, Laura would sing Krista's praises, his mother would give a dismissive comment, Laura would retaliate, Keith would defend their mother, and all the while he and his dad would keep their heads down. If Dana found out first, he'd never hear the end of it.

Will peeled off the stickers and snapped the new socks apart. "I should probably give my folks the heads up first." And because

Dana would say that he'd shared plenty of things with her before informing his parents, he quickly added, "Anyway it's not as if I pried into who you are after."

"That's different," Dana said over her shoulder. "This is somebody you're not wanting to have a relationship with."

"All the more reason it doesn't matter who it is." He put on a sock and reached for the other. The door opened and in walked Keith, Austin riding on his arm. He took a look at the scene and scowled. "Am I interrupting something?"

"Yes," Will said. "Me getting dressed. Do you mind?"

"We're fencing along our line this morning, and he's taking all day," Dana said in a rush. "Are you decent yet?"

Will checked his phone. "Seven twelve is not all day. And I'm putting pants on."

Dana sidled up to Austin. "Good morning, little man," she cooed. "You ready to play?"

"He should be," Keith said. "Caught him climbing the safety gate on the stairs." He groaned. "It's like being on suicide watch."

Austin pitched himself forward into Dana's waiting hands. She smacked a kiss on his chubby cheeks. He wiggled down and beelined for Will's hot coffee. Practiced, Will swept it away and replaced it with a small chip bag. Austin plunked down on his bum and set to exploring its crinkliness and potential to still have crumbs.

With Will more-or-less presentable, Dana shifted to watch Austin, while also speaking to Keith. "Show him how to use the stairs properly," Dana said.

"How? He'll go head over heels and crack his head open," Keith predicted.

"Get him to crawl backward on his stomach."

"Trust her," Will said. Dana was the oldest of five kids. Had practically raised the youngest two when her mom had died in a car crash.

"Austin and I can demonstrate for you tonight," Dana said to Keith. "When are you back?"

Keith did day runs for a local delivery company. "Probably no later than three. Thanks, Dana. I'd appreciate that." He plucked up Austin, who clutched Will's bag for all it was worth. "Nice one, Uncle Will. I buy him a fifty-dollar farm set and you win with a piece of garbage."

On his way out, Keith said to Dana, "See

you later," and to Will, "Get a shirt on." Will was about to fire off a wisecrack when he caught sight of Dana's expression as she watched Keith leave.

No.

Her dreamy smile faded as she took in his expression.

"Keith?" he whispered.

"Don't you dare breathe a single word."

Will raised his hands in surrender. "I won't. Just don't go setting yourself on fire."

She yanked on her ponytail. "I feel as if I am now that you figured it out."

"Not a word. I never would've guessed you and Keith—"

"You don't have to say it. I'm not his type. I'm too tall, too flat, and my eyes aren't blue. I don't like gifts. I'm not a girly girl. We agree on farming but what does it matter when we each can run our own? Believe me, I've hashed my stupidity out in my mind a thousand times over. But I love him, and he doesn't have a clue. And—" she glared at him "—he never will."

Dana was wild-eyed and Will wished things could be different for her, for Keith. He slung his arm around her shoulder. "I'm sorry my brother is as dumb as those posts you hauled over. At least, you got me."

Dana did exactly as he'd hoped. She screwed up her face in revulsion, and pushed him away. "Keith's right. Get a shirt on."

"YOU SHOULD GO with a full updo," Alyssa told Laura. "You've got the hair for it, and when will you ever get the chance again?"

Laura turned from her reflection in the spa mirror to Krista. "What do you think?"

Krista hated the updo she'd created. Yes, it had taken a full hour to perfect every twist and exact placement of the flowery pins. Yes, it was a phenomenal hairstyle that she'd snapped photos to upload onto her website. But it wasn't Laura. It wasn't the country girl with thick waves lapping her shoulders, the sun catching her dark red glints amid the thick brown. Will's hair.

But Alyssa was right. When in her life would Laura ever dress like this again? Both sets of eyes were fastened on her. Laura's, uncertain and Alyssa's, challenging.

Krista took a deep breath and plunged in. "I think that this is a once-in-a-lifetime shot at having hair that's an absolute showstopper. I also think that you'll come down the aisle and

Ryan won't know who he's marrying because you'll look so different from the real you. So this is your choice. Be stunning or be real."

"Be stunning," Alyssa said. "You can be real every other day of your life. Ryan will marry you anyway. As your maid of honor, trust me on this."

Laura patted her upsweep of curls, turned this way and that, her mouth twisting as much as her head.

"And the photographs will be forever," Alyssa said. "When your hair is back in a scrunchie and unwashed, you'll be able to glance at the photo of your wedding and remember how you once shone."

"Is there something in-between?" Laura asked Krista. "Something real but different?"

"Of course," Krista said. "There's a half-do. Lift up half your hair and let the rest fall free. Or we could let it all down and bling it up or—"

"No, no, no." Alyssa was shaking her head. "Halfway says nothing at all."

Except halfway defined Laura. She was the peacemaker among the circle of friends. When they were teenagers, Krista would've been as frustrated as Alyssa with Laura's hesitancy. Battered by sharp-tongued colleagues and so-called friends, she now appreciated Laura's tact. Decided to practice it.

"How about we try it first?"

Laura's lines of distress lightened.

"Sure, girl," Alyssa said with a tight smile. "Let's do it your way and see how that turns out."

Krista gritted her teeth against Alyssa's sarcasm. Laura snuck Krista a pleading look and Krista gave her a reassuring smile. After all, she wasn't the one who had Mean Girl for her maid of honor.

"Here," Alyssa said, crowding against Krista. "Let me take a few pics before you destroy it."

People who say painful things are in pain themselves. You can't control what people say but you can control your response. Krista reminded herself of these truisms Mara had taught her when dealing with Phillip. But she was still annoyed at Alyssa for intruding on Krista's private evening with Laura. Krista had brought munchies and the makings for virgin daiquiris, but then Alyssa had asked Laura if she could come. And, of course, how could Krista refuse? Wasn't Alyssa a friend, too?

But their friendship skated on thin ice. In their final year of high school, Alyssa presented Krista with a business plan to launch their own media marketing company based in Spirit Lake. Krista still remembered the thick cardstock paper Alyssa had printed the plan up on, complete with Roman numerals for headings and subtitles like Executive Summary and Revenue Projections. And at the top of each page, a logo with the initials of their first names entwined. KA Promotions. Instagram and Pinterest had launched that year, and both Krista and Alyssa were avid users. It was like a secret girls' club between them as they snapped photos, posted, followed, linked, liked, loved, commented.

But Krista had participated for fun. Still, she read the proposal and couldn't disagree with its contents, so she'd agreed to become a partner. Eight months later, Krista got an offer to study makeup and costumes in Vancouver, and signed over the company to Alyssa.

You're a flake, Alyssa had pronounced and set about growing her company.

While Krista…well, Krista had proven Alyssa right. She'd bounced around jobs and places. And whenever she'd bounced back to Spirit Lake, Alyssa would find a way to remind her of the opportunity she'd missed.

Once, three years ago when Krista was between both jobs and places, Alyssa had offered her a position as an employee. By then, Krista had discovered at least what she *didn't* want, and declined. *Have it your way*, Alyssa fired back. It was their last private conversation.

Alyssa's phone buzzed and a soft smile appeared. "Your big brother," she said to Laura, "has a question about the ride."

Krista unwound Laura's hair and was about to ask Alyssa how her nephew was doing when Alyssa added, "I'm also handling all the marketing and promotions for the rodeo."

"That's awesome," Krista said. "The rodeo must be a great gig for you. You know so much about it."

Alyssa scowled. "Are you saying I won the contract because of my relationship with the family? A fair amount of your business has come your way because of a Claverley."

Krista had only meant that Alyssa's ranching background made her a natural fit, but Alyssa seemed determined to misinterpret everything. "True," Krista muttered, "true." And kept her focus on touching up Laura's thick, russet waves.

Alyssa gave a satisfied smirk at Krista's

humbleness. "Here's what Will texted. 'Why photos of me?'" Alyssa giggled. "He's so silly." While Alyssa texted a reply, Laura gave Krista an anguished look of sympathy.

Krista shrugged. She'd become good at masking her hurt. Laura turned to Alyssa. "So...uh, have you and Will gone out?" Will wasn't the only Claverley aware of Alyssa's crush. "Not that it's any of my business," she added hurriedly. Despite her casual tone, her fingers were gripping the chair arms.

"Waiting for him," Alyssa said. "It's not as if I haven't dropped hints." She waggled her phone. "Just suggested that we meet for coffee to talk."

"Will never gets the hint," Laura said, her grip relaxing. "I bet he's never asked a girl out, probably because he doesn't have to."

Unless it's to get a fake girlfriend. Krista found herself ever so fascinated by beads. Best to stay mum about anything to do with the rodeo. Laura's silence on the subject led Krista to believe that Will hadn't told his family about their arrangement yet. He'd better get on with it because she hated keeping secrets from Laura, especially one that had to do with her own brother.

Alyssa tapped her phone on her lips. "You think I should make the first move?"

Do that and he'll reject you like he did me. Krista had no idea how to save Alyssa pain without betraying what Will had told her in absolute confidence. But what kind of friend would she be to let Alyssa walk into this blind?

She set down the thread of beads. "I just realized I should text Mara. She—we're out of milk."

Krista opened a text conversation with Will. Good thing they'd exchanged phone numbers a week ago. Krista here. Thought you should know Alyssa wants to ask you out over coffee. She was about to hit Send, when she added, When will Laura know about our arrangement?

There. She'd let Will do the heavy lifting. The less she was involved, the better for all. She returned to the far simpler job of making Laura beautiful. Her phone buzzed. Will had sent a thumbs-up sign. Whatever that meant.

Alyssa got a message next. She sighed. "Will can't come for coffee. A cow's got bloat."

Krista wasn't even sure if that was possible. "Bloat?"

"It's like gas," Laura said. "But if they lie down, it's almost impossible to get them up and they die. He has to deal with it."

Will, hero to cows everywhere. And master dodger of awkward human interaction.

"Krista?" Alyssa said. "I was going to send you the picture of Laura's hair but I can't find you on Instagram."

"I'm not on it."

"Why not? Didn't you used to be?"

"Yeah but I closed my account a few months ago." *Please Alyssa, let it go.* From the way Laura bit her lip, she seemed to be thinking the same.

"That doesn't make sense," Alyssa pressed on. "You need a presence there if you want to grow your business."

"I might later," Krista said and snapped in another row of beads. Yeah, the half-do got her vote.

Alyssa was a dog with a bone. "Why aren't you on it? You were there before even I was."

"Let's just say it went sideways. Friends were no longer friendly."

"You mean that thing with your Toronto

ex?" Alyssa shrugged. "Gotta take the good with the bad, girl."

Leave me alone, *girl*. Krista kept her mouth shut. Laura didn't. "They were really mean, Alyssa," she said quietly.

"I don't know. I read the comments. I thought some of them were funny."

Laura spun her head to Alyssa with enough force to dislodge a clip of beads and send them skittering across the floor. "No. They weren't."

"The ones with the blow-up doll in Krista's nightie? The doll posed at Starbucks? At that hair salon? Laying tile? C'mon. It was priceless."

Laura gripped the leather arms of her chair. "It wasn't. It was horrific. Don't you remember?"

"Yes," Alyssa said peevishly. "I remember Krista crying to you about how mean her ex was. But she was the one who broke up with him."

"Then you might also remember," Laura said, "that while she was here for her aunt's funeral, he threw her stuff into the garbage." Laura with her hair now lopsided and jammed with metal hairpins looked a little unhinged.

Alyssa rolled her eyes. "Maybe next time

she'll have learned her lesson about how to break up properly."

Right here, Krista thought. *I'm right here.*

Laura's knuckles were white on the chair. "And what's that supposed to mean?"

"She can't keep picking people up and leaving them behind when it suits her."

"Is this about her boyfriends or you?"

Alyssa bit her lip and Laura spun away from the mirror to face her. "Thought so. What this is actually about, Alyssa, is that people like being around Krista more than you, more than me for that matter, and we should be glad she counts us as friends."

"If she's such a friend, why did you pick me as your maid of honor?"

"Because she wasn't around for me to pick."

"Exactly! She wasn't around for you."

The two were practically nose to nose, both breathing heavily. "Well," Laura said, "she is now."

"What do you mean by that?"

"I don't want you as my maid of honor anymore. I want Krista."

Alyssa snapped straight as hurt and anger swept across her face. "Fine, then. If that's what you want. Or if that's what Krista has persuaded you to want." She held up her phone with her texts to Will. "You're not the Claverley I want to be with, anyway."

CHAPTER FOUR

LAURA SAGGED IN her chair the second Alyssa banged out the door. "What have I done?"

Krista expelled her own shaky breath. "Give it a couple of days and then talk to her. You know Alyssa. It'll blow over and she'll be your maid of honor again."

Laura shook her head, further fragmenting Krista's creation. "It's not possible to take back those words. And I don't want to." She met Krista's eyes. "This has been building for a while."

"Oh?"

"Alyssa's a good friend unless you're here. Then she becomes some dark witch."

"Maybe she's jealous of our friendship?"

"Possibly. But she couldn't wait to crow about what happened to you. She's even told me the details before you did. And then when I avoided social media because I couldn't bear to see you being humiliated, she'd update me via text with every especially awful comment or post. She'd say it was awful, too, but then she'd add stuff like 'Krista has met her match' or 'Not surprised.'"

"I shouldn't have been," Krista said. "And I did meet my match. Listen, I didn't realize you were dealing with this. It's not me you should be lucky to have as a friend. I should be on my knees to you."

To cheer Laura up and because it was true, Krista dropped to her knees on the hard floor. "I love you and pledge my loyalty to you, Laura Claverley, even if your hair looks as if my nieces styled it."

Laura cracked a small smile. "You will be my maid of honor, then?"

Krista sat back on her haunches. "Won't that prove Alyssa's theory that I get what I want?"

"It's what *I* want."

How could she refuse Laura who had just defended her?

"What about the dress 'n' things? Alyssa is really well organized, you have to give her that. And the wedding's only two weeks away."

"Let me figure all that out. Please, Krista, it'll be so much fun. And this way, Alyssa is away from Will. He's not into her, you know.

You'll be opposite him in the wedding party instead."

Oh. That made the arrangement between her and Will a little sticky. Thrown together at Laura's wedding and then not a month later, acting the part of a couple. Laura—all the Claverleys for that matter—might conclude Will and Krista really were dating. She better set the record straight right now.

"Laura, there's something I should tell you about Will and me."

Laura gasped, squealed. "You two are dating."

Krista blinked. Wow. "Not exactly. You know how Dana is usually his fake girlfriend at the rodeo? Well, Dana can't do it this year, so he asked me."

Laura shook her head, beads rattling. "Why you?"

"Because I'm not Alyssa."

"That makes sense." She smiled slyly at Krista. "You're so going to hate it."

Krista grinned. "Big scary horses, poop everywhere, country music. What's not to like?"

"So why did you accept?"

"A way to get my name out there. If I'm not on social media, I need to do something.

Maybe get a hat made up or a pretty shirt or something."

Laura clapped her hands. "We always have food vendors. You could have your own spot, too."

"Uh, that might clash with my official fake-girlfriend duties."

"Maybe Will Claverley's special girl is giving out pedicures."

Krista caught Laura's excitement. "Speed·pedicures by donation. All proceeds to the children's hospital. It'll promote me and the ride." She'd take a loss in supplies and set-up but would gain future clients and build her name in Spirit Lake and beyond.

"Alyssa will have to come crawling back to you," Laura said, a witchy tone to her voice. The peacemaker was on the warpath.

Krista hated that she was the source of rancor between the longtime friends. "Laura, you don't have to pick sides."

"It's not about picking sides. It's about making a stand for what's right. And—" she fluffed her curls "—what's right is this half-do." The hairstyle Krista could deliver. But being Laura's right-hand man for the most important day of her life? Alyssa was right. Krista had been a flight risk, time after time.

Opening her spa had put a screeching halt to all that. She'd worked hard to keep her dream business afloat. She'd have to work every bit as hard to keep Laura's faith in her.

"MAUDE STILL HASN'T CALVED," Will unloaded on Keith as they rode their mares across the pasture to check on the Claverleys' orneriest cow. Every year it was the same. The Black Angus ate grain and hay and grass, swelled out until she looked as if she was about to birth half a herd and then didn't drop her single calf until after all the others were turned out to pasture.

Keith had his eyes on the rest of the herd. "She'll sort herself out. C'mon, we should head back. Mom needs me to take over with Austin."

"Why? What's happening?"

"Dad got last-minute tickets to Alan Jackson in Calgary. She has to get ready."

Another date. They'd always made time for each other, but since their mother's spa session, the two were like newlyweds. It should be he and Keith acting that way, not their parents.

A warm day, Goldie and Blackberry didn't care to hurry. Neither did Clover, who padded about, shoving her canine snout into every gopher hole. Even Keith, who was always on the move, let Goldie pick the pace. It was his day off and Keith was where he wanted to be.

Their dad seemed willing to let them take over the ranch, but Keith had always resisted. Will wondered if it was because his younger brother disagreed with Will's intent to expand the horse operation.

"What do you think of Laura's new maid of honor?" Keith said.

Laura and her mother had had a back-and-forth about it a couple of days back during which he and his dad had hid out with the horses. "Not my concern," he said.

"She also told me that Krista's playing the part of your rodeo girlfriend this year."

"Yep."

Keith pulled down on the front of his hat. "You and Dana have a falling-out?"

"Not that I'm aware of. She didn't want to do it this year, is all, and I'm okay with that."

"Why doesn't she?"

Will shifted in his saddle to take a good look at Keith. Was his too-busy-to-think brother sparing a moment for Dana? The two wouldn't do all that badly as a couple. They both loved farming; they both had the same ideas about it; she was good with Austin; they'd known each other since they were kids. Maybe all that was needed was for Will as his big brother to prod him in the right direction.

"Apparently she's interested in someone who's coming to the rodeo, and she doesn't want to give the impression she's with me."

"Who?"

"She wouldn't say." At first, anyway.

Will let Keith mull on that up and down one short hill. "Must be one of the contestants. Didn't think they were her type."

Keith was definitely bothered by the notion of Dana with someone. "Could be. Could be one of the food truck operators. Or the clown."

"Shut up," Keith said easily. "I guess so long as it's her idea, that's fine. Otherwise considering how long Dana and you have been friends, it wouldn't be right to pass her over for somebody like Krista."

Will understood what his brother was getting at, but his hackles rose even so. "What are you implying?"

"I like her well enough, but she's not suited for life with you."

Pretty much the conclusion he and Krista

had settled on, but that others saw it too… well, it was kind of disappointing. "I get that. We're dating for a few days, pretending to anyway, and then it's over."

"Don't forget Laura's wedding. You two are going to be together most of the day, and then we have the rehearsal coming up, too."

And just like that, Will felt better. "I forgot. There's that whole dance thing we'll have to figure out."

"Which Alyssa had down pat."

Only because of a couple of private sessions in which Will had spent as much time dancing around her advances as doing the dance itself. He should have come right out then and there, and told her plainly he wasn't interested. He'd tried to hint at it. He'd asked her if she was seeing anyone, and she'd perked up and said no and why was he asking? Too late he realized his question implied interest. But he wasn't sure how to let her down without hurting her. Krista had warned him about the coffee date but he'd sidestepped it until he could figure out what to say. Coward. Krista probably agreed.

"I'm sure Krista will catch on to the dance quick enough," Will said.

"But why even ask Krista to replace Dana?

Why do you need a fake girlfriend, anyway? Why not use a real one?"

"Because I don't have a real one."

"You could with Alyssa. You'd have to be blind not to see she wants to go out with you."

"Maybe Laura and I feel the same way about her."

"Better choice than Krista. Take it from me."

Will bristled. "What? There some history between the two of you?"

"No. But you've got to recognize the similarity between Krista and Macey."

"Other than the two are both blondes, no, I don't."

"How about the fact that they both hate farming—no, the entire outdoors, and they always want everything their way."

He thought of Krista's insistence on not missing any part of the pedicure. It wasn't so much her way, but the right way. "Seems to me," Will said, "you're being a little excessive."

"Am I? You warned me about Macey, and I didn't listen. All I'm doing is handing your own advice back to you."

They were at the corrals now and Will

leaned down to open the gate. "First of all, we're not dating."

Goldie carried Keith through the opening. "That's what you keep saying. But how come you asked her to be your fake girlfriend in the first place? You go off to get a gift certificate for Mom and you come back two hours later with a fake girlfriend. Which you don't even mention until Laura finds out from Krista herself."

Blackberry, practiced for years on farm work, held tight as Will pulled the gate closed. That kind of teamwork was why he trained horses.

"Because I'd half forgotten about it." Except every night and morning when he rubbed his bare feet together.

"But why her?"

"She mentioned she wanted more clients, and I figured this way we could kill two birds with one stone." He didn't mention their discussion was over a pedicure. If Keith needed any proof that Will had lost his mind over Krista, permitting her to rub lotion on his bare feet would blow his cover wide open.

Keith shook his head as he dismounted. "She sweet-talked you into it."

Will followed suit. "No, it was my idea.

I had to talk *her* into it. Can't you give me some credit? I'm not as stupid as you were."

"I was stupid," Keith said, uncinching the straps, "but I'm not anymore. It'll be a cold day before I ever marry again."

Dana sure had her work cut out for her. "Not every woman's like Macey," Will said.

Keith swung his saddle off. "Question is, how can we ever be sure?"

Wasn't that the million-dollar question? Not that it mattered with Krista. They were both clear that they didn't care about each other, not like a real couple.

"You ready?" Will said from behind Krista.

"Not a clue. I hope your boots have steel toes."

"You wouldn't step all over your good work, would you?"

Before Krista could answer, Janet called the wedding party to attention. They were gathered in the Claverley rodeo dance hall to rehearse the wedding dance. "We'll do it without the music first," she said, "then with it, and finally we'll review any part that needs extra work."

Which would be every part in her case.

The five girls were strung out with the

guys matched up behind before a low stage where the DJ would be, tonight represented by Janet's ancient boombox. It was early evening, the perfect time for a walk along the lake, or to sit on her deck unwinding with Mara. Not to be untangling her feet among this choreographed ensemble.

"And one…"

"Do what I say," Will whispered in her ear. Calm. Playful. Her breath steadied. Her nerves reacted well to that combo.

"…two, three, four. Vine to the right. Vine to the left," Janet Claverley called to the wedding party. "Remember, girls, you will be wearing your skirts. For those of you—Krista and Laura—not wearing them tonight, pretend you're lifting them. Let's start at the top."

"I swear," Keith muttered as they shuffled back to their starting positions, "this prancing around is enough to turn every man off marriage."

His sister glared at him. He shrugged. "All I'm saying is why can't we dance like normal?"

"Because," Will said to Keith warningly, "this isn't your wedding."

Krista agreed with Will but the parts of her

brain responsible for coordinating movement wanted to high-five Keith.

Janet clapped her hands and gave the start-up count. "Vine to the right. Vine to the left. Right forward. Left forward. Turn clockwise. *Clockwise*, Krista. Left forward. Right forward. Turn counterclockwise. No, the other way, Krista."

Even with Will's whispered instructions and his hand guiding her, she felt as if she'd crashed onto the stage of a dance troupe. Krista had watched the video of the dance a million times, but tonight Janet was throwing in variations that seemed to come straight out of *Dancing with the Stars*. It didn't help that everyone else had been practicing for weeks and had probably been able to country dance the day after they started to walk.

As the music segued into the bridal dance, Laura, in Ryan's arms, peeked over his shoulder at Krista. Her worry lines had reappeared.

"I'm stressing your sister," Krista murmured to Will.

"Don't worry. The wedding's not for a while yet."

"A week this Saturday, Will."

"Oh."

"Yeah, oh."

"Well then, you're screwed." He paused. "We're screwed."

"I'm making you look bad, aren't I?"

"I'll live."

She searched his face. Calm and composed. He really didn't mind. "I don't want to screw it up for Laura."

"She'll forgive you. No one will care."

"*I* will care. My job is to make other people look good, but this is taking it a little too far. I'm the wonky wheel on the shopping cart. The loud drunk in the church. The—the—the—" She floundered to describe exactly how bad she was.

"The ex-rodeo rancher in the spa."

He had her there. "Your feet recovered yet?"

"My toes curl in horror every time I put my boots on. They've gone all soft and spoiled."

"Bring them back anytime and I'll indulge their every wish."

"Because my toes want what my toes want?"

Krista broke into laughter, surprising herself at its unintended flirty drift. She'd not dated since leaving Toronto. Her heart had needed a break. But if she could find someone like Will, someone laid-back—only less… country—she might try again.

The rest of the party was drifting off. "If you want, we can practice now."

It would be a good idea, but she wasn't sure if she should take him up on the offer. It might send mixed signals about their relationship to the others. And yet everyone could see she needed help, and she really didn't want to mess things up for Laura.

"If you've the time…"

"Hey, Mom," Will called. "Can you leave the music? Krista and I are staying to practice."

In unison, everyone turned to them. Laura grinned. Janet and Keith frowned. Two out of three Claverleys disapproved of her. She'd no idea how Dave weighed in. Hard man to figure out. Like Will.

"Oh well, I suppose," Janet said faintly.

"See you all later," Will said. He sounded like when he'd been guiding her movements earlier. Steady and a titch bossy. In short order, the entire group was filing out as neatly as travelers through a turnstile, leaving the entire floor to Will and Krista.

WILL WAS A natural teacher. He switched on the music. "Otherwise it's just walking in all directions."

He sang to her, low and punching up the

beats to signal the turns, humming through the instrumental riffs. He had a voice that could land him a stage in front of a crowd of buckle bunnies.

Not that she would tell him that. He'd think she was coming on to him. He'd break off his fake arrangement and she'd lose her best opportunity to rustle up clients. Not to mention dealing with a second rejection.

As it was, his every touch crackled through her. Her senses jumped at the push and pull of his fingertips as he coached her away and then closer to him.

"I bet," she said, "that if I stayed trained to your hand, I'll be good."

"You're really going to let me lead?"

"Of course. I can't be trusted on my own, that's clear."

"Leading will be a new experience for me."

He must be referring to dancing with Alyssa whose type A personality prevented her from letting someone else lead. And if Will had let Alyssa dominate on the dance floor, he'd likely not taken charge in their personal relationship. She debated speaking to Will as he walked over to kill the music.

In the sudden quiet, he strolled back, his boots on the plank floor beating out a slow rhythm. Her own heartbeat kicked up. No. She made up her mind. "I'm going to say something, okay?"

He gestured to where wall panels reached waist-high, a series of uprights continuing to run up to the overhanging roof. The open-air spaces between the uprights allowed for a view of the rodeo grounds, barn and, to the west, the dipping sun. He leaned his elbow on the ledge of one opening, adjusting to take the weight off his bad shoulder. Before she could ask about his injury, he said, "Shoot."

Right. She was sticking her nose into his business enough without going into his medical history. "Has Laura told you much about her fight with Alyssa?" She was no-go territory among the bridal party. During the past week of preparations, the group texts were dead quiet on the sudden change in maids of honor. Whatever Laura wanted, the rest of them were more than happy to give.

"Nope. And she said she doesn't plan to. I guess she's still invited to the wedding."

No-go territory among the Claverleys, too, it seemed. "And how do you feel about that?"

"It doesn't affect me. Are you going somewhere with this?"

Krista had to tread carefully. She didn't

want to betray her friendship with Laura, but she also wanted to warn Will about Alyssa's intentions.

"The thing is, the fight between Laura and Alyssa was mostly about me, but your name came up."

Will winced as if she'd flicked dirt into his eyes. Poor Will. He really hated being the center of attention. She followed his gaze to the yard below. It was pretty. Deep shadows stretched from the barn, the fences, the trees, mellowing the edges of the day and softening harsh colors. Then there was the setting sun. She'd moved around a lot—first with her nomadic parents and then again as an adult—and seen sunsets around the world. This one might not be as majestic as one in Hawaii, but there was something to be said for its low-key splashiness. A free nighttime show for anyone to watch.

Will shifted beside her, his shoulder skimming hers. "Looks like the sky got into your nail polish."

Changing the subject away from Alyssa and him. Then again, there was definite appeal to discussing a sunset with a handsome cowboy. What right-minded single girl wouldn't? Only, she had a job to do. "Before things went south, Alyssa said that she's been dropping hints that she'd like to date you."

Will rolled his shoulders. "Yeah. I got that impression. I tried to set her straight without hurting her but it backfired."

"You need to tell her straight-out. Otherwise this situation will blow up in your face." There, it was finally out there.

Will removed his hat and gave his thick hair a fierce scrubbing. What she'd love to do with that hair. By way of styling, of course. "But we haven't even gone out. Won't she get the hint after a while?"

"How long has she been chasing you?"

"Last few months for sure. She took me to the movies on Valentine's Day. Some sort of singles celebration," she said. "I didn't get the hint until Keith explained it to me afterward."

Krista puckered her lips not to laugh, but his eyes drifted to her mouth. He squeezed his eyes shut, as if that flicked dirt was getting ground in. "Why can't she say what she means?"

"Why don't you?" Krista said. "Man up and tell her you're not interested. A little honesty now will save you a whole lot of pain later."

Some of her own bitterness edged into her

voice. They both studied the sunset. The brilliant oranges were gone, faded to bands of purples and pinks.

"Speaking from bitter experience?" he said softly.

She could brush it off, but maybe if she shared her experience he would understand the urgency. "My ex from Toronto. Things between us weren't going well. And when I decided to stay here, I broke things off between us. He got nasty."

"Laura said he slandered you on Facebook and Instagram."

"She told you about it?"

"Not at first, but at the time she was moody and thumping around, checking her phone every half hour. This whole ranch shrinks right up when Laura clouds over. She explained what was going on. Not all, I'm thinking, but enough."

Will and his whole family knew about her humiliation. Had she really believed it would be otherwise? Had he seen the pics of her nightie on the blow-up doll? Phil's innuendoes?

"It's finished now."

"I've got a head gate he could be fitted

into. A whole lot of manure for him to get a close whiff of."

He'd given this some thought. And she was a—a not-quite friend. Imagine his fierceness if she was…someone closer. "There's something about the breakup I haven't told anyone. Something I've only now realized myself.

"I always knew in my gut that Phil and I weren't meant for each other. I tried to like what he liked, do what he did, because I had no idea what I wanted for myself. He's a set designer and photographer in Toronto, and he used his connections to land me a sweet contract as a makeup artist. I felt I owed him, so I helped him with his work, even though I had zilch interest in locating napkin dispensers for a restaurant scene or artistically strewing garbage in a back alley.

"We started struggling. I should've broken it off then. Instead I let him think I still cared. When we broke up, he was hurt. And I can understand why because I'd never been honest with him. And I don't want you to make the same mistake I did."

He regarded her, his hair a mess from his hat and head scrubbing. "You think I'm a liar and a coward?"

"I think," she said, "you'd rather sit on a

bucking horse for ten seconds than cause someone else the slightest discomfort for even one second."

"But that's not how life works, is it?" Will rubbed his cheek and gave his hair another scrub. She couldn't resist smoothing an especially spiky tuft, and he leaned into her touch. They froze. Their eyes connected. He straightened, and she quickly brought her hand down. Will slapped his hat back on. "You think she'll come after me?"

Krista blinked, getting her head and heart back in place. "Not the way Phillip did. I'm more worried about how it will affect the friendship between her and Laura. I've already driven a wedge between them."

"You're not to blame for that, either. They both speak their minds."

"Yeah, but Laura admitted that when I'm around things get heated between them."

Will swept his hand over his face. Was that a smile he was hiding? "You have a way of riling people up."

Krista sighed. "And here I thought my talent was getting people to relax."

His voice softened. "Oh, I'd say you're talented there, too."

For the second time tonight, Krista felt her

heart rate jolt. "Yes, well, thank you. So, uh, you'll consider what I said?"

Will looked off to the fading sunset and opened his mouth. Clamped it shut. "I'll talk to Alyssa. First opportunity I get."

Which would be Laura's wedding. If Alyssa came. Will seemed to think along the same lines. "But maybe not the wedding. Last thing anybody needs is a scene on Laura's day."

He could be stalling, but he did have a point. And really, she'd done her part. The rest was up to him. "Agreed. Besides, there'll be enough of one when I take to the dance floor."

Will grinned, turning to retrieve the mini stereo. "Nah, I'll make you look good."

Will, Krista resisted saying, you'd make any girl look good.

CHAPTER FIVE

LAURA'S WEDDING WAS at the unheard-of hour of 11:00 a.m., which meant Krista's feet hit the floor at six to prepare the salon for the bridal party. They sailed in from their breakfast at Penny's shortly before eight. Then she worked flat out on their hair and makeup. Three bridesmaids and the bride.

"But what about you, Krista?" Laura said as Krista swiffed on a faint layer of blush to her cheek.

Krista swung her ponytail. "This is it. Sleek yet fun."

Up popped a worry line. "Are you sure? It seems…plain."

"I am your maid," Krista said. "I'm not supposed to outshine you."

"It'll be practical around the horses," Caris added. She was Dana's sister, and her wedding was set for three weekends from now.

Horses? Nobody had told her there'd be

horses. Laura's eyes, six inches from Krista's, widened in alarm. "Oh no."

The bridesmaids—Caris, Raine and Jenna—turned as one to Laura. "You didn't tell her?"

"I forgot," Laura moaned. "I'm so sorry, how stupid of me! I was thinking more about the dress and flowers and catering…and about all the other arrangements."

Krista took a deep breath. Then another. True, she was nervous around horses. Okay, she was petrified but her fear was groundless. Nothing bad had ever happened with them, and she'd recovered from bad things that really *had* happened, so why should this be any different? In this very salon, she had vowed to herself that she'd stick by Laura. Now was her opportunity to prove it.

"Tell me the plan and we'll work something out."

"We decided to ride our horses to the ceremony. The guys, too. Then the horses will be part of the photo shoot afterward. All of us know horses…before…" Laura's voice trailed off.

The bridesmaids, in various stages of undress, looked as uncomfortable as Laura. No. If anyone should feel awkward, it should be Krista.

"Is there a horse I could possibly ride?"

"Mom might be able to give you hers," Laura said. "She's quiet."

"The horse isn't the problem," Caris said quietly. "It's the rider, Krista. Do you know how to even turn a horse?"

Krista's grimace was answer enough.

"That would work," Raine said, "if we were going straight on a trail, but we have to line them up. Get them in formation."

"And," Jenna said, "we have to bring them around behind the guests, so you'll have to keep the horse on the rein."

"So I won't be part of it," Krista said. "I'm fine with that."

"But Ryan and his guys will be there with their horses," Laura said, her voice squeaky with panic. "If you're not there, it won't match up, or Will might have to sit out to make it match. And he's part of the party. Plus the horses are already getting saddled up and decorated. We talked about rehearsing that part of the wedding, but that would've meant loading and unloading the horses from everybody's stables. But at least then we would've remembered about Krista, or at least I would've—"

Krista laid her hand on Laura's shoulder.

"We got this. How about someone else takes my reins?"

The other four girls exchanged looks. "I mean, it would look a little funny, because well, most people can ride," Laura said.

"But I could go first," Caris offered, "and lead her horse."

"What do I care if I look like a two-year-old?" Krista said, "Better that than I try to do it myself and spook the horse."

Except it was Krista who felt spooked when she took in Janet's gray mare, Silver. Why did they have to be so big?

Laura got on her ride first. The bridesmaids arranged the skirt, the back mantling over the horse's haunches. Krista held the bouquet while the other women fluttered about. By unspoken consent, they'd let Krista stay away from the hooves and shaking heads.

But Silver was…nice. She stayed quiet, yielding to all the fussing, her dark eyes bright with interest. And her eyelashes…oh man, to die for. So when Laura was declared done but her skirt was bunched in one place, Krista felt brave enough to step forward and flick it straight. Laura's horse stamped; Krista yelped and jumped back. Square into a stinking pile of horse crap. Her splurge—a pair of shoes she intended to have until she was eighty-two—were ruined.

All four of the bridal party looked at the smelly mess of her shoe in horrified dismay.

They'd wisely worn running shoes, and Caris even had an old denim shirt on to keep her upper half clean until the last minute.

Their collective sympathy made her heart swell with gratefulness that people outside of her family cared when even little disasters came her way.

"Listen," she said, "tonight after a couple of drinks, we're going to be laughing about this." She slipped off her shoes, treating the soiled one like the toxic waste dump it was, and tossed them against a corral post.

Will might soon wish he was opposite Alyssa again.

"If you can ride a horse bareback, I guess you can ride it barefoot."

WILL WATCHED THE arrival of the bridal party from his place beside the groom and the other guys. They stood along one side of the assembled guests with their backs to the hitching rails where their horses already waited. The guests, a good hundred or so, turned in their outdoor chairs to watch the main event—the arrival of the bride—camera phones rolling.

Raine and Jenna came first in harmonizing colors of pale pink and yellow, pausing their horses for photos.

Keith nudged Will's elbow. "Dana wants you."

Will scanned the guests.

"Fifth row. This side. The end."

Dana sat with Austin on her knee, tapping her hand. What? Will looked down at his hand.

"Doofus." From Keith. "She wants to know if you remembered the ring."

How did Keith figure that? Will checked, smiled back a yes. Dana's attention flicked to Keith, who must've signaled something, because she sucked in her lips to stop a laugh. Fine. If the one thing they were doing together was laughing at him, so be it. Raine and Jenna moved on.

Then came Caris in matching pink and yellow leading Janet's horse ridden by Krista. Well, barely ridden.

"Who's the one in blue?" Jasper, one of the groomsmen, said.

"Alyssa's replacement. Krista," Keith whispered.

"She ever been on a horse?" Jasper cracked through the side of his mouth.

"Doesn't look like it," Keith beside him answered.

Krista swayed in the saddle with a two-fisted grip on the horn, despite Silver's easy walk. His mother watched, her smile fixed. Caris taking the lead rein was not a bad plan for most horses, but Silver liked to know who was in control, otherwise she'd put herself in charge. And from the backward bent to Silver's ears, she didn't think Caris's horse made the grade.

Caris stopped for the requisite pictures and Silver obediently stopped, too. Krista sat astride the horse, unlike the others who had managed sidesaddle easily. They'd probably advised Krista to sit that way for greater stability, but it meant her skirt was hitched up to midthigh and she had to keep one hand pressed between her thighs so the material wouldn't rise any higher. Some pictures those were going to make. Also—

"She's barefoot," Ryan commented.

A dangerous option when you and the horse weren't partners. Or even acquainted. Krista adjusted herself in the saddle, her heels tapping Silver's sides.

Silver, trained to respond to the slightest touch, stepped forward, the lead rein slipping from Caris's hand. Silver walked straight past Caris's horse and kept going, away from the entire event. Caris moved her horse up to Silver to recapture the rein but, tired of following, Silver showed her haunches, not letting Caris close.

Caris hurried to secure her horse to the hitching rail likely planning to return to Krista. Meanwhile Krista was attempting to get Silver to move toward the rail, but her pulls on the reins confused the mare. She snorted and didn't budge.

A titter arose from the horse-savvy crowd. A bunch of people laughing at Krista when she'd had no say in this predicament. Will felt a rush of annoyance with his sister. Why hadn't she warned Krista? He would've been happy to give Krista pointers.

He started toward Krista but his dad was already on the move. He strode across in that easy way of his and picked up Silver's lead rein. He spoke to Krista. Her reply made his father break into a full smile.

He said something back and the two of them chatted like old buddies as his father led Silver to a large lilac bush beside the hitching rail. All three disappeared behind the bush, and when they came around the other side, Krista was on the ground. His dad, ever the gentleman, hadn't let the crowd witness her probably graceless dismount.

He should've been there instead. Krista was his sort-of date, after all. Beside him, Ryan straightened. His bride had arrived.

Will barely recognized his sister on the back of her palomino. She was all white and ruffles as if she'd dropped into a cloud like the ones floating in the blue sky above. Will leaned close to his best buddy's ear. "Just so you know, I've already got a brother but I only have one sister."

"Thinking the same," Keith said from his other side.

Ryan nodded once. "Understood."

Laura dismounted and Krista risked stones and splinters to rush over and do the last-minute fussing with the dress and bouquet. The other girls assembled to begin the procession but Laura was losing her nerve. Even from where he stood, Will noticed the bouquet shake. Krista had seen it, too. She came right up into Laura's face. Will remembered doing the same for Laura before toboggan rides, the big math final, the barrel race. Reminded her to break it all down, to keep her eye on the goal.

Krista wrapped her hands around Laura's bare shoulders. Those talented hands that infused serenity into whomever she touched. *Do your thing, Krista.* Sure enough, Laura's eyes lifted to look past Krista to Ryan. Her goal. Krista gave Laura's shoulder a quick rub, and Will felt it in the soles of his feet. Laura nodded and Krista hopped to her place in the bridal procession.

All eyes were on Laura as she walked with her dad down the aisle, but Will was distracted by Krista and her bare toes, right to where they stopped across from him.

Painted blue, her toes waggled. He glanced up to find her grinning at him.

Barefoot, her hair in a ponytail, and wearing a pretty blue dress, she looked like a whole lot of fun. Keith cleared his throat pointedly. Will ignored him. He wasn't marrying Krista, but that didn't mean he wasn't going to enjoy walking back up the aisle with her on his arm.

KRISTA'S ARM TUCKED into his as they approached the reception line, Will leaned to her ear. "You short a pair of shoes?"

Krista looked down, mock-gasped. "Oh

man, I was wondering what everyone was staring at. You wouldn't happen to have another pair on you?"

He patted his suit pockets. "Straight out."

"Never mind. I'll raid Laura's closet before the pictures."

"I can run you back to your place. It'll take under a half hour."

Will was prevented from getting Krista's reply by the formation of the reception line which placed the wedding couple between him and Krista. After a long procession of clasping sweaty palms and hugging perfumed aunts, he finally regained Krista. "How about it?"

"Shoe shopping in under a half hour? That'll be a new world record."

"I believe in you."

His faith turned out to be well-founded. Will had assumed they'd go to the fancy shoe store downtown, but Krista dug in her heels because she couldn't afford another pair there. When he started to protest she'd firmly said no, he wasn't paying and no, she wouldn't consider paying him back. Then she'd asked him to please take her to Walmart. She had an idea which turned out to be a pair of white sneakers with two artificial blue daisies attached to the laces.

"Blue's good," Will said. "Matches your eyes."

She wrinkled her brow. "Uh, Will. They match the dress. That's the point."

Her point, maybe. He was making an entirely different one. "Not sure about white. They don't seem practical."

"There are no blue shoes, and it's practical to buy shoes a color I can wear with other outfits."

"Point taken."

He began to doubt her rational side though when she opened her phone on the way back and began muttering to herself.

"What's that you say?" he said extra loud as if she was talking to him.

"My speech. I'm doing the bride's toast. And you're doing the toast to the groom."

"I am?" He did know but it was worth it to see her half die from an anxiety seizure before she realized he was joking.

"I'm not sure why I'm worrying," she said as they got out from his truck. "If you screw up, it's not my problem. I just don't want—"

"To ruin it for Laura. I understand."

She didn't, either. At first the phone in her

hand shook so hard it was all Will could do not to jump up to the podium and hold it for her. But then she set it down and turned to Laura and poured out her heart. The two of them and half the room were bawling by the end.

Dry-eyed, Keith whispered to Will. "First she melts hearts, then breaks 'em."

Keith didn't know Krista.

Will and Krista nailed the dance, or at least they didn't goof up so bad they stole from the main attraction, Ryan and Laura. At the final song beat, Krista beamed up at him. "All right, I think we can finally have fun."

"You haven't been?" He meant to sound lighthearted, but he detected his own regret.

Krista's gaze lingered on him, probably wondering if she'd hurt his feelings. "Today was way better than I ever believed possible," Krista said. "Better than how it started with Silver. All I could think about was 'What if I break your mom's horse? She will kill me. Wait, no she won't have to because I'll do it for her.'"

Will laughed, and she broke into her terrific smile. This was why it had been so hard to refuse Krista all those years ago. He felt so good around her.

"Thank God I'll never have to get on a horse again."

And there it was, his reason for why he'd refused her. Age difference aside, he couldn't be with someone who didn't love horses. They had no future then or now. But that didn't mean they couldn't move deeper in another direction.

"About this fake girlfriend thing," he began, stopped. This was harder than he supposed. What if she blew him off?

Her smile wavered. "You saw me in action and changed your mind?"

"No." Far from it. "Might have to work around your equine skills, but I was thinking that given how well today went, there's no need for us to fake at being friends."

Krista reached her arm around his neck— and then he felt her flip down the back of his shirt collar. "Yeah, I think we blew that by standing here on the dance floor while everyone else is dancing."

Will took in his surroundings. They were like rocks amid a stream of moving people. He edged them off the floor. Krista seemed about to speak when Alyssa appeared.

"You two looked pretty good out there."

He'd made a point of sidestepping her

whenever possible today. He didn't want to deal with her, not when he was busy with Krista.

"Thanks," Krista said. "Will made us look good."

Alyssa gave him the once-over. "I believe it." She was coming on pretty strong, right in front of Krista, who had wiped her face clear of its earlier liveliness and was now neutral.

"A couple of rough spots for you, Krista," Alyssa continued.

Now why did she have to bring that up? "Krista did just fine, if you ask me. And I ought to know, seeing as how I was right there with her."

Both women startled. What did he say so wrong? Krista said in a rush to Alyssa, "I'm glad you came. Have you had a chance to speak to Laura? Other than after the ceremony, I mean?"

Laura was sitting at a table of aunts and uncles. Ryan was doing his hosting duties at another table with his family tribe. Alyssa's mouth twisted. "She's got plenty of company, I'd say."

The DJ struck up a song Will liked. He could teach Krista this one, easy.

But Alyssa moved between them. She wore

a dress with giant pink flowers, so it was like a garden had sprung up in front of him. "Still remember the two-step?" Alyssa asked.

"I do," he said and he had no choice but to dance with Alyssa. Otherwise, his brush-off might lead to a scene he'd promised Krista he'd avoid, and quite honestly didn't want to create. He watched her wander off to have her own fun while he pretended not to miss her. Odd how he didn't have to fake having fun with his fake girlfriend.

Fake girlfriend and for-real friend.

KRISTA TURNED HER back to the dance floor so she didn't have to watch Alyssa in Will's arms. That might appear a tad obsessive. She and Will were only friends, after all. Very new, straight-out-of-the-wrapping friends. But—the way he'd hesitated to dance with Alyssa, shy and worried, as if her reaction really mattered—something more was there.

Or she simply wanted there to be more. She forced her gaze to drift among the guests at the tables, lighting on Dana and Keith. A toddler in an adorable dress shirt and pants was standing on Dana's lap. Austin, Keith's boy. He started stomping on her lap. Keith didn't waste a second but swept up his son and calmly began threading his way among the tables to the exit, Austin howling and kicking as if his dad was kidnapping him. Dana watched them uncertainly and then dropped back to her seat.

She looked lost and lonely. Krista found herself going to her, even though they were little more than acquaintances. But hey, misery loves company.

"That cute dude knows his mind," Krista said.

"More like he's out of it. It's a half hour past his bedtime and he refused to nap this afternoon with all the excitement and noise, so now he's overtired."

"Keith's got a handle on it."

"He refused my help. Told me to take the evening off. Enjoy myself."

Austin had been perched on Dana's lap during the ceremony, Krista remembered. "You babysat him the whole day?"

"Not the whole day. Keith helped when he could, but it's his sister's wedding, so I wanted him to have a break, too."

So this was why Dana had declined being Will's fake girlfriend. She and Keith were a thing. "How long have you two been dating?"

Dana's eyes widened. "We're not dating. We're just…friends."

Another couple caught in the slick ground of Friendland. "I'm sorry, I misread that. You two seemed…a couple."

Dana brightened. "You think?"

Ah. "You'd like to be…close to Keith?"

Dana colored. "That obvious, is it?"

"No. You two work well together, is all."

"He really got burned by his ex. All women are off-limits now."

It was none of her business but she couldn't sit on the obvious, either. "You are different," Krista said quietly. "He trusts his son with you. He's known you forever."

"Yes, and that's the problem. To him, I'm another family member."

"If you keep acting like one, then that's what he'll keep on believing."

"What do you mean?"

Who was she to give romantic advice, given her bust with Phillip? Except she'd learned the importance of honesty. "Define yourself differently. Like how you refused to be Will's fake girlfriend this year."

"He told you about our arrangement?"

That man. Not honest with Alyssa and now he was holding back on his best friend. Dana would find out soon enough. "Yeah. After you turned him down, he asked me."

Dana's eyebrows nearly lifted clear off her face. "You?"

"I know. After today, people will say Will's crazy to take me on as his girlfriend."

"What? You agreed?"

"Yeah. He sweetened the deal by saying I might pick up a few clients."

"You two are using each other?"

"Sort of. Are we using each other if we both know we are?"

"I guess it's fine. Let me warn you that you're in for an exhausting five days during the rodeo. He used to pay me back with concert tickets, flowers, dinner. It was like we were dating, he was that grateful."

"The girls come on that bad?"

"As bad as Alyssa with him right now."

Krista stole a glance. Alyssa was dancing close, despite the looseness of Will's hand on her spine. She was a good dancer, way better than Krista's hopping.

Dana leaned close. "Does Alyssa know, by chance?"

"No. Not yet." Hopefully she wouldn't, either. Not until after Will had talked with her.

Dana sat back. "That's a ticking bomb."

"One Will's reluctant to be anywhere close to when it goes off."

Will's best friend studied Krista. "But you're saying that we both need to get out of our comfort zones."

"That's my experience, Dana. You have to know what you want first."

"I want four kids by age thirty-five. But I'm already thirty, and not a father for them in sight."

Krista grinned. "You've already got one kid. The father just doesn't realize it."

The music ended, and without thinking, Krista searched the dance floor for Will. There he was, scanning the tables. For her? Alyssa was tight against him.

Dana tapped her arm. "Will seems to be looking for you. You're his new comfort zone."

That was what he wanted from her. Friendship. A comfort zone. And that's what she'd accepted. Except somehow it left her wanting more.

FIVE DAYS LATER, Krista was seated at the deck table on the covered front porch of Bridget's house. Krista's sisters had been staring at her all night.

She'd had enough. "What? What?"

"What do you think, Krista?"

"Oh, quit that, Mara. I hate when you psycho-people make us say what you already know."

"It's like with Isabella's math questions," Bridget said, referencing her oldest daughter. "Show four ways that six plus five makes eleven."

"Okay then, Krista," Mara said, nestling into her deck chair. "Show me four ways that you've fallen for Will Claverley."

Krista swirled the red wine in her glass. "I can't even show you one. It *is* possible to like a guy but not want to be with him. Dana and Will, for example."

Mara crossed her legs and swung her foot. "It's possible. Not entirely convinced in this case."

"I already explained our situation weeks ago and there's no point rehashing it."

An SUV with a logo for Penny's on the passenger door pulled up. Jack, Bridget's husband as of four months ago, got out. It had kept Krista believing in true love when her adopted sister and her newfound cousin had taken a second chance on each other.

Bridget and Jack had a routine that even the presence of her and Mara on their weekly

Thursday night meetup didn't alter. First, the kiss. Then the exchange of comments on how good or tired or hungry the other might be. Next asking after their adopted daughters, Sofia and Isabella, who had gone to bed a half hour ago. And only then would they open the conversation up to anyone else in their presence.

Bridget brought Jack up to speed. "Krista was about to tell us four ways she's fallen for Will Claverley."

"I know Will," Jack said, dropping into the last deck chair as he cracked the tab on a beer. "He donated their dance space for a charity event I did with Penny, years ago." Penny was not only the deceased aunt of the Montgomery sisters but also the biological mother of Jack. "Nice guy but isn't he big into rodeos, horses, the outdoor life?"

"Exactly," Krista said. "Nice guy but we've got nothing in common."

"Here, let's flip it around," Bridget said. "Show me four ways that *Will* has fallen for *you*."

"Same answer. None, because he hasn't."

"I'll start," Bridget said. "He submits to one of your pedicures even though he doesn't like them."

"I'd like one," Jack said. "Why haven't you given me one?"

"I will, when you pay for it. Which Will did."

"Why would he pay for something he doesn't want?"

"It was part of a package for his mother. I didn't want to rip him off, so I persuaded him to give it a try."

"One," Bridget repeated.

Krista turned to Jack. "Okay, a man's perspective here. What do you think?"

He raised his gaze to the porch ceiling. "All you'll get is my opinion, because every man is as unique as a snowflake and needs to be respected for their individuality."

"You're trying to get out of this."

"Yep."

"Just be honest."

"Three words a man absolutely should not believe a woman means."

"I promise I will not disown you," Krista said.

"Your first time together and you talked him into putting on pajamas. I'd say you got some pull with him."

"That's not—"

"He did an extra one-on-one practice session with Krista to teach her dance moves for the wedding," Bridget told Jack.

Jack seesawed his head. "Cutting her from the pack. Happens in bars all the time."

Bridget held up two fingers. "Then on the wedding day, he drives her into town to pick up shoes because she ruined the first pair, even though Krista had told him she could take from Laura's closet."

"Using every opportunity to be alone with her." Jack smiled at Bridget. "Best seven minutes of the day."

He and Bridget kissed, even as she raised three fingers to Krista.

"And four—" Mara joined the take-down of Krista "—he agrees to break up with a girl he's not even dating because Krista asked him to."

Jack broke off his kiss. "That sounds messed up, Krista. How does that work?"

Krista glared at Mara. "For a therapist, you should know better than to twist the facts. I suggested to Will to be honest with someone he doesn't want to date but who clearly has feelings for him."

"I get where Mara is coming from," Bridget said. "Will's also giving the all-clear signal that he's open to a relationship."

"That pretty much wraps it up," Jack said. "He's into you."

"Except he told me he *wasn't*. We have an understanding from way back."

Jack frowned in confusion. "Later," Bridget said.

"Wait," Mara said. "Isn't this the same guy that you accused of not being honest because he hadn't been clear with Alyssa about his feelings for her?"

Mara was leaning forward. Too much like a detective grilling a prime suspect. "Yes," Krista said cautiously.

"Then if you agree that he isn't always honest about the things he *doesn't* say, isn't it also possible that he isn't being entirely honest about the things he *does* say?"

Three "gotcha" smiles surrounded Krista. "If you saw me and Will together," she said desperately, "you'd get how mismatched we are."

"Invite him to our Canada Day barbecue, then, and we'll see for ourselves," Bridget said. "Deidre will be there, too. Time she weighed in."

Krista had to actually unpack her mother's suitcase to stop her from flying east to tear a strip off Phillip. "Definitely not. It'll send the wrong message. She'll grill him as if we're dating. And we're not. We're just friends, okay?"

They smiled indulgently, like when the kids said something cute and naive.

"Now look," Jack said, "at who's not being honest with their feelings."

CHAPTER SIX

IT BECAME CLEAR to Krista after Laura's wedding that she needed to get back in the social media game. Three of the six clients she'd booked from the wedding had asked how they and their friends could follow her. Ringing silence on her website suggested that Phillip had grown bored.

Still, when she set up a Facebook page for the spa, she put it under Bridget's personal profile. She posted artsy shots of the shop with a "hello" discount for a manicure or pedicure to first-time clients. After texting her clients for their permission to post pictures of their finished hands and feet, she watched her follower list grow, her likes uptick and her discounts "loved."

Then she had a sneaky, buzzing thought. What if she were to check up on her Down East peeps? No, bad idea. She was setting herself up to be hurt, and this time it would be totally her fault. But she couldn't shake the impulse, even after she closed down her computer and mopped the floor. It was the ice cream cake for the dieter, the whiskey for the alcoholic. The Facebook search for the trolled victim.

She rationalized her craving. She could prove to herself that she was healed. That she could face her greatest fear and move on. In fact, she wouldn't be able to move on if she didn't. Mara would agree, if asked.

In case things went sideways, she closed the curtains of the spa, flipped the sign to Closed and moved the tissues closer. She started small, calling up the profile of a friend of a friend. Krista scrolled through pictures of the other woman's vacation in New York, the Summer Concert Series in Toronto. One photo included a friend who Krista often had drinks with. Krista clicked on the tag and was bounced over to that friend's page. Nothing much there…same shots of the Summer Concert Series, snaps in clothes the friend had designed until…there, Phillip. He was shown with his arms around a different girl than the one he'd rebounded off Krista with. Another blue-eyed blonde. He clearly had a type. He'd moved on, well on.

Krista checked in with her emotions as

Mara had instructed her to do. A few licks of shame, but she felt ready to rip off the bandage. She typed in his name and tapped Search.

There he was. With a new profile pic of himself and his latest cutie-pie, temples touching as he'd done with Krista.

Little emotional waves rose and then crashed, but nothing breached Krista's peace. Like how she withstood memories of her father who'd passed from a stroke five years ago, and her aunt who'd died in a car accident last fall. It hurt, but time had padded the blow. She'd moved on before and she could again.

For kicks and giggles, she typed in Laura's name. Wedding pics bloomed all over her timeline, including a big one of her and Ryan for her cover image. Wasn't she on her honeymoon, too busy to be updating her profile? Krista settled into scanning through the pics. She'd have to show them to her sisters. The picture of her on Silver, riding barefoot, the dreamy ones of Laura and Ryan caught off guard, so much in love.

And then…one of her and Will.

She'd been trying to dismount from Silver after the photo shoot. Will had guided Silver into place for her time and again during the shoot. She had hoped to at least get off on her own but because of her tight skirt, she ran the risk of flashing everyone.

"Don't even think of it," Will had said, striding over. "You can't hop off like the horse is a fence."

He'd held up his arms. "Ease yourself off and I'll take you the rest of the way."

"No," she said, and then whispered through her plastered smile, "My skirt will ride up."

He grinned. "You mean even farther?"

She'd instinctively clamped her knees together which made her appear even sillier.

"C'mon. Hands on my shoulders. If Silver's like her owner, she's had enough of today's nonsense."

Krista had smiled down at him and that was the moment the camera had captured. Her hands on his shoulders, his hands on her waist, lifting her down and the two of them laughing about what a horse might be thinking.

Except in the image they appeared to be two people madly in love. Which they weren't.

Only more proof that social media twisted the truth.

On impulse, she searched Will's name. There were loads of recent pictures, but the text running with them didn't sound a bit like him. Here I am at my sister's wedding. Isn't she beautiful? A good enough photo of Will and Laura smiling together, but no way would Will ask that question. He wouldn't care what other people thought; he knew his sister was beautiful.

In a separate post was one of Alyssa and Will. He stood, hands on hips, but Alyssa had squeezed herself tight against him. Krista could make out dancing couples behind them—and from the angle, it appeared Alyssa herself had taken the picture. A good friend and I two-stepping to "Nobody but You". Good times, great company!

"Oh, gag me," Krista said aloud. Alyssa had posted that. Alyssa, queen of social media and organizer of the Claverley Rodeo, had appointed herself his social media manager. Ten to one, Will hadn't even seen this post.

Alyssa would've needed Will's permission to take control of his account, but he'd probably handed it over ages ago and gone back to his bloated cow or fence posts.

Krista felt a rush of annoyance with Will. He was tied to Alyssa deeper than probably even he realized. She was tempted to call him but she'd already done her bit. Time for Will to do his.

WILL DIDN'T SEE the photo of Alyssa and him until Dana showed it on her phone. She'd driven up in her truck with the posts they'd need to finish the fence. Hopefully before the day got too much hotter.

"I thought you weren't interested in Alyssa," Dana said accusingly.

"I'm not. Alyssa must've posted it herself."

"What are you going to do about it?"

Will hauled the post through the tangle of open wire, ignoring the twinge in his shoulder. He'd begun to think that he'd have to ignore it for the rest of his life. "Not much I can do now that it's up."

"You could ask her to delete it." Dana pocketed her phone and dragged a fence post from her pickup. "You can tell her that the picture gives the impression you two are dating, which you're not. You can tell her to leave you alone. You can take back control of your Facebook page. Why did you give it to her in the first place?"

Will relieved Dana of the wood. "Branding. She wanted the same look for my personal page as the Claverley Rodeo, or for them not to clash, or something like that. Made sense at the time."

Dana reached for a second post. "Will. This

crosses the line. Krista's right. Alyssa has got to go."

Will shoveled loose dirt from the posthole. "Krista talked to you about Alyssa and me?"

"At the wedding. She's worried for you."

That was supposed to be a private conversation between Krista and him.

"Don't pout," Dana said. "I'm the one who brought up the subject. She figured out my stupid feelings for Keith, and I was trying to distract her. She has a way of getting you to say things you hadn't intended."

Or doing. It'd taken her less than a quarter hour to get him in pajamas and soaking his feet in a tub of salted water. "Tell me about it."

Dana held the post while he tamped dirt around the base. Each drive sent shocks straight to his shoulder. He needed to refill his painkiller prescription.

"She saw us together and asked me about my relationship with Keith. I can't lie to save my soul, so the next thing I know we're best buddies."

"Krista replaces you as my fake girlfriend and me as your best friend."

"She keeps it up and she'll replace Laura as your mom's daughter."

"That I gotta see," Will said. On the wedding day, he'd caught his mother looking at him and Krista with a worried expression. Even after Silver was back safely in the barn.

"It might if you don't watch yourself." One hand steadying the post, Dana held up another photo. The glare from the sun blackened the screen so Will shaded it with his hat. And a good thing his face was hidden from Dana as he took in the sight of him lifting Krista from Silver. She was laughing, her head bent to him. And the emotion on his face…well, it was exactly what the photographer had tried to capture between Laura and Ryan. Way better than him and Alyssa.

He handed Dana's phone back and picked up the ten-pound maul. "Good photo."

"Hardly seems as if you're faking it at all."

Good thing Krista wasn't on social media. He didn't want her…misinterpreting. "We weren't. I mean, we were just having fun."

"Will. You were all over her, all day. You want to date her for real?"

No. His intention going into his next relationship was to make it a forever one, if possible. He and Krista were entirely incompatible. That was why they could be so free and easy with each other, because they didn't take each other seriously as romantic partners.

"Being with Krista is like being with you, Dana."

She waved her phone in his face. "You and I have never been like this."

"That's because you know how to get off a horse."

Dana's voice lowered. "Is that all it is?"

Will got a lump in his gut. Similar to when he'd told her she couldn't break sixteen seconds on the barrel race and she'd let fly with a 15:87 posting. He was about to lose.

She tapped on her phone and shaded it with her own hat this time, probably so he couldn't hide his reaction. The ten-pound maul nearly slipped from his grip. It was another picture of him and Krista. Dana had taken the shot. Krista was smiling at the camera. Will was turned to Krista and he looked as if he thought himself the luckiest guy in the world.

"You didn't post that pic, did you?" he said. If Keith or his mom saw it, there'd be no living it down.

"What should it matter if you two are faking it?"

Because everybody who knew him would take one glance at that image and understand that he wasn't faking a thing. One posted photo could be passed off as a fluke. He could tell a funny story about how the city girl had been about to fall off the horse. Krista would back him up. But a second one? Where he looked dead serious except for that little smile, the same one his dad wore in the photo of him and Will's mom at their twenty-fifth wedding anniversary.

"Thanks for keeping it between us," he muttered. "No chance you'd delete it?"

"Not a one." She slid her phone once again into her back pocket. "Never know when I need ammunition."

"I thought we're friends."

Dana picked up a string of wire to reattach to the new post. "Not the way you and Krista are."

No use arguing more. She was determined to think what she wanted. Even if it was absolutely dead wrong.

THE NEXT EVENING when Alyssa came into Penny's to meet Will, he wished he were anywhere else. Alyssa wore a short dress and heels, her hair all curly around her face.

Decked out for a date. He'd come in clean skin and a clean shirt. Maybe he shouldn't have chosen Penny's. Open in the evening on a limited menu, mostly drinks and desserts, he'd chosen the place because it was more conducive for close conversation than the commercial buzz of the chain restaurants. But now he realized Penny's was far too quiet and... intimate. Besides which, their server was Jack, Krista's brother-in-law. Will didn't want Krista to get wind of how this went down. He wasn't even sure if Jack knew about the fake arrangement.

They could've gone out riding, but that's what his parents did together, what you did with someone you were dead serious about.

At least he'd selected the same table he'd had with Dana instead of a cozy booth. Alyssa took the chair opposite. Her lips were a glaring barn red. "I see you've ordered already."

"A coffee," he said. "What can I get you?"

"A glass of red, please."

Like a discreet five-star waiter, Jack presented the wine and took their dessert orders. Apple crisp with double vanilla ice cream for him and the lemon cheesecake for Alyssa. He bet Krista would've gone for the mint chocolate crème brûlée. Fresh and cool and sweet.

He and Alyssa made small talk. At least, Alyssa made talk, while he kept to the small as he found himself in the exact position he'd been in with Dana a month ago—trying to figure out how to bring up what he really wanted to say. Alyssa wondered if he wouldn't mind posing with Jacob for pictures to post on social media. Will liked her nephew and agreed. Then she asked if he had any pictures of himself from his days when he was Jacob's age to give it a human touch, to appeal to the older crowd. He couldn't quite see the connection, but he gave Alyssa the benefit of the doubt and said he'd ask his mom what was in their albums.

But it was when she suggested a photo shoot of him and Jacob on horseback with Alyssa joining in as the aunt that he put the brakes on.

"Jacob up to riding yet?"

"Are you kidding? My sister can't keep him down." Alyssa wrapped her overdone lips around a forkful of cheesecake.

"Maybe after the rodeo."

Alyssa frowned. "No point doing it after. Trust me, I'm the professional."

Will pushed around his melting ice cream. "I don't doubt your professionalism. Except I saw the picture of us you posted on my Facebook page. I think it gives the wrong impression about us."

Alyssa cut off a thin delicate sliver of her cheesecake. "And what impression would that be?"

She was not going to make this easy for him. "That we're dating."

She gazed pointedly at their table, their surroundings. "Isn't that what this is?"

"I didn't intend it that way," he said carefully. "Though I can see how you might have assumed that. I'm sorry," he added for good measure.

She twirled her fork. "You don't want everybody to believe we're dating when we're not, and you especially don't want me posting pictures of us together when we're not."

Relief rolled in like breeze through a hot truck cab. "Yes, that's exactly what I'm saying. Thank you for understanding."

"No problem," she said. She cut off another fine slice of cheesecake. He shoveled crisp into his mouth.

"Good crisp," he said. "How's the cheesecake?" Look at him making small talk.

"A little dry but okay," Alyssa said. "Dana tells me that she's not your fake girlfriend this year."

Will slowed his fork. Had Dana also mentioned that Krista was filling in? "Yeah, she has something else going on."

"Well, then," Alyssa said, "given that everybody already thinks I'm your girlfriend, how about we just continue on?"

Will's crisp stuck in his throat. "You want to be my fake girlfriend?"

"Yes." Her foot brushed against his leg, glided away. Maybe accidently, but he was beginning to realize that not much about Alyssa was accidental.

"Did you purposely post that picture to set us up as a fake couple?"

"Will," Alyssa said, "we danced together at the wedding. That's all the picture says. A picture doesn't lie."

Images rose in his mind—of him reaching up for Krista like a man with his bride. Him staring at Krista like a shmuck in love.

"We are good friends, aren't we?" Alyssa persisted.

"I guess."

"Then what's the harm?"

Will fixed his gaze on the shared wall between Penny's and Krista's Place. Was Krista there right now serving up another pedicure to some other unsuspecting guy? Melting another rancher's wife with her massage? He swore he could smell her fresh hay and grassy lotions from where he sat.

Riding on the calming memory of Krista's scents, he said, "The harm is that I've already got a fake girlfriend."

Alyssa's gold-brown eyes drilled into his. "Who?"

Better she heard it from him. "Krista. Krista Montgomery," he added unnecessarily. But saying her full name made it sound more like a formal arrangement between two partners. Not the fun-filled, close experience it was.

Alyssa mashed a slice of cheesecake under her fork. He hadn't fooled her. "When did you plan this?"

"Can't say the exact day. Couple of weeks at least before Laura's wedding. Maybe three."

"Maybe three? Was I still Laura's maid of honor when you two decided?"

"I think so. Listen, Alyssa, the two aren't connected."

Her fork clattered to her plate. A couple glanced over. So did Jack. "Are you really that stupid, Will?" she hissed. Hissing was good. She was keeping her voice under control. "Krista set you up."

Exactly what he'd wanted to avoid—dragging Krista into this.

"How do you figure that?" Will said. "I'm the one who brought the idea to her."

"That's what you think. But did you decide on your own that you wanted Krista to be your fake girlfriend, or were you talking with her and suddenly it came up?"

He couldn't remember. He knew that at some point he wanted to have a reason to see Krista again. "I guess," he admitted, "it came up."

"And then she plays up her problems with the horse at Laura's wedding and you are happy to help. Isn't it obvious that she's using you?"

"I have my own brain."

"I really wonder." Her expression became eerily calm. "Tell me, Will, what made you decide to have this little talk with me?"

"As I said, it was the picture on Facebook. And to be honest, others noticed it, too."

"Others? Krista, by chance?"

He was tired of her innuendoes. "As a matter of fact, yes. She wanted me to be honest with you because she believed the longer I put off telling you, the more I was going to end up hurting you."

Alyssa's eyes brightened with tears. "You're a little late for that."

Will felt horrible. He was humiliating her in a public place. "Do you want to go?" he whispered. "We can leave together. Go for a walk. Finish talking."

She shook her head. "Why drag this out?" She hooked her purse over her shoulder. "But I feel sorry for you. Krista will promise to work with you, be there for you. She'll build you up and make you believe you two can take on the world. And then she'll move on. Leave you wondering what went wrong. That's our sweet little Krista Montgomery."

CHAPTER SEVEN

DANA HAD TO admit she'd never looked more beautiful than she did for the wedding of her sister, Caris. Not without a good deal of backup in the form of a sensational maid of honor dress, and hair and makeup by Krista.

"I don't recognize myself," she whispered to her own reflection in the spa mirror. She touched one of her many curls cultivated into full plumpness from her usual bed of natural waves.

"Don't you dare put a baseball cap on it," Krista warned.

Dana leaned closer. "Is it my imagination or do I see a bit of blonde?"

Krista squinted. "Definitely a light brown."

Oh well. Nothing was perfect. Dana pulled at her strapless dress front. Krista tutted. "And none of that, either. You've got enough to hold it up, trust me." Krista tilted her head. "You're not used to so many eyes on you."

Dana breathed out, shot a look at her bodice to make sure nothing became dislodged. "Hate being under a microscope. Should I ever get married, it's elopement or whoever can fit into the living room on a Tuesday afternoon."

"You know," Krista whispered so the rest of the bridal party couldn't hear, "today might be the perfect time to clue that future husband in about your plans."

Dana fiddled with the carnation on her wrist corsage. "I couldn't."

"Why not? Love is in the air."

"He'll think—he's not ready."

"Isn't that for him to decide?"

"I suppose—but I don't want to lose what I already have."

"But what if you gain something more?"

There was that. And lately, maybe because of all the weddings, or seeing the way Will and Krista were together, something important was building inside her, something close to an overwhelming obligation to take a risk. "I will try."

But as the events of the day unrolled, there was precious little time to think, much less talk to Keith. During a pause in photos, he searched her out to coordinate the next item in the itinerary, and she liked how he lingered by her side longer than necessary. They'd stood together at the edge of the lawn in an unusually awkward silence. At least on her part. *Speak from the heart*, she reminded herself. But how to say, "Keith, I love you. Will you marry me and be the father of my kids?" She didn't have Krista's moxie.

Keith himself broke the silence. "Will tells me you—"

Right then, Caris called for them to rejoin the others for group shots. Keith slipped his suit jacket on again. "The show continues."

Walking back together, Dana forced herself to say, "When I get married, it'll be fast and small."

Keith gave her a sidelong look. "When? You got someone in mind already?"

Now was her chance, closing fast as they were steps away from the rest of the wedding party. "Yes, actually. I do."

He looked at the wedding party, tightened his tie. "Good, good. Anyway, duty calls."

She could believe that he didn't care about her love life, period. She could also believe that he just didn't care about her love life with someone other than him. When she spotted him alone at a reception table scrolling on his phone—her hair, makeup and dress still good to go—she chose the latter possibility. She armed herself with a vodka cooler from the bar and ordered her feet to cross the dance floor to him, brushing past Will and Krista, neither of them noticing her or for that matter, anyone else.

Maybe she could have a little of what they had.

KRISTA HAD NOT intended to dance with Will. They weren't expected to. And after the traditional initial dances, he disappeared. She had hoped to touch base with him about the Claverley Rodeo, but that was almost two weeks away. Plenty of time yet.

She ducked into the hall foyer for a quiet place to send pics to Sofia. Her niece shared Krista's passion for fashion and she'd promised to forward a few pictures before the girl's nine o'clock bedtime. Except she wanted to bling the pics with effects. She was tapping a spray of stars above Will's hair when the DJ let go with the same song she and Will had performed with the others at Laura's wedding. Her feet instinctively shuffled in time.

"You remember the steps." Janet had stepped into the foyer. She wore a pale gray dress inlaid with a giant pink peony that spread from a side seam around to the front. Striking, as was everything about Will's mother.

Krista felt childish in her yellow sundress. "Will's a good teacher."

Janet fixed Krista with a steady look. "Always there to give a helping hand."

"I couldn't agree with you more," Krista said. Okay, that came out a little strong. Janet made her nervous, had since she was a teen. Janet had always been a mother bear around her family, and seemed to believe Krista was out for her cubs.

Janet waved her hand at the coat closet. A very nicely manicured hand. Janet had come in this past week for a touch up to her manicure, completely separate from Will's Mother's Day package she'd yet to book. "Are you leaving?"

Krista hadn't any intention but then again, what was she staying for?

"Yeah, been a long day."

"I bet." Janet paused. "You did a wonderful job with the hair and makeup. You have a real talent for making people feel good."

That was unexpected. "Thank you so much."

"A skill set completely different from mine as a co-owner of a ranch. And a rancher's wife."

Pieces fell into place. Janet must've seen

the photo of her and Will with the horse and assumed that Krista was crushing on Will again. "I couldn't agree more. You saw me at Laura's wedding. I'm totally useless around horses. I don't even know what a bloated cow is. The country is something that I just drive through." How else to say she had no designs on Will?

As luck would not have it, the son in question entered the foyer and came immediately over. He'd done away with his suit jacket and tie, and his shirtsleeves were rolled up to reveal tanned, muscled arms. She felt that old tug of attraction, rather inconvenient, given Janet was studying them both. "Mom. Krista. I finished loading up a few of the extra tables. I thought you two would be dancing."

"No," Janet said. "I'm stepping out for a bit of fresh air. Krista said she was leaving."

Will frowned. "Really? I was hoping we could sort out things about the rodeo."

Janet's mouth thinned. "And that stupid ride you insist on doing."

"Mom—"

"Your shoulder is still damaged, and you're acting like nothing ever happened."

"I've got it under control."

Janet flipped up her hand. "You're not

going to listen to me. I'll leave you two to talk."

When Janet exited, Krista turned to Will. "What's this about your shoulder?"

"It's been acting up a bit."

"Translation from cowboy talk—it feels as if a car ran over it."

"I'm good."

She stepped in close, looked right up into his face. He stood his ground. "You're not lying to me, are you?"

He switched on the slow-burning Claverley smile. You could roast marshmallows over that smile. "You concerned about me?"

She didn't want to be. Ever since her sisters had disputed her honesty about her feelings, she'd deliberately not contacted Will all week. It proved harder than she'd expected, and now that he was right in front of her, she had to fight the urge not to cling to him like a buckle bunny. "You haven't answered my question."

"I did. You chose not to believe me. It's *my* question you haven't answered."

He was evading her, but she didn't have the right to demand a medical update from him. "Of course, I'm concerned. But I won't pry.

Let me finish sending this pic to my niece and I'm at your service."

"What picture?" His voice had sharpened.

She held up her screen showing the bridal party.

He peered at it and straightened. "That's fine."

"What did you think I was going to send?"

He rubbed the back of his neck. "Just curious. I didn't realize there were fireworks going off above my head when you took the picture."

"They're always going off with you around." Whoa. That came off more like an innuendo than a joke. She hurriedly sent the picture. "You wanted to talk about the rodeo."

She looked up to find him studying her. He eerily reminded her of his mother. "We can talk about the rodeo another time."

Nice one, Krista. She had come on too strong, and he was wisely distancing himself from her. "I guess I'll go."

"Dance with me instead."

Krista's heart missed a beat, as her feet no doubt would. "Don't you have tables to haul out?"

Will took her hand. "If they need me, they can just look for the fireworks."

KEITH SET ASIDE his phone as Dana approached. "Hey. Austin only went down a half hour ago, the babysitter said."

Dana took a seat beside him, her bare shoulder grazing his shirted arm. It was natural that they would sit close to hear each other above the music. "Yikes. Remember back when I covered for you in March?" He'd had a rare overnight haul, and she'd stepped in when Janet and Dave were vacationing in Mexico. It was eleven before she could convince Austin to sleep and then he'd been raring to go at five in the morning.

"I know. The later to bed, the earlier to rise. I might head out. Try to get a few hours of sleep in before the Austin alarm goes off."

Now or never. Start anywhere.

"So earlier today, before we were interrupted, you were saying something about Will talking about me...?"

Keith pulled on his already loosened tie. "Nothing important. Not my business."

But her business. He was curious about her. She reined in her jolt of hope, took a swig of her cooler. "Go for it. I want to hear what Will has been saying about me."

Keith pushed aside a paper plate smeared with the chocolate remains of the wedding cake. "He said you refused to run interference for him at this year's rodeo."

"Yeah, the gig got old." Dana kept her voice casual. He wouldn't bring that up unless he was interested in her private life. "I decided to maybe try becoming a girlfriend for real. Not his," she added quickly, in case there was any doubt.

Keith glanced at her, more at her hair, and then away. It probably looked strange, not like Krista's blond, bouncy curls. Dana gazed out at the dance floor where she spotted Krista and Will. They might've sensed being watched because Krista waved and Will grinned. Both knew her deepest secret. Krista went on tippy-toe and whispered into Will's ear.

"One of the rodeo contestants?" Keith broke into her thoughts.

What? How did he figure that? "No!"

"Will said it was somebody who came to the rodeo."

What was Will up to? "What else did Will say about me?"

Keith looked at his brother. Will and Krista were edging off the dance floor and out the side exit, hand in hand. Keith gave a snort of disgust. "He better watch himself."

"Why? He and Krista are good together."

"They might look good, but there's more to a relationship than that."

A reference to his irresponsible ex. "Krista's different than Macey."

"I'm not so sure. She has the same talent for making a grown man stupid. Will was smart enough to step away from Krista when he was twenty, but now—"

"What? He never told me about that."

"I don't think he told anybody else. I noticed the two of them started avoiding each other way more than necessary, and asked him. He neither confirmed, nor denied. But now, he seems to have changed his mind."

"Or maybe," Dana tried to steer the conversation back to them, "maybe he realized that he'd passed up something really good and now that he has the chance to make it right, he isn't going to make the same mistake twice."

"Talking about him or yourself?" He blew out his breath. "Sorry, Dana. None of my business. You can get involved with whoever you want."

What to say to that? He clearly wasn't offering to fill the position.

"Though," he added, "you've already got a particular somebody in mind."

He wouldn't keep circling back to the question, if he wasn't interested on some level. *Go for it*, her heart commanded her head. She felt the same coiled tension before the buzzer sounded at the start of a barrel race. Where anything was possible.

"What if," Dana said, her heart galloping, "I were to say that the particular someone was you?"

THE COOLNESS OF the evening pebbled Krista's bare skin as Will led her around the edge of the dance hall to an empty bench. The blooms of a nearby white lilac bush scented the air. It was peaceful, even romantic.

But Will's mind was on something else. "I'm worried about Dana. Keith will refuse to date her, and he won't be diplomatic about it, either."

On the dance floor, she'd told Will that she'd urged Dana to open up to Keith. Will had not reacted well, hauling her outside. "I'm sure that he's got some Claverley charm." Which was confessing that Will had it. But he'd seemed unaware of the compliment, sidetracked by the supposed disaster going on between Dana and his brother.

"Won't outweigh his bitterness toward

women." He rubbed his hand across his face. She could make out the faint scrape of his stubble under his palm. "If I'd known you had figured out Dana's feelings for Keith, I would've warned you not to encourage her."

"Did Keith actually tell you he wasn't interested in Dana?"

Will hesitated. "No. And if he could bring himself to be interested in anyone, it would be her."

"Then give them a chance."

Will dropped to the bench, elbows on his knees. "Look, I'd be all for them getting together. But with Keith, it'll take a while. If Dana makes a move now, it'll scare him off. I know my brother."

"Or it'll be the wake-up call he needs to realize that there are good women out there who genuinely care for him and his son."

Will raised his head to meet her eyes. "You just can't help interfering, can you?"

Ah, the root of his frustration. Keith and Dana weren't the only couple she'd meddled with. She drew her sandal through the loose gravel. "Jack said you and Alyssa met up. And that you left separately. I'm sorry it didn't go well."

"I might've told her about you being my

fake girlfriend. I guess she was angling for the position and figured you cut in."

He looked so uncomfortable, caught in the middle of a catfight. Poor guy. Krista aimed to sound dismissive. "We've got history. After high school, she talked me into becoming partners in a marketing company, even though my heart wasn't in it. Not a year later, I walked away from it and she hasn't really forgiven me. Turned her down again a few years ago. She believes I'm a flake."

"And you think she's got a point?"

"No! I mean, maybe once…" She plucked at the daisy petals on her sundress. "Why do you say that? Do I give that impression?"

"Not in my eyes. You're working your tail off to make a success of your salon, even going so far as to take on this arrangement between us."

"But for a lot of years, I was exactly what Alyssa accused me of. I jumped from one job to another, one country to another, for that matter." She paused and then fessed up. "Had way more than one relationship."

"Oh." He cleared his throat. "So I wasn't the only one you asked out?"

Since she insisted on honesty from Will, she needed to give fair turnabout. "You were the only one who refused me." The only one she'd cried about not getting.

"Just so you know," he said softly, his mouth close to her ear, like when he'd whispered the dance steps to her at the rehearsal. "Riding bareback was easier than saying no to you."

Keep it light, Krista. "It's okay," she said. "I recovered."

"But I hurt you."

A statement of fact she couldn't refute. "What's the saying? 'What doesn't kill us makes us stronger.'"

He looked back through the door. Inside, Dana was opening a vein for Keith, and Keith—she could only hope he showed common sense.

Will touched his knee to hers. "You know, there's something to be said for not forcing people into hurting others in the name of honesty."

"In other words, I shouldn't have pushed you into hurting me. Thing is, I was pretty cocky back then. I didn't believe you would turn me down. Or that I would be hurt."

"Dana's taken the bigger risk, then, because she's well aware what could happen. And the thing is, Krista, not everybody's as tough as you."

She twisted to get a better look at him.

Not even a glimmer of the famous Claverley smile. "Me tough? You're crazy."

"You call yourself a flake because you walk away from things you no longer want. That's courage, Krista. Hardest thing about riding bronc is the dismount. That's when the majority of injuries happen. There's no avoiding it for us riders, but people will go through life getting bucked around and not having the nerve to break free. You're not one of those people, and that's a good thing."

Krista felt winded. Will Claverley, bronc rider champion, thought *she* was brave. "Oh. I—thank you." The corner of his mouth turned up. A very kissable corner. She gave herself a mental shake. "But Dana has it in her, too. To be brave."

"I'm more worried about my brother. Macey bucked him off hard. He's back on his feet, but definitely not back in the saddle." He paused. "How about you? After that Toronto guy, are you back in the saddle?"

Was he wondering if she was dating again? "I'm on my feet, maybe, but I'm not dating."

The other side of his mouth kicked up. "For real, anyway."

Enough of the hot seat. "What about you? I take it you're not dating anyone seriously?"

"Not at all, actually." He grew interested in gravel she was scuffing around. "I kind of made up my mind to find someone I could picture for the long-term."

"You're looking for a wife?"

"You could say that."

Of course, he would be. He was sharing his plans with her because that's what friends, totally unsuited romantically for each other, do. "Oh."

"That was always my plan, you know. Have my rodeo career and then carry on at the ranch."

"Is that…what you want?"

"What I've always wanted. That's why I didn't think it would work between us in high school. You'd be off sooner rather than later, and I knew I wasn't going anywhere."

Krista laughed to show how little his rejection had hurt, how his current pursuit of a serious girlfriend mattered nothing to her. "I was only asking you out, Will. Not to marry me."

He turned to face her. "Maybe. But even then I realized dating you would be way more intense than I could handle, and I didn't trust myself to land the dismount." He twined his finger around one of her curls. "I admit sometimes I wonder if it might've been worth it."

She fought to draw a full breath, though it came out like a gasp. "We both know I'd make a lousy wife."

"You might be right about that." Well, she had wanted honesty. His hand fell from her hair. He stood, tugging her up with him. "You and me might not work, but how about we go inside and see if we can get my stubborn brother to hang on for the full count?"

DANA WAITED FOR Keith's response. Had she misread the situation entirely? Anything was possible, and in this case it was as if her horse had balked at the first barrel.

At her question, Keith had turned sharply to her, shock and disappointment on his face. He looked away. Fiddled with his phone, stared hard in the direction of the bar, watched the whirling, twisting dancers. Dana's insides jolted downward.

She couldn't back out now. She'd have to sit here and let him give her the no-can-do speech.

He finally faced her. Well, her hair. "I'd say you could do better, Dana. You are better.

You know my life. I work all day, and then I'm a dad the rest of the time. I'm pushing thirty and live at home. You shouldn't settle."

He was giving her the old "It's not you, it's me" letdown. She picked at the label on her bottle. "I'm not settling."

"And you can do a lot better than a rodeo guy. Will has told me stories about what they'll do on the road. Don't sell yourself short."

Where was that coming from? "I'm not—"

But Keith was on a roll. "I've always wondered why Will didn't snap you up."

"He tried. I said I only wanted to be friends."

Keith glared at the door Will and Krista had left through. "When was this?"

"A few weeks back."

"And now he's hooked up with Krista. A rebound."

Dana was relieved he'd steered the conversation to Krista and Will again. "I don't think it's a rebound."

"She's entirely unsuitable to be his wife. It won't last more than the summer, I bet. So long as he doesn't—" Keith broke off, but Dana mentally finished it. So long as he doesn't get her pregnant. That was what happened with Macey. Keith had married her, a quick slapdash affair that everyone had attended, plastering on smiles and not bothering with extended warranties on the gifts.

"Krista's caught up with her business. I don't anticipate problems there." Then again, what kind of relationship expert was she? She'd just let her own heart get stomped on. She picked up her cooler and drained the contents in one go. When she lowered the bottle, Keith was frowning at her.

"You've not had too many of those, have you?"

He was giving her an out. Blame it on the alcohol and save both of them embarrassment.

"Probably. Didn't sleep much last night. And big day today. Didn't eat much. I should…let you go home."

"If you don't mind…"

"Sure. Go." Before she ruined Krista's makeup and started bawling right here, right now.

She waited until he disappeared through the doorway before beelining for the bar.

On her way across the floor, she spied Will and Krista slipping back in. Krista spotted her, waved and started toward her. But Will caught her arm. Good move. Right now, as unfair as it was, she couldn't stand the sight of pretty Krista. Or Keith's brother, for that matter.

CHAPTER EIGHT

Where are you?

WILL'S TEXT CHIRPED as Krista turned into the long driveway of the Claverley Ranch. She was supposed to have been at the ranch an hour ago but a chatty client proved hard to shoo out, and then she'd had to dash to her apartment, throw on something a girlfriend of a rodeo champion would wear before hustling out there.

The suspension on her low-riding car took a beating as she bounced along the freshly mowed land between the arena and road, now functioning as a parking lot for a hundred or so vehicles. Friday night and Spirit Lake's top-ranking outdoor summer show was set to get underway. Top-ranking according to Alyssa's buzz, anyway, which glossed over the town's jazz festival, youth festival, sailing festival, beach volleyball playoffs—all of which Krista had attended instead of the rodeo when she'd lived in Spirit Lake. A rodeo featured wild horses and mean bulls and rocks-for-brains cowboys.

Yet here she was, picking her way across a mosquito-thick pasture to be with one of those cowboys. And kind of excited. She'd not seen much of Will in the past two weeks. They'd made their plans via text or quick calls. She'd seen him only once when he'd dropped off boots Laura had wanted her to have. White and studded silver with intricate rainbow threading, they were on her feet right now as she texted: I'm here. Where are you?

East end of arena by the gates.

Wherever that was. She'd walk to the arena and ask someone.

Families with blankets and lawn chairs were forming a settlement on the sunny grass slope opposite the covered bleachers. It might make a decent weekend outing for Jack, Bridget and the girls. She sent Bridget a photo, as Keith came along on a horse big as a hill with Austin tucked in front of him on the saddle.

And this, Krista thought, is why farms

ranked high for accidents. Though she couldn't deny that Austin seemed totally at ease up there in the curve of his dad's arm.

Keith slowed to a stop. "Here to meet Will?"

"On my way to him now. Uh, which end of the arena is east? Asking for a friend."

To his credit, he kept a straight face as he pointed to the other end. "He's there in the big white hat."

So he was, and she noticed there were already a couple of pretty little things within arm's reach of him. She also noticed Alyssa on his other side.

"I better beetle on over there."

"Ready to be Will's girl?" Keith didn't crack a smile. In fact, he sounded as if she were lowering herself onto a bull.

"Sure. How hard can it be?"

"Not bad. Saturday's the peak period." As if buckle bunnies were an infestation.

"I'll slap them down."

He grinned, the wide Claverley smile that came straight from Dave and the four generation of Claverleys that had called this land theirs. It was a living Claverley heirloom, and while Krista thought Will wore it better, Keith was a contender. "That's what Dana used to say."

"She here?" Krista kept it casual, unsure if Keith knew she'd encouraged Dana to reveal her feelings.

"Not yet." He adjusted Austin's baseball cap against the sun. "She usually comes for the barrel racing. Dana won every year before she retired a couple of years ago." His pride in her was unmistakable. You didn't feel pride for someone you didn't care about. Maybe there was still hope, if Keith shaped up.

Austin pushed up on his cap, twisted to gaze up at his dad. "Dana?"

Keith couldn't have looked more surprised than if his horse had talked. "He said, 'Dana,' didn't he?"

"Loud and clear."

Keith's arm tightened around Austin. "Good work, son. Your first word."

"First word? Wow. That's something to celebrate." Krista felt an upwelling of pride herself, and she hardly knew the little guy. "You'll have to tell Dana."

Keith played with the reins. "I guess."

"It will make her day." It would also give Keith a reason to contact Dana. If he was searching for one.

Krista's phone chimed. Can you see me?

"I better go. Will's antsy."

She left Keith frowning at his phone. Tell her, she silently urged.

THE TWO BUCKLE BUNNIES had edged alongside Will as Krista arrived, their skirts high and their tops low. They looked like twins, or else they shopped at the same place and shared the same makeup. Alyssa glared at them.

Time for her to step up. She skimmed her hand across his lower back, lifted his arm and ducked underneath. "Hey there."

He grimaced. Had she played it up too much? They hadn't talked specifics but some physical contact made sense. He squeezed her shoulder and tucked her closer to his side. Ha! Krista flashed a smile at the girls.

But then Will's arm slipped down to her waist in a loose hold. Very loose. Well, his choice. Out in the arena, a performer was defying gravity on her horse. She was extended sideways from the saddle, long golden hair streaming out as her horse galloped around the perimeter of the arena. The crowd in the stands and on the grassy slope opposite whistled and clapped. As horse and rider passed in a rush of muscle, pounding hooves and sequins, Krista joined in the applause.

She was about to remark on the act when she noticed tension around Will's mouth and eyes, like a horse had backed onto his foot and he was determined not to react. "What's up?"

He rested his boot on the bottom rail. "I'm good." He added, his lips grazing her cheek, "Glad you're here."

Nobody could've heard him, so why say it? His attention pivoted to the equine goddess who was now standing on one leg atop her cantering horse. "Will. Do you know the main difference between her and me?"

"What?"

"Everything."

There, his mouth softened. "I'm up next on the stage," he said. "They're about to make an announcement about the ride I'm doing tomorrow." He patted his pocket. "I'm supposed to say something."

"Ah. And you'd rather ride a bull that throws you into a pit of hungry boars while under attack from murder hornets."

"Something like that."

"What are you supposed to talk about?"

"The reason for the ride, and then to ask people to open their wallets. 'Call to action' it's called. Alyssa's written something up for me."

Of course Alyssa would've micromanaged Will's every step. "Hold on to the mic like you would the leather strap thingy and read right to the end."

Will's lips were twitching like an invisible butterfly kept landing there. His hand on her waist tightened. She leaned in. All part of the act. "You'll rock this. Just be—"

"Yourself. Speak from the heart, right?"

"Speaking of speaking, Austin said his first word. I heard it myself."

Will finally broke into a full smile. "Is that right? What was it?"

"Dana."

His smile faded. "How did that go over?"

"I left Keith staring at his phone, deciding whether or not to text Dana with the news."

"And let me guess. You suggested to him that he should."

"It's big news! Wouldn't you want to know if Austin had said your name?"

She wouldn't get her answer because Alyssa tapped his arm. "Time to go."

Will did that lip-grazing-cheek thing again. "You'll wait here?"

Krista was sure her cheek had scorch marks. "I might move around an inch or two, maybe go to the dance later."

She could feel his full smile against her cheek, a reward for her sass. Yep, Will's smile took top honors. His hand fell away from her waist and he reached up to adjust his hat. Tension tightened his features.

Krista finally connected the dots. He wasn't sending mixed signals. He was in pain. "Will. Your shoulder. You've hurt it."

"It's fine. It's stiff from the work I've done this week setting up fence panels and moving stock in. I've got a physio appointment next week. All's good."

"But it was hurting last week, too. At the wedding. You acted as if it was nothing. And now you've pushed it too far. You could seriously reinjure yourself, if you're not careful. Are you sure you should be doing the ride?"

"Krista. I'm not going to cancel the ride. Too many people are counting on me. Alyssa, Jacob, the hospital kids…no."

"I'm not saying you should cancel…just postpone it."

He shook his head. "Krista, I'll see you later." He headed for the announcer's booth.

He was being stubborn. Krista had to go directly to the source. She caught up to Alyssa as she was about to follow Will.

"Look," Krista said, "I don't know if you're aware, but Will's shoulder is not good."

Alyssa stepped well within Krista's space. Clear intimidation. "It's been 'not good' for a year now. I've been aware of that longer than you."

Krista took a step back. "I understand. Only it seems to have gotten worse."

"Is that what he's told you?"

"In not so many words. Janet's also worried."

"She loves to worry. What's your point?"

"He's doing the ride because he doesn't want to let you down. But if you assured him he could postpone the ride if necessary, he might do it."

Alyssa's eyes widened. "You're telling me that I should throw the charity ride because Will has a sore shoulder?"

"It's serious—"

"What happens to the kids in the hospital is serious, Krista. Life-or-death serious. The money the sponsors paid is serious. Your opinion is not. Unless Will comes to me and says he's pulling out, nobody will stop it from happening. Not even you, Krista Montgomery. Now I've got a show, a serious show, to run."

Alyssa disappeared up the stairs. Krista finally understood Janet's fear for her son. It was squeezing her own heart, and there was nothing she could do.

"AND NOW I'LL turn it over to the star, two-time rodeo champion and Spirit Lake's number one cowboy, Will Claverley!"

Amid hoots and hollers, Alyssa handed Will the mic. "Your speech is in your pocket," she ground out through a plastered smile.

Shoot, he'd forgotten to have it ready. He fumbled in his shirt.

"Sorry about this," he muttered into the mic. "I guess I figured I had to give the nod first."

The Friday night crowd—off work and with beers in hand—laughed.

Alyssa's script in hand, he scanned the lines again. When he'd read it earlier, it had sounded like someone trying to imitate him. Which, given it was written by Alyssa, made sense. He probably couldn't have done better on his own.

Settling his focus on the stands where all the major donors of the ride were seated in the VIP section, he caught sight of Krista on a platform at the bottom.

Speak from the heart, she'd said.

No. He'd stop and start like an old truck. Best to stick to the script.

"First, on behalf of the Claverley Family, I want to thank you for coming to the Fifty-eighth Annual Spirit Lake Pro Rodeo. We start planning the next rodeo the day the last one ends—" not literally true but close enough "—and we're always looking to make it bigger and better."

Actually, there'd been a fair amount of family discussion about how it had gotten too big already. His shoulder was acting up because they'd had to erect far more temporary pens for the stock than they'd capacity for.

"This year it's my great honor to be doing a special celebrity ride." Some celebrity he was when Krista probably didn't even know what he was champion in. And hadn't seemed interested in knowing.

He searched the stands for her again. She wasn't listening to his speech. Instead, she was taking a picture of a family, trying to squeeze in everyone from the grandparents down to the babies. She took a step backward. If she didn't watch, she'd fall right off the platform, a good ten-foot drop. Weren't there supposed to be portable benches underneath? He was sure he'd asked to have them in place. How had that slipped inspection?

He focused on his page. "I first heard about the Calgary Children's Hospital when Alyssa told me about her nephew's harrowing journey with cancer. I—" Krista was right on the edge. Nobody seemed to have warned her. He lowered his sheet. "Krista Montgomery. Please step away from the edge."

Krista lowered her phone, registered the drop and stepped forward. She waved at him and grinned. He felt a lift, that same lightness as when she'd hung his arm around her shoulders and the stress and scramble of the week had fallen away. "We'll have to deal with that drop. Someone else might be as oblivious to danger as my girlfriend."

He stopped. He'd said Krista was his girlfriend, not to whomever they happened to bump into, but to the whole crowd. Hundreds.

From the distance of sixty, seventy yards away, Krista cupped her hands around her mouth and yelled, "Honey, those someone elses are called cowboys!"

The crowd roared.

Alyssa edged up to him. "Just finish the speech," she hissed.

It was impossible now. He'd gone so far

off track, it didn't make any sense to continue. He'd spent all day looking forward to being with Krista. Since Caris's wedding, he'd counted the days to when he'd see her next. He had missed her bright chatter, the way she walked with so much bounce her hair lifted off her shoulders, the way her hands felt on his aching shoulder. The anticipation had carried him through the worsening pain in his arm.

He'd made plans for what they'd do when they were together again, what he'd say. He'd started to wonder if Krista might not make the lousy wife she'd claimed at the wedding. They'd both grown in the past ten years, including, it appeared, his feelings for her.

And today, when she'd slipped up beside him, fitted herself to his length and smiled up at him as if there was no place she'd rather be…well, he was sure it wasn't all one-sided on his part. Her as his fake girlfriend was now an excuse until he found a way to convince her to be his real one.

The crowd had quieted, waiting for him to finish.

Be honest.

Speak from the heart.

"Krista just told me some great news. My

nephew, Austin—some of you might've met him already. He said his first word today. I won't share what it was because it was somebody's name and we're hoping to connect with her first. But I gotta say, my nephew's one smart kid. Because he said the name of someone who isn't technically family, but Austin has already figured out that family's more than people with the same last name. And that's how I see us all here tonight, and the way I see those kids dealing with illness head-on at the hospital. Here's to hoping we can help all of us, and all of them take a step away from the edge."

The crowd broke into applause and after a hasty thanks he happily relinquished the mic to the rodeo announcer.

He didn't stick around. He had bleachers to move into place and then—Krista.

FROM WHERE SHE was handing out her business cards in the VIP section, Krista glimpsed Will and his crew do a final check on the portable bleachers. She'd have to motor through her spiel faster to get back to him so she could play the part that he'd announced to the entire audience.

His broadcast of their personal relationship had made it way more real, something she couldn't escape from. She sensed people's inspection, scrutinizing her every move and word. A kind of rodeo reprise of her social media debacle.

"Hi there," she said to a woman in denim and diamond earrings, a glass of wine in hand. "I'm Krista Montgomery, offering Speed Spa Saturday over by the food trucks tomorrow. A ten minute pedicure for ten bucks. All proceeds go into the same bucket as Will's charity ride."

The woman winked, tucked the card inside her purse. "I like your game. You better hurry along. Your guy's waiting."

So he was at the bottom of the stairs. He gave a little chin lift. She was tempted to drop the cards and rush to him, but what then of her business? She held up ten fingers to indicate how much longer she'd be. He took out his phone and sat on the bleachers. He'd wait but she was on his clock.

She was done in eight minutes. Will watched her descend, his gaze fastened to her, not unlike how Ryan had bound his attention to Laura coming down the outdoor wedding aisle. Krista felt the betraying heat of a blush and when Will reached out his hand and she took it before everyone gathered here today—*Stop: he's playing to the crowd. That's all.*

"Come," Will said, "I've got something to show you."

He led her around the arena to the horse pens. "If you're taking me to a horse," she said, "you know I'll say that it's big and beautiful and please, please, don't make me come any closer."

"No," Will said, "not a horse. At least, not today."

At the top of a dirt access lane by the dance hall, the food trucks were lined up to sell burgers, ice creams and jerky. Krista scanned the area for a likely spot for her to set up her spa booth. Nothing. It would all be noisy, smelly or both. She looked over her shoulder as Will pulled her along. That stretch of grass by the fence might work.

"Will, what about—"

"Here," he said at the same time, "what do you think?"

She followed the direction of his outstretched arm. There, on the hill, tucked among cottonwoods, stood the white gazebo from Laura's wedding. The white and blue gauzy curtains still hung, fluttering in the breeze.

Krista had no idea what he was going on about.

"It's a ways away from the traffic, but I figured you'd prefer privacy and people can still see it from the trucks."

He had made a spa for her. They'd not seen each other all week, but he'd been helping her to succeed.

"No, it's…perfect. But how did you move it?"

"Same way we got it into place the first time. Set a pallet on the bale forks and lifted it up. It's not eight feet across, no heavier than a bale. Come."

He tugged on her hand which he still held and which she'd made no attempt to remove. For appearance's sake, of course.

Will highlighted additional features of the gazebo as they stepped inside the airy hexagon. "The blue barrel over on the side is for the waste water, and I set up a hot water urn—" he drummed his fingers on the metal side "—to the generator for your basin. There's a cooler for cold water, too."

"Absolutely wow. Thank you. This is way beyond the call of duty. Not that you had to do anything at all," she added hastily.

"Didn't feel like a duty," he said softly.

There was no one around and he was acting as if they were still a couple. Maybe it was easier for him to stay in the role all the time. "You better not have busted up your shoulder doing this."

"I repeat. Pallet, bale forks."

Krista assessed the interior for her purposes. All the wedding paraphernalia had been replaced with a wood patio table, the urn and two lawn chairs. The chairs were wooden with thick cushions in blue and white stripes.

Krista spun to Will. "These are from Janet's deck. I noticed them at the wedding. She'll kill you if she finds out you took them."

"She already found out. She and Dad were sitting on the other two when I came in for them."

"She let you take them?"

"No, but Dad did." Will sprawled on a lawn chair and indicated the other for her.

She sat down gingerly, still not believing her luck. "I always liked your dad."

"Everybody does. He doesn't have an enemy in the world."

"Good way to live," Krista said absently, mentally staging the space with her product and gear.

"The only way to live," Will said, "if your

last name is Claverley. We built this place on hard work and a reputation for fair dealings."

The rack of pedicure lotions she was imagining collapsed at Will's casual arrogance. "And Montgomery. My sisters and I run businesses, too. Bridget runs a third-generation family restaurant, you know. The Claverleys didn't invent honesty."

Will pulled himself up in his seat. "I didn't mean any offense, Krista. Just filling you in on my family."

"Because of the fake couple thing? The more I learn the better I can play the part?"

His eyes locked onto hers. "Because I want you to know me better so you can feel closer to me. Because I wanted to bring a bit of my world into yours."

Krista at once melted and jerked to attention. Will was up to something. Even from this distance, the rodeo announcer's voice still floated up to them, calling out entrants. The patter between him and the rodeo clown and the crowd's easy laughter at their jokes were like a TV show running in the background.

"Hey, shouldn't you be down at the arena? Networking or whatever you call it when a bunch of you lean on a fence."

Will relaxed into his chair, stretching his

legs into her space. "My phone's on if any-body needs me."

"Good," Krista said. "Time you gave your shoulder a rest anyway."

"You know," he said, "outside of my fam-ily and Brock, my old rodeo buddy, you're the only person today who's asked about my shoulder." He hooked his boot under her ankle. She supposed that a particularly astute eye might gaze up the hill, along the stairs to note his casual yet intimate move.

She nodded at where their ankles crossed. "This for the fakery bit?"

"I'm not faking anything right now."

He had to be, because otherwise it meant— no, things were clear between them, but—the gazebo, the public declaration of her as his girlfriend—he was making this far too real. Except hadn't they agreed that they weren't suited?

"Exactly. I'm the girl who can't ride, has no idea what a bale fork is, much less how you make them."

"Horses aren't a big mystery."

"Maybe not to you, but I know more about life on the moon than about them."

"You been to the moon?"

Relieved they were in safer territory, Krista

settled into her chair. "Nearly. Mara and I traveled every continent with my parents."

"Every continent? Including Antarctica?"

"Yep. Only for three days, though, when I was eleven."

"Laura was always telling us your stories about traveling around. I guess Spirit Lake was pretty dull when you came here for high school."

"Yes and no. My parents still took us on trips during the holidays, but I also got excited to come here where I already had friends and family."

"Outside of the rodeo circuit, I haven't been anywhere."

"You're thirty. You must've been somewhere."

He squinted, as if trying to remember. "I've been out to my dad's cousins' ranches."

"Ranches? As in plural?"

"One in British Columbia and then there's another in Ontario. There's another one out in Nova Scotia. But that's a fruit farm. Haven't been there."

The Claverleys were a dynasty. "The Montgomery properties extend from Penny's all the way to my shop and then one story above.

Do all the Claverley ranches have horses, except for the fruit farm, of course?"

"Even the fruit farm. Horses, cattle, some grain."

"So… I was wondering…do you make hay?"

Will smiled. "We have a section of hay, yes."

"You realize that I have no idea what you just said?"

"How about I take you around one day?"

"Sure." Except one day would happen after this weekend when they were no longer a fake couple…or anything, for that matter. She centered on where her white boot rested on his dark brown one. "So we would revert to friends status at that point, right?"

His hazel eyes bored into hers. "No. More." She sucked in her breath. He wanted her as his girlfriend, his serious, maybe-marriage girlfriend. Ten years ago she would've leaped at the chance. And hadn't her imagination just converted coming down the stairs of a rodeo stand into a wedding scene?

But…her bulging salon calendar wouldn't fit into his strict ranching routine. Gauzy gazebos aside, she needed to be in town five, six days a week to run her business, and he couldn't exactly bring the ranch to her. Which meant he'd expect her to come to him. And now that she'd found her passion, she wasn't about to give it up for crazy big horses and bloated cows and bales. Neither could she ever see him caring about lotions or nail polish. A relationship might work if they both had a common passion—cooking, squash, traveling—but they didn't. She would have to pretend an interest or he would, and that would not end well.

She opened her mouth at the same time a distressed shout and gasp rose from the crowd. The rodeo announcer came on. "Rider Brock Holloway is down. Our paramedics are coming in now."

Will bolted to his feet. "I've got to go."

Brock must be the rodeo friend he'd mentioned. "Do you want me to come?" she called after him.

"No," he said over his shoulder. "I'll catch up with you later."

He slipped through the fence and ran down the dirt lane. She should follow him, regardless of what he said. To do what, though? Play the part of the rodeo champ's girlfriend or be his real one?

CHAPTER NINE

As Krista emerged moments later onto the grass slope overlooking the arena, she spotted Janet, arms crossed, standing alone, eyes fastened like everyone else's on the drama below.

Krista joined her, if only because she didn't want to be alone herself. Janet glanced at her before returning to the rider with two paramedics crouched beside him. Two rodeo attendants hovered close, and there was Will crossing the arena to the group.

"Last year," she said quietly, "I stood in this exact same spot when Will was there flat on his back."

Already fretting over Will's present injury, Krista couldn't conceive of the desperate waiting Janet must've endured. "It must've been horrible."

Janet gave a tight nod. "I saw him go down. I had no idea if it was his head, spine... I couldn't do a thing. Just watch. And pray."

Tomorrow it could be Will down there, again injured. And she would be forced to watch him ride, as his dutiful girlfriend. Her stomach lurched.

Janet gusted out her breath. "I was so thankful it was only his arm. And collarbone. But his arm was broken in three places and his elbow shattered. A year on and his shoulder's still out of whack."

Krista resisted voicing her own worries. Next to Janet's lived experience, hers would sound weak, even insincere. "So, the rider. He and Will are buddies?"

"Good friends. Except when they're competing."

"Really? I have a hard time picturing Will as competitive. He always seems so…laid-back."

Will's mom looked at Krista square-on. "You haven't seen his determination when he gets something stuck in his head. There's no shaking him loose."

No. More. Will had made up his mind. He'd expect her to…and fast.

She was saved from having to respond to Janet by the paramedics easing Brock into a sitting position. As one, Krista and Janet released their breath while the crowd broke into encouraging applause. The clapping rose to a roar as Brock rose to his feet and walked with the paramedics, Will close.

"Good," Janet said. "I don't have to call his family."

"That's your job?"

"The hospital always calls, of course, but we always like to let them know we're thinking of them and help out if we can. The families are often hours away, some out-of-province, out-of-country once. Only had to do it twelve times in thirty-three years, but the tradition is that the 'matriarch' does it," Janet said, with a twist of her mouth.

Krista imagined that if she and Will—well, if they took it to the next step and then the steps proceeded to marriage, the job would eventually fall to her. What if—

"Say, Janet, has there always been a Claverley in a rodeo?"

"All four generations have had at least one, usually more. If not here, then somewhere in Alberta."

"So every generation of Claverley mothers has had to stand here and watch?"

Janet gazed out over the scene. "Every single generation. Watch and pray."

That decided it. If it wasn't bad enough that

she was a poor fit for country life, she did not have the guts to watch her husband, much less her children, get maimed—or worse. And stand by helpless.

She demanded honesty from Will, but she was telling herself the biggest lie. The simple fact of the matter was that for all he called her brave, she didn't have what it took to love a strong, determined family man like Will Claverley.

"Now I'm praying," Krista blurted out. "That it rains tomorrow so Will doesn't have to ride with a hurt shoulder."

Arms still crossed, Janet's pretty nails dug into her flesh. "That makes two of us."

"Krista Montgomery. You the one Will told to step away from the edge?"

Krista looked up from wiping her basin to find a man who seemed to have stepped out of a cowboy poster. Tall, square-jawed, great teeth. Only discrepancy was the sling and cast on his left arm. "I am. And you must be Brock Holloway."

"The one and the same." He held up her card. "Here for the best ten minutes of my day."

She'd hoped to sneak a break to answer

a string of texts from Will and her sisters. Since eleven thirty, rodeo goers had filed in for their speed spa pedicure. She'd never seen so many naked toes in her life. But hey, this was Will's friend. "Step right up."

While Brock made himself comfortable in the lawn chair, Krista inserted a fresh liner into her basin and poured in warm water.

"Quite the operation you have here."

"Will set it up for me."

"He always had a head for details." Brock reached down to haul off his boots but his bandaged arm made it awkward.

"Here," Krista said, "let me." It was like pulling lids off rusty cans but finally his feet were free, his socks sliding off, too.

She perched on her stool. "Roll up your pants if you can and drop your little piggies into the water."

He did so, Krista assisting with his jeans, and then leaned back. "This is worth the ten bucks right here."

She set his foot on her lap and took up her file. "Thought you'd be resting somewhere else today."

"Home's a camper out by the bush over there." He pointed over his shoulder in the general direction of the temporary parking lot. "I'll head out in a couple of days but can't drive while I'm on the sedatives."

"You and Will can compare injuries."

"No use. He'd win hands down."

Brock, Krista realized, was the perfect one to ask for details. Like her, he wasn't family but…close. "You…you were there when it happened… Will's fall?"

"Yep. I'd already ridden and was back with the others watching. He'd come away with a clean ride. The outrider was coming up alongside but the horse threw in a sudden twist and Will went flying and then the horse kicked him."

"How bad was it?"

"As bad as it gets. Torn tendons. Broken collarbone. Will has had I don't know how many surgeries."

"Five." It was Will. He walked into the gazebo, completely disregarding that she was with a client. "You're a hard woman to get a hold of. Thought I'd come in person."

This was the closest they'd been, since they'd sat together in the gazebo. Last night, Will had texted to say that he planned to go to the hospital with Brock, and she'd been secretly relieved that he'd not wanted her to accompany him. She wasn't at all sure how to tell Will that she didn't have the guts to launch a relationship with him.

"I got your texts and was about to answer when your buddy took off his boots."

Will pulled the spare lawn chair from its place against the far railings and dragged it across so it was crowded right close to Brock and Krista.

"You're butting in on my time," Brock said, swapping out one foot for the other at Krista's direction.

"I could say the same," Will said. "Krista's off duty."

"How do you figure that?" Krista said. She didn't even know there was an end to her day. Not that she needed any more work. She'd rustled up four bookings and two more wanted to chat about autumn bridal parties. One had even inquired about a Christmas party. Her fake girlfriend arrangement had paid off beyond her wildest hopes. It had also complicated her personal life beyond belief.

"Because you haven't had a break in five hours. You're wiped, and we were in the middle of a conversation which your client here interrupted." He stared pointedly at Brock. "And seeing as how he lives two hours south of Calgary, he won't become a regular."

"Not so fast," Brock said, lifting both feet onto Krista's lap, where she patted them dry. "I'd come up regular for this treatment." His eyes widened as Krista applied her massage. "Very regular," he said and slumped back, closing his eyes.

Will looked ready to send his buddy back to the hospital with further injuries.

"You ready to ride tonight?" she asked by way of distraction.

"Hopefully it'll happen. There was a hailstorm west of town. More are expected. Even chance it'll get rained out."

The best news today. But Krista kept her face absolutely neutral under Will's fixed gaze. Still, her expression must've conveyed enough. "You'd be happy, wouldn't you?"

"I'm not going to deny I care more about your health than a charity ride. I get the importance of the charity, but a delay of a few weeks won't change the long-term outcomes for the kids. It will change yours. There are lots of people behind the kids, but no one for you. Except your mom and me, it seems."

Brock cracked open an eye. "Maybe after I'm done here, you could give him a shoulder massage."

"My shoulder's fine," Will growled and said to Krista, "You done with his hoofs?"

She wasn't but for the sake of harmony, she lowered Brock's feet onto the mat. "All done. Anytime you're out this way, drop by. I'll give you my good-guy deal."

With excruciating consideration, Brock gentled the sock top over one set of toes. He raised woeful eyes to Krista. "Seeing as how I'm all hurt, would you mind helping me along?"

"All right, that's it," Will said. He snatched up Brock's boots, stepped to the gazebo entrance and flung them. "Go fetch."

Hilarity lit Brock's face but he wiped his expression into one of indignation when Will turned back. "Hey, you've no right to—"

"Go," Will said. "You're not using my girlfriend to pull on your boots."

Brock pulled himself to his feet with an exaggerated sigh. "Fine. So much for the Claverley hospitality. Good to meet you, Krista." He paused. "Hey, Will."

"Yeah?"

"Krista's right. This—" he pointed to his bandaged arm "—might be my wake-up call. You already got yours. Time to answer it."

Krista faced Will as soon as Brock left.

"Anybody who cares doesn't want you on the back of any horse tonight."

"So you admit that you do care about me?"

"Of course. We're friends." She reached down to remove the liner from the basin, but Will wrapped his hand around her arm. "Krista, you're big into honesty. So here it is. I haven't faked a thing since you nearly took a tumble off the platform. I doubt I even was before then. I want whatever there is between us—and there is something—we've both known that for the past ten years, to get real and play itself out, whichever way it goes."

Man, he could talk a line. "We can't do this. You want a serious relationship and I'm not it. I'm not Claverley wife material. Not even close. We're not built to last."

"Whoa. I'm not proposing marriage, Krista. I'm suggesting that we no longer pretend to pretend."

A real good line. He was so tempting. *Kiss him*, that stupid, wild part of her said. "I can't believe I'm saying this but you're not being practical. I'm no more compatible than I was when you suggested the fake relationship. In fact, our lack of suitability is what made this fakery perfect, according to you."

Will was staring at her lips. She pulled back and he blinked. His eyes went to hers. "We need to find a quiet place and hash this out."

"Will, this is a quiet place. I've given you my answer."

"The answer you *think* you should give. It's the same one I gave ten years ago, and here we are in the same place again, so how about we come up with a different solution?"

"This is the great Claverley fair deal talk in action?"

"I've seen you in action. You got a bit of the Claverley already in you."

"My, aren't we presumptuous."

"Look, we both enjoy running a business—"

"Three months hardly counts."

"It does to me. You like my family, and they like you."

"You talked to your mom and Keith lately?"

"They don't hate you, which is a start."

"I beg to differ, but we'll leave that for now. But remember, there's my family, too."

"I'd be happy to make their acquaintance."

"Yeah, well, Jack and Bridget, they already invited you over for our Canada Day barbecue. I said it wasn't necessary because we were just pretending. Then."

"So if you were to invite me, it would mean we weren't pretending?"

For better or for worse… "Yes."

Will took her hand, glided his thumb along her knuckles. "I'll make you a deal. How about you and I drop the fake part of our relationship for tonight. If all goes well, we'll stay together until after the barbecue with your family. That's what, two weeks from now? We survive that, and we'll see if we're good for another two weeks."

"Our relationship is on a semi-monthly lease?"

"At first, then month to month, then…" He shrugged.

"Then I fall off a horse one too many times and you come to your senses."

"Or you don't and I never do."

"Huh." That was the best response she could manage, her heart was banging around so badly. She should run from him now before she did it later, like she'd run from jobs and guys for years.

Or she could be braver than she'd ever been before. "I'd say, Will Claverley, that if you can stick your backside to a bucking horse for ten seconds, I didn't stand a chance."

He grinned and kissed her cheek, by her mouth. Her lips twitched, as if he'd missed his mark. This time when his eyes went to her lips, she gave in to what they both wanted and touched her mouth to his.

"It's been a pleasure, Krista Montgomery," he said when their lips finally parted.

Her teenage hope had come true. Only, how long would it last in the real, grown-up world?

THE CRACKS OF thunder barely registered above the music from the band. Will would check the rain gauge outside the house before going to sleep tonight. Every quarter inch would help the hay, though it wouldn't help the odds of the ride happening. Already rained out for this evening, it wasn't likely to happen tomorrow, the last day of the rodeo.

Krista might get her way yet. She was tucked against his side, his arm around her waist, studying the dance moves of a white-haired couple. Will recognized them. They lived and breathed the rodeos, and probably spent the winters practicing their dance moves. Krista was shuffling through the steps. She'd disappeared after they'd kissed, then reappeared for the dance in a full rodeo getup of skirt and boots but with a flowered shirt and a fake flower in her hair. She looked half Hawaiian, half cowboy. On her, it worked.

"Do you want to dance?" He nearly yelled in her ear, the throb of the two-step rising up from the floorboards into his boots.

She shook her head, her curled hair grazing her bare shoulders. His fingers itched to tug a curl and see if it would spring back into place. "Not unless you're in for major embarrassment. Those two should run a studio."

He decided to grow up a bit, and dragged his attention off her hair. "They are pretty serious. They have their own YouTube channel."

"Really? Wait. You know them?"

"Their names. And we've spoken. They're rodeo regulars. You register faces first and then put names to the faces. It's a circuit for a reason."

Krista surveyed the room and said, her breath stroking his ear, "So, how many people do you know here?"

"I'd say a good third. Not all by name necessarily but enough to say hello to."

"In that case," she said directly to his face, close enough for him to read her lips, "why haven't you done the rounds with me?"

Because he didn't want to share Krista with anybody, not when they'd only become a couple about five hours ago. They were still in this gray zone, where to the outside world they were supposed to be pretending to be a couple but in the private world really were together. The public and private were theoretically the same, but Will still felt not quite right about it all, like a gate latch that hadn't fully hooked into place.

Until then—he tightened his arm around Krista's waist—he wanted to keep her to himself as much as possible. "I thought you'd prefer not to have to go through the motions with people you don't know."

Her lips grazed his ear this time when she spoke and he felt it right down to his boots. She could find a way to tickle his toes without touching them. "Those are exactly the kind of people I want to meet. A stranger today, a client tomorrow."

She had a right to push her business, but there ought to be a limit. It was ten at night.

He was about to suggest she close up shop

when she tilted her face up to his. He kissed her, her mouth stilling and then moving against his, moving to form words. "Will, I hadn't—we—" she broke contact and glanced around. He didn't care who saw but when she stiffened, he followed her gaze to Keith, watching the dancers, too. One in particular, it turned out. Dana was in the arms of a rider. Will placed him as a middle-of-the-pack entrant, there for whatever money he came into, but mostly for the good times. Keith looked ready to pile-drive him. He wondered if Keith had told Dana about Austin's first word.

"Have you talked to Dana?" Krista asked him.

Will shook his head. "Not about Keith." He took in Krista's determined gleam. "I figured I'd mind my own business."

"Keith's not business, he's family. You talked me into dating you. Can't you train your powers of persuasion on that bullheaded brother of yours?"

He shouldn't get involved, but Keith was screwing up bad. "If I talk to him, will you promise to stay out of it?"

A swift smack of a kiss was her answer. Good enough for him. He pulled her in for another when up popped Alyssa with her camera phone. "Hey there. Just taking some shots to post."

Krista posed for the shot, but it was clearly that— a pose with none of the curvy softness of moments ago. He hoped there wouldn't be a scene. Then again, the music might drown them out, and if they had to take it outside, the weather would also drown them out.

Alyssa sidled in closer, as the music stopped and the band announced a set break. "We'll likely have to cancel the ride."

No surprise there. Sales would take a hit for tomorrow, but they'd run a profit. After nearly sixty years, the ranch could absorb the occasional hit.

"But I was wondering if you'd consider rescheduling."

"Of course." Beside him, Krista stared pointedly at his shoulder. The pain was under control thanks to a full dose of painkillers.

If Alyssa noticed, she didn't let on. "I lined up the ride for Okotoks."

"Okotoks? That's good."

"Even better than here, actually. It's closer to Calgary so we could draw interest from there. Get a lot of sponsors and buildup before the event."

"When is it?" Krista asked.

Alyssa's lips tightened. He'd better find a way to end this conversation soon, while things were going smoothly. "It always happens the middle of August," he said. "Plenty of time."

"Yes," Alyssa said. "Plenty of time for Krista to make sure your shoulder is in working order."

"Perfect," Krista said. "And plenty of time for you to make plans with Will when I'm not around."

A not-so-subtle jab for Alyssa to move on. Alyssa delivered Krista a vicious glare, immediately masked over with a bright smile. "Just wanted to check with you to make sure that'll work."

The lights came on for a short break and Alyssa glided away. But Krista was no longer his happy girlfriend. Or his alone. Because now everybody was taking advantage of the break in the music to mosey over and chat. So much for keeping Krista to himself.

WILL'S TEXT TO Krista arrived at eight thirty the next morning. We're officially rained out.

Good, she thought and snuggled deeper under her puffy covers. He could give his shoulder a day of rest. Do you want to meet up?

Maybe later. Full day wrapping up at the corrals.

So much for taking care of his shoulder. She browsed through the internet until she discovered a grisly image of torn shoulder tendons and sent it to him with Have a great day!

I'm so lucky. Now I have both a mother and a girlfriend.

His girlfriend, though she hadn't gone on a date with him yet. Perhaps she should remind him that Dana got concert tickets and flowers for playing the part of a girlfriend. As his real one, she could negotiate her own fair deal.

Krista heard Mara in their apartment kitchen. Mara moved like a thief, slowly and quietly, afraid of making a mistake. Last month she'd broken a glass. Krista only discovered it when she'd stepped on a tiny shard in her bare feet, and Mara had confessed, deeply apologetic that she had missed it. Krista's reassurances that it could've happened to anybody didn't fly with Mara.

Did Will know about Mara's deteriorating blindness? Krista had told Laura, so probably. But it was also probable that she had a thicker file on the Claverleys than he did on her family.

Unable to stop herself, she scrolled through her photo stream of the pics she'd taken of herself and Will at the rodeo. There weren't many and her thumb hovered over the delete button on a couple that showed her gazing up at him as if he were the sun and the moon. She left them because, well, who knows when they might come in handy?

There were others perfect for promoting Krista's Place. On her laptop, she created an image of Will and her with catchy text about the monies raised and posted it to Instagram. She'd been posting on Instagram for a couple of weeks now, and gotten nothing but upbeat replies, as well as hearts and thumbs-ups and shares. Life really did carry on.

She shut her laptop, took up her phone and padded barefoot into the kitchen and straight to the coffee machine. Empty.

"Make a full pot," Mara said over the

whirr of the blender. "Mom's coming over for brunch."

"When?"

The apartment buzzer let off its foghorn call. "Now."

"You didn't tell me."

"Because I didn't hear you come home last night. Besides, you weren't supposed to be here this morning, and you've only just now made an appearance."

"Sound logic is no excuse," Krista said. "Did you tell Mom about the fake girlfriend thing with Will?"

"I'm not doing your dirty work," Mara said.

"I guess I better since there's an update."

Mara hit the cancel button on the blender and in the silence asked, "What happened?"

There was a knock on the door. "Later," Krista said and jumped to answer it.

She was greeted by cheesecake rimmed with fresh strawberries. Krista's insides went as squishy as the dessert. "Are those strawberries from Aunt Penny's garden?" The garden technically belonged to Jack and Bridget now, since they owned Aunt Penny's house, but to everyone it was still Aunt Penny's even though she'd passed away eight months before.

"Yes, they are," their mother said, sliding the dessert onto the counter. She enveloped Mara and then Krista in a hug of Bali cotton and incense. "Now tell me quick what you've been up to, so we can have a slice."

Krista balked. How to confess to her family that she was about to launch into a hopeless relationship? "Mostly busy with work."

"At some convention promoting your spa?" Mara raised her eyebrow.

"Did I say convention?"

Their mother opened her phone and read, "'Hey, Mom. Sorry I can't call. Busy working a convention. Will talk Sunday.' And here it is. Sunday. What gives?"

"The quiche is ready to take out of the oven," Mara said. "And I've made the salad dressing. How about we wait until we're seated before we hear her news. Meanwhile, Krista?" Mara pointed to the still-empty coffee maker.

"Right." Krista hopped to it.

"I'm afraid you inherited the absentminded gene from your maternal side," her mother said. "Your father eventually shooed me out of the kitchen. This is about the third cheesecake I've made in my life that wasn't burnt or a soup."

"Oh, I don't know. I expect to make a profit this month at the shop."

Their mother's eyes crinkled with pride. "Good for you, which proves that you've inherited another gene from me. The FIUYMI gene which is—"

"Fake it until you make it," the sisters sang together.

"Now, then, Krista," Mara said once they were seated, "perhaps you could explain to us how the fake-it gene is expressing itself in your life."

Krista explained to her mom how in pursuit of obtaining new clients, she had happened upon a gig as a fake girlfriend with Will Claverley.

Krista's mom emitted a chirp of surprise. "Janet Claverley's son?"

"Yes. You know his mom?"

"Of course I knew whose house you spent your teenage years at. We went to high school together. She always acted as if she were better than anyone else. And yes, her daughter is more like her father. That's why I didn't mind you hanging out with Laura."

Krista recalled the live pain on Janet's face as she'd recalled watching Will get hurt in the arena. "I admit she still has an edge to her, but she does care about her family."

"She does. Whatever belongs to her is the best. Everyone thought it odd when she took up with Dave Claverley, rodeo bad boy."

"Dave Claverley? Bad boy?" Not the man with the gentle voice who'd broken from the wedding guests to help with Silver. "He made Will come to me at the spa and buy Janet a gift certificate. Doesn't seem bad to me."

"We've all mellowed, and full credit to them for making a life together when we were all betting it would be over in a matter of months."

"That's what happened to her other son," Krista admitted, and the three of them cleaned off the quiche as they discussed Keith's lousy love life and his stupidity with Dana.

"Anyway, Will said he'd talk to him," Krista said. She wondered if she'd broken some code of confidentiality between Will and her by discussing Keith's affairs. Then again, she couldn't imagine muzzling herself around her family.

"Ah, onto the firstborn goes the burden of

keeping siblings in line," their mother said, crunching on lettuce. "Mara, this dressing is amazing. I need the recipe. No, forget it, I'll never make it. So, how was it, Krista? Pretending to be in love with a Claverley?"

Krista eyed the cheesecake.

"Don't even think about it," Mara said from across the table.

"It went pretty well. We mostly hung out, let people take pictures of us, danced, which was pretty much him walking me randomly across the floor."

"Was his family in on what you two were up to?"

"Oh yeah." Krista could almost taste the sweet crush of strawberries on her molars. "Though I'm not sure Will has filled them in on what happened yesterday."

She paused and her mother rolled her wrist in the universal "go on" gesture.

Krista let it fly. "We've agreed to date. For real. For two weeks."

Mara and her mother exchanged glances; Krista made a lunge for the cake. It was Mara—slow, methodical Mara—who slapped her hand away. "Not nearly enough detail."

"What do you want to hear? We like each

other, but I warned him it wouldn't last because we are so different. We agreed to try each other out until after the Canada Day barbecue and then take it from there."

"How very…" Their mom trailed off.

"Boring," Mara finished.

"It's not boring," Krista said. "It's being honest about our chances. And Will agrees. Now can I have my cake?"

Mara set it before Krista. "But you have to serve us first."

"That boy just wants a foot in the door," their mom said. "But you are taking caution to an insane level. Of course, you two will end things if it's not working out, but why put a deadline on it?"

"It's not a deadline. It's a renewal date."

"Different name, same beast. Are you worried about Phillip?"

"That part of my life is over. I've received no hate mail on my website and no snarky comments on my social media. See?" Krista opened her phone to show them the post of her and Will on Instagram.

In the space of an hour seven comments had popped up. Probably Laura and other friends.

There was Laura's, congratulatory and

complimentary with an emoji row of hearts, smiley faces, a cowboy hat and a dollar sign.

Alyssa with Thank you for your support! Bland but professional. She had also shared to the Celebrity Ride page with the comment, Will poses with his latest special friend. Okay, accurate but it made Will sound as if he went through women like tissues, and it made her seem…disposable.

Alyssa had shared the image on her personal page and tagged Krista's Place, making the post available to all her friends. One friend, in particular. Lindee, Phillip's right-hand warrior in the charge against Krista.

Oh, that poor cowboy! He has no idea who he's hitched himself to.

"Oh no," Krista murmured.

"What? What?" her mother and sister pressed. Krista shook her head and continued to follow the trail.

Lindee had shared Alyssa's post and the comments were coming in fast and furious.

Krista's back to taking the innocent for a ride!

There's gold to be dug in them thar hills.

WARNING: Proceed with caution, cowboy. That was accompanied with a poison symbol.

"Krista! Tell us what's going on," her mom commanded. "Or, at least, put that phone away and eat your cheesecake."

"Cheesecake isn't going to fix this," Krista murmured. She showed them the feed, stunning Mara and her mom into sympathetic silence.

Mara picked at a strawberry. "What are you going to do?"

Hide. Remove her page, and wait until the storm blew over. Except this time the attack wouldn't only affect her. Now Will was involved. The Claverley family, the celebrity ride sponsors, the list went on. Such was the power of social media.

Her throat blocked up, her cheeks flamed. Her fingers twitched at the urge to rebut all the comments, to tell her story. But she'd gone down that road before and it would only add fuel to the fire. Then again, if she didn't take a stand, her past would always hound her. There would always be someone out there ready to grind her into dust for simply existing.

"I will fight them," she said. "I don't know how but I will."

Her cheesecake still sat prettily on her plate. The trolls were a thousand miles away. The cheesecake was right here. Her family was right here. "But first, we eat cheesecake."

CHAPTER TEN

KRISTA STARTED HER fight with a phone call to Alyssa. The other woman picked up after the fourth ring. There was laughter and loud male talk in the background. Was Will one of them?

"Alyssa, sorry to bother you—"

She gave a mild snort which Krista chose to ignore. "But a social media issue has come up that I wanted to address before it harms your clients." Appealing to Alyssa's self-interest had been Mara's idea. Positioned across the room in support, she'd given her some other pointers, which Krista had written down on a pad she now kept on her jittering knee to bolster her confidence. Their mother had left because she couldn't promise that she wouldn't rip the phone from Krista's hand and tear a strip off Alyssa. Krista suspected her mother swathed herself in hippie gear and incense in an effort to disguise her inner red-eyed monster.

"What is it?"

"I noticed that you shared a picture of Will and me."

"It's a good photo."

"It is, and that for me is not the issue." Krista strained to keep her voice calm and diplomatic. "Unfortunately, in sharing it on your personal page, my former connections in Toronto have identified it and have posted comments that are…demeaning to me and—"

"Not this again," Alyssa interrupted. "Did someone accuse you of being a Barbie doll and your feelings got hurt?"

Krista had anticipated this response and referred to Mara's notepad. "This isn't about me. It's about Will and by extension the charity ride."

There was a pause. "What do you mean?"

"There are some comments about Will now, too, and they're not flattering. I thought as the promoter of the ride, you might consider damage control."

"I'll have to read these comments," Alyssa said. "What do you want exactly?"

"It might be best if you remove the post."

There was a second pause. Krista imagined Alyssa's stony expression. "When I get a moment, I'll take a look."

The moment must've arisen quickly, because Alyssa called back even before Krista had time to relay all of her conversation to Mara. "I've read the comments and they're not doing Will any favors, so I deleted the post. It usually takes a while for the deletion to affect the shares, but it should disappear in a few hours."

Relief percolated through Krista like a cool rush of water. "Thank you for understanding, Alyssa."

"Yeah, well, I did it for the sake of the ride, not you. I should've known better than to bring you into the picture. Literally."

"I thought everything had died down," Krista said, trying not to sound defensive. "And I wasn't aware you were friends with Lindee."

"After what she just pulled off, I wouldn't exactly call her a friend."

Krista dug her teeth into her bottom lip to prevent her from screaming that this was the kettle calling the pot black. "Well, lesson learned. I hope this is the end of it."

Except it wasn't. Later that day, she spotted a comment with a link to Phillip's Facebook page. Weird. He usually relied on Instagram to troll her.

There on his page, he'd resurrected the Krista doll with the pink pouty lips and poufy blond hair. He'd dressed it in a cowboy hat and an outfit straight out of the closet of a buckle bunny extraordinaire. The quip: She rides again! There was a hashtag for the celebrity ride and another for buckle bunnies. Great. Phil had portrayed her as exactly the type of woman Will avoided.

Only there wasn't just one inflatable doll. Beside the Krista doll was one that looked like Sheriff Woody from *Toy Story*. Will. A comment balloon floated over the Krista-doll. "How do you like me so far?" Will-doll: "Please don't ruin it by talking."

Phillip had depicted Will as cruel and shallow. But her ex was clever. Two dolls, two caricatures. No names, so no use complaining to Facebook.

"If he doesn't reference us by name, there's no harm, right?" Krista asked Mara.

Even as she spoke, another Instagram post from Phil appeared. It was the one Krista had posted. He'd found her again.

Krista takes a cowboy for a ride. Another one bites the dust.

"Oh, Krista," Mara sighed. "What a horrible thing to say."

"I sometimes wonder if I made him that way."

"No one has that kind of power over someone else. As much as we'd like to think so."

Krista posed her pen over the notebook. "What should I do? Never mind. You'll just turn it back to me."

"You shouldn't ask me what I want you to do, because it's highly illegal and is driven by protective rage. Is there a sister's equivalent to a mother bear?"

"The three little sister bears?" Krista offered up.

"We know who the big bad wolf is," Mara said. "To mash up the fairy tales."

Krista hated to do this, but… "I should make a second call."

After she and Mara had brainstormed several pages of notes, Krista made the call, her fingers shaking. Not unexpectedly it went to voice mail. She left a long, winding message that was cut off by the tone. She waited a half hour and called again, leaving a simple message to call her.

"So much for that," Krista said. "Phillip won't call. Why would he?"

"Why would he not? Murderers return to the scene of their crime, don't they?" her mild-mannered sister replied.

Her sister's uncharacteristic venom cheered Krista somewhat as she drove out to see Will in the late afternoon. She'd left a few items at the Claverley house and had thought to bring lotion samples out to Janet and Laura. At the ranch driveway, her phone rang. Phillip. She parked her car halfway off the shoulder and was connected by the third ring.

"Thanks for calling back," Krista said right off the top. She wished she had Mara's notes in front of her.

"I was a little surprised you called at all," he said. She could tell he had her on speakerphone. Was someone else listening in?

"I wouldn't normally but as you heard on my message, I thought it best."

"I couldn't follow what you were saying. What's your problem?" She could hear the smile in his voice.

He knew exactly what her problem was, but he was going to make her repeat it for the sake of his audience. Krista bit back her anger and said, "I am sorry I hurt you, Phillip. I didn't realize how much I had until your reaction on Facebook…and again now."

There was a fraction of a pause. "Don't assume you have that kind of power over me, Krista."

"It's not power, Phil," Krista said. "I mean, it's the kind of power we give anyone when we enter into a relationship with them."

"Been talking to your psycho sister lately?"

"My psychologist sister," Krista clarified, not able to keep the sharpness from her voice. "I am sorry for not discussing our relationship sooner with you, and breaking up with you over the phone was not…kind."

"Nearly a year of my life flushed away with one phone call."

"I'm sorry." It wouldn't do to point out that it had also been a year of her life.

"You tried to make a fool out of me."

"That wasn't it."

"Of course it was. Run across the country to your family, drop me and never have to face our friends, our coworkers. Leave me hanging. You humiliated me, Krista."

He was alone. No way would he allow anyone to hear that confession. "So…the doll… the posts…the comments, it was all because you wanted to get back at me for making you look bad?"

"What did you think it was about?"

"I thought it was because I made you *feel* bad."

"I could've dealt with that at home with a few bottles. But this was about my reputation and you knew it. If you didn't, Krista, that's almost worse because it shows how clueless you were.

"We were in the business of appearances. Makeup, costumes, sets. The way things look is all we have between us and the rest of the world. Tear that down and the world attacks."

Krista gazed out her side window at the Claverley Ranch. There were still a few horse trailers, but largely the place had returned to its usual quietness.

"So you tried to tear down my world, the way you thought I'd torn down yours."

"Thought? I didn't dream up the stares of pity, the drop in invites to parties, the drying up of gigs. No one wanted me without you. They seemed to believe you were the better one."

"I had no idea," Krista murmured. "I always assumed you sort of…let me tag along. Cut me in for a share as a favor."

"You had a whole lot of wrong assumptions."

"But the doll, that's wrong, too."

"That doll was a brilliant stroke of genius on my part."

"Why did you stop? No, I only need to know why you started again. This guy, Will, he has nothing to do with us."

"He has everything to do with it. Believe it or not, I'm doing you a favor so you're not wasting ten months of your life like I did."

Leave it to Phillip to paint himself as a paragon of virtue. He should have his own superhero movie. Hypocrisy would be his superpower. "How's that?"

"This cowboy of yours is no different. Appearances matter to him, too."

"He's not like that," she said but as soon as the words left her mouth, she remembered how much value he placed on the Claverley name, the ranching tradition.

"Has he seen the posts?"

"No."

"Because you know what his reaction will be. Once he realizes that being with you is a liability, he'll drop you faster than hot crap. Nobody likes to be made a fool of, Krista."

Phillip was wrong. She'd been totally honest with Will about their chances, and he'd still wanted her. If anyone was under the microscope, it was her. She would stick by Will

and see this through. "That's what you want, right? For me to be humiliated the way you believe you were?"

"I don't believe it. I lived it. Yes, I want you to be humiliated. Your business destroyed and more than anything, your love life ripped apart. Just as you did to me."

Beneath his scorn, she could hear his pain, still raw after eight months. They'd almost been broken up for as long as they were together, and he still hadn't let go. And even though she had shed relationships and jobs like muddy clothes, she had no idea how to make him let go of her. No experience in how to make a heart no longer want, to change it into a forgiving heart.

Still, for the sake of Will and Alyssa and the charity ride itself, and for the sake of all she'd built at her salon, she tried one more time to reach Phillip. "Could I ask you to at least remove the posts and not put up any more?"

"You could always ask."

She thought of another idea. "Phil, if I were to come to Toronto and talk to you in person instead of over the phone, would you then?"

"If you got down on bended knee and begged?"

Krista swallowed. "Yes."

"Could I post the video of you doing it?"

"No!"

"Then no deal."

"You don't want this to end, do you?"

"Sure I do, Krista. Only I'm the one who gets to say when it will."

WILL TOSSED DOWN two anti-inflammatories, lowered himself onto his bed, positioning his right shoulder on its own pillow. He wrapped two ice packs around it like saddlebags. At the first prickle of cold, he closed his eyes in anticipation of cool peace.

Then came a rap on his door he didn't recognize. Alyssa, probably. "Come in."

Hinges squeaked and footsteps lightly followed. "Hello?"

Krista, cuddable in shorts and a T-shirt with threads of every color running every which way across the front. He scrambled up but it was too late. She spotted him, his pill bottle and the ice packs. He braced for her to let loose on him. Instead she sighed. "Oh, Will. Glory wounds of the firstborn, is it?"

"I don't know what you're talking about, but it sounds better than a screaming bunch of busted muscles."

She came over and dropped a kiss on his forehead. He would've preferred one on his mouth but he'd take it. "Go on, lie down."

"I'm good—"

"Lie down." And he did. She knelt on the mattress beside him, beefed up his shoulder pillow and squared his ice packs into place. She really did know how to make a guy feel comfortable.

She gave her tanned legs a satisfied slap. "There. Now, did Alyssa talk to you today?"

Will blinked at the sudden change in topic. "Briefly. About the ride. That she'd be in touch if I needed to make any appearances." Krista cringed at the word. "Why?"

"She didn't mention the post of you and me on Facebook?"

His free hand reached for his phone kept in a leather holder on his belt. "No, but I take it she should have."

She put her hand on his, her touch cool and solid, its own kind of ice pack. "Too late. It's been deleted. There's another one. A far worse one."

She unrolled the whole story, showing him pictures of the Krista and Will dolls, the rude comments and the upshot of her phone call with her ex. She plucked at the fringe on her shorts. "I'm so sorry about all of this."

Will silently cursed the ex for crushing his bright, fun-loving, Krista. "It's not you who should be sorry." He drew her hand onto his stomach and covered both of her hands with his. He meant to offer comfort but could feel her touch seeping its own healing strength across his belly. "You really do have talented hands." He intended to sound lighthearted, flirtatious. Instead it came out like a vow.

She gave a faint smile. "So I've been told." She frowned. "I guess we should develop a plan."

They should, but not until he'd gotten his old Krista back. He stroked her hand with his thumb. "Who was the first to tell you?"

This time Krista's smile didn't seem forced. "An actor.

"There came a point when I knew that I wanted something Phillip couldn't ever give me. She was having a hard day. A bunch of retakes was pushing back the schedule, she was distracted by her sick toddler at home. The director called a break for her to get a makeup change. She was in tears when she hit my chair, which isn't great for makeup. She said, 'My feet hurt.' She'd been all day

in these four-inch stiletto boots, a size too small. I helped her out of her boots and I gave her a massage. By the end, she said, 'You've got the hands of an angel, Krista.' And that's when I realized my calling."

"It worked on me. It worked on my mother." Will lifted her hand in his. "It's working on me right now."

She squeezed his hand. "Phillip did not want me pursuing that dream, and I was almost giving up on it when I came out for my aunt's funeral, and she'd given Mara and me a place to set up. It was an opportunity I couldn't walk away from."

"I see." Her motto, "The heart wants what the heart wants," was her declaration to the world, then, that her spa was her dream. But if she'd left one guy to pursue it, would she leave him, too, if she had to make a choice?

And since he was dead set on living here on the ranch, could he blame her for that choice? *We aren't built to last.*

Except he could learn from where Phillip had failed Krista. He could find a way to let Krista have her dream and a life with him, too. He wouldn't make her choose, because, well, he didn't want to have to choose between her and his life, either.

"Listen," he said, "about Phillip, I'm not sure we should do anything further."

"Did you not hear a word I said? Phillip has me in his social media crosshairs and now that we're together, you are, too."

"It'll blow over like it did before." Blow all away, so he and Krista could have a decent start together.

"Yes, it will. Eventually. All things come to an end, but not before serious damage is done. The Celebrity Ride is a full two months away. People have lost their reputations and jobs after twenty-four hours of Twitter storms. Look, you have done absolutely nothing wrong, but, thanks to Phillip, there's a sector of social media who thinks you only date dumb blondes. How is that going to look to your sponsors? Forget that, how badly is that going to blacken the Claverley name?"

"The Claverley name can weather a little bad publicity. We've been around a long time."

"And you're always going to have loyal customers that know you and the rest of your family personally. And your cattle and horses don't care about social media, either. I get all that. But going forward, you said you want to get more into breeding horses. Won't you

have to increase your social media presence for that? All this stuff will follow you, Will. What happens on the web, stays on the web."

That stopped him. He didn't want some knothead in Toronto trying to ruin his family and his future. "I take it you have a suggestion?"

Krista met his gaze squarely. "It might make sense if we maintained a…distance."

Will sat up in one motion, ice packs tumbling off. "Not happening. That's giving in to that mob. That's letting them rule our lives, get between you and me here on my bed, on this ranch, on this Sunday afternoon. No way."

She sighed. "You're making it very hard for me to take the high road, here. I don't want to cause trouble for you, Will."

If he could stand the pain in his shoulder, then he could stand anything she dished out. Especially if it came with her.

"There may be some very good reasons why we don't belong together, Krista. But what the world out there throws our way isn't one of them."

Alyssa's warning popped into his mind. *She'll build you up and make you feel as if you two can take on the world. And then she'll move on.*

"Hard," she whispered. "Impossibly hard."

No. Alyssa and Phillip were wrong. They'd make this work. He swooped in for a kiss on her soft lips. "Now that's a message I'd like to get out there."

JANET LISTENED TO Dave making small talk on their evening horse ride. It wasn't like him, but neither was her silence. She usually chatted nonstop, and it suited them both. She had never been good at holding out with Dave, and she'd held her tongue for nearly a week now. It was killing her.

Dave rambled to a stop, and they finally rode together in silence. Janet took in the clop of the horses and the throaty calls of frogs from a slough, the beat of the lowering sun on her cheek and the breezes carrying the herby scent of hay and grass. Two calves were tucked together in the tall grass and with a slight press of her knee, Silver adjusted her course to skirt them.

"Now that is what Silver deserves," Janet burst out, patting her horse on the neck. "Someone who trusts her."

"All right," Dave said.

"I was almost glad when she made a fool of herself on Silver at Laura's wedding. I thought, 'Good, now Will can see for himself just how preposterous the chances of their relationship are. It will never go beyond fakery.'"

"We're talking about Krista," Dave deduced.

"Yes. Her." Janet sat even straighter in her saddle, if that was possible. "She has her hooks in Will."

Dave didn't answer right away. He stared out at a bunch of cows grazing together. She expected he was looking for Maude and her calf. They'd noticed the cow had what appeared to be a light sprain last night.

Janet gave her prognosis to steer him back to the issue of their son's choice of a possible wife. "She seems better. No worse."

"Better check on her." Dave slipped from his horse and handed Janet the reins. Not that it mattered with Goldie. She'd not go far without Dave. He pushed on Maude's haunches to get her walking, his eye on her front hoof. From where she sat, Janet judged her prognosis to be dead-on.

"Swelling's down," Dave said as he swung

into the saddle again. "Problem's fixing itself for a change."

"I caught them together in Harry's House, kissing."

Dave pushed back on his cowboy hat and gave her a reproachful frown.

"I didn't realize she was there! I saw her car parked next to Alyssa's, so I assumed Krista was with her at the arena. I'd gone down to ask Will about bringing the lawn chairs back down from the gazebo. I knocked, opened the door and wham!

"She scuttled off and Will denied nothing. He said that they'd decided to take their relationship to the next level."

"Well," Dave said, "he's done this before. With other girls."

"Not with Krista!"

"What's your problem with her in particular?"

"Have you heard about what happened with that man she was with Down East?"

"Sounded to me as if *he* was the problem."

"That only proves she makes bad decisions when it comes to men."

"Are you saying our son is a bad decision?"

"In this case, yes. As she is for him. What can Will possibly be thinking?"

"Maybe he's not," Dave said, turning his horse for home. Silver followed without a cue from her. Smart horse.

"That's what I'm worried about. I don't understand her appeal when he has other obvious options. I asked him about Dana and he said she's already interested in someone else."

"Hard to believe that there's a better choice than Will out there."

"I agree, but he refused to reveal who it was. And he made it quite clear that he and Alyssa didn't have a future."

"You're worried that he'll end up in the same situation as Keith," Dave said.

"How can I not worry? Krista is not as shallow as Macey, I'll give her that, but Will and Krista, they are oil and water, fire and water."

"And yet Will's got his heart set on our little Krista," Dave said with a smile.

"She's not 'our little Krista.' She has her own mother and sisters, a cousin and nieces."

"Yeah," Dave said equably, "but after all these years of her eating at our table and sleeping over with Laura a piece of her is still ours."

Janet twisted in her saddle to get a better look at the man she thought she knew inside and out. "You don't mind that they're together. You actually *like* the idea."

"She's different," Dave said, "and different is good."

"Different? From the man who refuses his steak if it's not medium well and served with homemade barbecue sauce. When we went to Mexico, you couldn't sleep on the plane because you were seated to the right of me instead of to the left like in our bed."

Dave shrugged. "Point is, I got on the plane to Mexico."

"True," she conceded. It was in celebration of their thirty-fifth anniversary last year.

"And I wore sandals every single day there."

"Also true. Your poor toes had never been exposed to the light of day before."

"Yep." Dave grinned, that incredible Claverley smile that always made her believe things weren't as bad as they actually were. "I hear there's a new place in town where I can expose them again."

"She's gotten enough of our business."

"Maybe she'll give me the family discount."

Janet spluttered, incoherent again, but Dave's grin remained unmoved.

CHAPTER ELEVEN

WILL FELT MORE than his shoulders tense as Krista and Alyssa took in the latest from Krista's ex on their phones. "When do I get to read it?"

Not that he'd get more than a glimpse, given he was point man on Austin patrol right now. Keith was on his way home from an all-day haul that was running late, and Will's parents were out on their horse ride. Their time alone. Fed, Austin was toddling around the back lawn, Will following like a bodyguard to make sure small stones, grass or too much dirt didn't make their way down Austin's gullet.

"Here you go," Krista said. Austin had his fists clutched in the neck hair of Clover, who saw Austin as her human pup. That would buy him time to look away from the boy. Will took Krista's phone. A meme of two inflatable dolls sat together on a fence, a superimposed sunset of oranges and purples in the background. The Krista-doll, perky in a buckle bunny outfit of pink and tassels, held a rope lassoed around the foot of the Will-doll slouched in chaps and a plaid shirt. The speech balloon above the Krista-doll read "Don't you just love kids? I love them like cupcakes." His reply was a thought cloud: "Kids are accidents that permanently injure my life."

He thrust the phone back at Krista, too angry to speak. Where did that piece of scum get off accusing him of hating kids? Austin was edging to Clover's tail. Will closed the distance between him and Austin, Krista right there with him in silent support.

Alyssa followed. "The hospital is all about kids who have had accidents. We can't be represented by someone who is caricatured as calling kids themselves accidents. And wow, that permanent injury bit—" She shook her head. "We've got to hit back. It's already had five shares and it's only been up for a half hour."

This had not been the first meme or the first online attack, either. Phillip had set up a website and created an entire dreamy life featuring Krista-doll and blogging about her country hick boyfriend. They'd had titles like

How My Man Lassos a Post, What Makes a Horse Go Vroom-vroom, and Riding Off into the Sunset—Backward. Each blog came with a meme widely distributed on social media. Each Will had absorbed, but this one would not go away after a few hours of working with the horses.

"Oh great," Alyssa said. "An email from Super-A Supplies. 'Our company draws its support from our family-oriented customers. Due to the ongoing media spotlight on Will Claverley, we regret to inform you that we will not be able to proceed with our sponsorship of the charity ride.'"

Clover, who made a living flushing cattle out of the bush, wove in front of Austin to herd him back to Will. Austin decided to try and crawl under Clover. Smart tike. "But I'm *for* family. I've never said a word against it."

"It doesn't matter who you are," Alyssa said. "It only matters what other people say you are."

Practically word for word what Krista had said. She was tapping her lip. "Nobody said anything until this latest meme, so they don't really care who Will dates. It's the family thing. So how about we focus on Will and family on the Celebrity Ride page and start a new narrative."

Austin broke around Clover, and gravity was carrying his legs down the slope of the lawn to the gravel drive where a face-plant would bring blood and howls. The dog and the three humans moved in accordance, but Austin was picking up serious speed.

Will nabbed him as his little rubber boots hit gravel. "Come on, buddy. Let's get you back in the pasture." He began to walk Austin up the slope. Alyssa and Krista regarded him with the same speculative expression. What had he done to put them on the same wavelength?

Alyssa's fingers were flying over her phone. "We'll go with a short video. Less than thirty seconds."

"Then a voice-over from Will, maybe some music," Krista continued, "if it's not long enough."

"What are you guys up to?"

Alyssa held up her phone. "Walk. I'll video you."

"You can't put Austin on social media. It's not right."

"Laura has already put him on Facebook," Alyssa countered.

True… "Okay, just the back of him."

Alyssa began to protest but Krista said, "That'll work. It'll come across more universal."

And so Will had the unsettling sensation of two single women filming from his backside, Austin riding on his arm. His good arm. He had yet to tell Krista the dire warnings of the physiotherapist. It was bad enough that his mother knew.

"Stop," Alyssa said. "Now to come up with words to neutralize Phillip's poison."

"Something natural," Krista said.

"But profound," Alyssa said.

"I can do the first, but not the second," Will said. "I'll say whatever you two decide."

"But that completely goes against the 'natural' part," Krista said. "Tell me, Will, how do you feel about kids?"

Will gazed at Austin, whose little hands were busily digging into his shirt pocket bumpy from his baggie of painkillers. The crinkling noise had Austin squeezing the pocket for all he was worth. Austin had never made strange with Will, like other babies with their uncles, because they were part of each other's daily routine.

He couldn't imagine a world without Austin, without kids, a family. When did Krista want to start a family? He wanted one, the sooner, the better. But she had her business, and she'd probably prefer to wait until it was on its feet. Only he couldn't see himself waiting years on end to carry around his own Austin or Austin-ette.

He brushed away a mosquito hovering around Austin's bare neck. He spoke to Krista, though Alyssa had her microphone pressed close. "Some people say kids are a pain, a problem, not worth the trouble. But I grew up with farm animals and there's not one of them that doesn't take care of babies. Even those that belong to others. A mother cat will nurse kittens if their mother dies. A stallion makes sure all the other horses get in ahead of him. The dog lies beside a hurt calf. Kids aren't easy, but even an animal understands you don't ever give up on them."

Krista's blue eyes were wide with…what? Bewilderment? Fear? Definitely not the excitement he'd hoped for.

"Aaand that's a wrap," Alyssa said. "I'm off to get this turned around. I should have it posted to the Celebrity Ride site in a couple of hours." Krista's head was still down and didn't rise until Alyssa was out of earshot. "That was nice, what you said."

"You want kids?" he said quickly, to get it out there.

She drew her finger down Austin's arm. "To be honest, they always seemed down the road. I've never had a serious enough boyfriend to consider having kids. My nieces, Sofia and Isabella, they're my first contact with kids and that only started eight months ago."

"Laura told us about them."

"You'll meet them at the barbecue."

He grinned. "Six days and counting."

Austin yawned. Will recognized that signal. "First yawn already. Three yawns and he's done for the day. We'd better get him in the bath quick." He caught Krista looking in the direction of her car. "Unless you have someplace to go."

"No," she said. "No better place."

He wished he could believe she wasn't just saying that to make him feel better.

"I SCREWED UP BAD, didn't I?" Will said as he and Krista got into his truck after the Montgomery Canada Day barbecue. The rest of her family were still around the fire, probably happy to see the last of him.

Krista shed her red-and-white beanie with moose ears—and yes, she made it look cute. "Um, well, it wasn't all bad. The girls adore you. I mean who can resist a guy with dogs, cats *and* horses. I bet they'll pester Jack and Bridget to take them up on your invite to come out to the ranch."

"Which I shouldn't have offered before checking with them." He pulled the truck away from the curb, relieved to put distance between Krista's family and him.

"I promised to give Sofia makeup before checking with them, too. It's small."

"And the whole steak thing. I meant it as a hospitality gift, but Jack made enough digs for me to regret it."

"I totally blame him for that one. He is overly sensitive that way," Krista said. "Penny's Place nearly went bankrupt last Christmas, and they're really only breathing easy now. I guess your gift was an unintentional reminder of a time when they couldn't afford to serve their house guests steak."

"What else did I do?"

Krista hesitated. "You did seem nervous around Mara."

That was the worst mistake. Krista had filled him in on Mara's deteriorating vision, how they had to watch not to put stuff in her peripheral vision. He'd overcompensated, reacted as if she were Austin. He'd jumped to reach for a plate, scooted his chair way back when she edged by and it wasn't until Jack outright told him that Mara wasn't deaf, that he realized he'd spoken extra loud to her.

"I was nervous," he confessed.

"Why?"

"Same reason you're nervous around my mother. You want to make a good impression."

"No, I don't."

No way was she getting away with that lie. "I don't believe you."

"I—" She stopped. "I guess I am out to impress. But why do you care about what my family thinks?"

He couldn't have this conversation and drive at the same time. Krista, he was discovering, demanded his full attention. He pulled over and faced her. "Because I want to impress you, Krista. And part of that is impressing your family."

"So that's why you told them about your

two sections of land and two hundred head of cattle?"

Gaffe number four. "I guess I wanted them to know that you hadn't made a mistake in choosing me."

This was where she was supposed to re-assure him that they weren't a mistake, that she didn't regret her decision and that she was ready to renew their relationship lease. Instead she leaned her head against the head-rest.

"Our entire relationship so far has been about keeping up appearances."

"We haven't really been together for very long."

Krista gazed out the passenger window so he couldn't see her expression when she said, "For ten years."

Will's head hurt worse than his nagging shoulder. "What do you mean? We didn't date."

"And why didn't we? Not because you weren't attracted to me, because you admit you were. But because I didn't fit your picture of the kind of woman you were looking for."

"Give me a break. You were hardly a woman. You were sixteen."

"And you were twenty. Neither of us was

full grown, but you already had the image of the girl you ought to date, didn't you? Even when it went against what your heart wanted."

What did she want from him? "I changed my mind. I grew up. So did you."

She tilted her head and her face softened. For a second, he thought she might touch him. He could really do with her hands on him right now. "You know what Phillip said about you?"

Will scrubbed his face with his hand. "I bet it wasn't complimentary."

"He said you're no better than him or me. You're all about appearances. At first I thought he was nuts, as usual. But now... I'm not so sure. Maybe he has a point."

There she was, letting that jerk govern their lives. "What do you mean? The promotional videos weren't my idea but if it weren't for them, there might not be a charity ride next month."

Krista nodded, conceding that much. The campaign had stemmed the withdrawal of sponsors, but there was still the sticky factor of the dolls out there. Phillip had lobbed more nasty memes, more asinine blogs, and his followers had spread them like a virus. Going viral was not always a good thing. But so far, he and Krista and Alyssa were putting up a good fight. Still, it went to show how many people got off on the cruelty of others.

"Believe me," he added, "all I want to do is be outside, away from the spotlight."

Krista nodded again, this time with a twist of her mouth. "Getting back to the real work of finding a suitable wife?"

If he'd not had such a nerve-racking evening, he might've trod more cautiously. Instead, he stepped right into the muck of their argument. "Nothing wrong with that. You're the one who believes you don't fit the criteria."

"I don't," she said. "But the only way you're going to find that out is if you see the real me."

"What am I seeing right now?"

"The real me. The one you're in a fight with. You want more of that for the rest of your life? And the real me is in that family you were on pins and needles with. Are you ready for more of that, too?"

Yes, the twenty-year-old him would've run at this point. The young, rational guy. The older Will, though, stared right back into her blue eyes and said, "Bring it on."

She blinked. "And in return, you're not to go out of your way to impress me."

That made no sense. "Krista, so long as we're together I will always try to impress you."

"Try not to."

"I will impress you with the real *me*." His stomach flipped at the idea.

"Didn't you hear a word I said? Be yourself."

"I'm always that way."

She touched him now, a hard poke to his chest. "You're always out to impress. You'd still be riding bareback if it wasn't for your shoulder. You still feel you have to impress."

He did miss winning. But it wasn't buckles or trophies he wanted now. He wanted top ranking with Krista. "What do you want from me, then?"

"Be Will Claverley as if I'm the only one around."

Will wasn't sure Krista really wanted that guy. That Will popped pills, had never traveled outside the rodeo circuit, thought a horse ride in a pasture was the height of romance. The real him was sore and boring. But if that bought him an extension on his Krista lease, then sign him up.

"Sure."

She touched him again, this time placing her soft lips on his. And it felt very real.

"DON'T LEAN FORWARD," Will offered from his position astride Blackberry.

Krista had no idea that she was anything other than straight. She sat back, and up shot Molly's head. Right, stay easy on the reins.

Will looked across the pasture they were supposed to arrive at the end of sometime before the snow flew. Well, she'd warned him that she would hand him the real Krista and he'd still insisted on this evening ride for a missing calf.

"Now what am I doing wrong?"

"Maybe not quite so far back."

Krista tilted forward a titch. "There?"

"A little more."

"There?"

"Try pulling your feet back." He watched. "The other way."

"Maybe," Krista said, trying to keep up a smile, "we stop and you show me?"

He agreed, but that operation happened in fits and starts. First, Krista was worried about pulling too hard on the reins, so Molly kept walking, and then because she pulled unevenly on the reins, Molly turned to face home. "I completely sympathize," Krista muttered.

Will dismounted in one easy swing and gave instructions, which were as useful as his earlier ones. His hand flexed in obvious restraint. Eventually with Blackberry's reins in one hand, he instructed her to let go of the reins and brought the horse to a stop by soft words and a tug on the strap that went behind her ears.

Still holding Blackberry's reins, he rearranged Krista's body.

"Now stay like that." He stepped away, as if checking for the squareness of a picture frame. "Shoulders down."

"I've taken dance classes that don't require as many adjustments."

He rubbed Molly's neck. "Relax, Krista. Molly's feeling your tension."

"She is? How can you tell?"

He shrugged. "She's getting a little tight in the face."

Krista had no way of checkingMolly's face, and she doubted she'd recognize "tension" even if she did.

"Put your weight into your heels," he said as he swung himself back into the saddle—no mounting block for him—his right foot arcing through the air and slipping into the stirrup like he'd done it a thousand times. Well, he probably had.

This evening ride was proving to be every bit as bad as Krista had feared. Silver was on loan to an equestrian stable, so Will had chosen Molly, Laura's horse. Except Molly was used to being ridden by an expert rider and she was confused by Krista's mixed signals. And Molly was definitely not used to plodding along. Neither was Blackberry.

Which didn't help any of them, horses or riders, feel less tense. If it wasn't for that poor, shivering calf with its soft pink nose, alone and scared somewhere, she would've begged off the second they'd cleared the barn corral.

Will had tried to ease her into it. He'd taken her out to the grass corral so she could become more comfortable with the horses. But watching for brown piles and keeping a sharp eye on the horses' massive haunches that could kick her into Tuesday had only made her jumpier than a rabbit. Will walked around these huge animals as if there was nothing to be afraid of.

"Aren't you worried that they'll kick you?" she'd asked. "I mean, even by accident?"

"No, you get a sense of where they're at, and what they're capable of. Like people, I guess. You must've met people and known if they were going to be dodgy or not."

"I think it's already been established I'm a poor judge of people. Men, anyway."

He smiled at her, that classic Claverley smile. "Your luck has changed." He put a bridle around a horse whose hair was a shade of red she'd recommend to clients, and then saddled up Molly to give them time to get to know each other, but Molly must've sensed that Krista was nothing like Laura. But would Will listen?

"If I can make a fool of myself at your family's, you can make a fool of yourself on a horse," he'd said.

Krista decided not to inform him about her family's conversation the night after the barbecue. Bridget, also stung by Will's supply of meat, reminded her of the great Claverley Legacy. They were one of the original settler families, they even had a block claimed in the town graveyard, there was a Spirit Lake street named in their honor and, of course, as everyone knew, there was the Claverley Park with its Western-themed playground equipment.

He cares about you, Bridget had said and

then shrugged, *but at the barbecue it was clear he also cares about being a Claverley.*

Sneaking a look at Will now, Krista knew that her horsemanship had failed the Claverley seal of approval. Even the horses didn't approve of her, and she wouldn't blame them if they voted her out of the barn.

Nor did it help her confidence that she wore a helmet and a Kevlar vest to protect against kicks and falls, both insisted on by Will. Even Keith let Austin ride with a baseball cap.

Feeling her body going out of position again, she wiggled. But Molly took it as a signal to break into a trot. Unprepared, Krista jolted along toward the bushes rimming a slough.

"Will. What do I do?"

He accelerated Blackberry to come up alongside Molly. "What exactly do you want to do?"

"First gear. I want her back in first gear."

"Okay, relax your thighs, pull back a little on the reins, whoa, whoa, duck—"

If Will had shouted, his warning might've registered but he kept his voice even and the overhanging branch smacked her in the face. She instinctively twisted to the side. Molly pulled away under the unexpected shift of her weight and with a yelp off went Krista, falling between the horses. Hooves flashed at her face; a knock on her helmet; she screamed. Now there were pounding hooves and one seriously long curse from Will uttered even now in a calm, even voice.

He spoke again, this time above her. "Krista? You okay?"

Nothing but blackness. She then realized that was because she'd closed her eyes. She opened them to Will's concerned face. Concerned—and from his flattened mouth, irritated.

"I'm good."

"Do you hurt anywhere?"

"My dignity is crushed beyond all repair."

"If that's all, then can you sit up?"

She did. Molly had run off and was now slowing to a walk. "I'm sorry."

"Yeah, well, I should've known it wasn't going to work out. Molly hasn't been ridden in a week, and she was raring to go. Bad call on my part."

He was being kind. "The trouble is that I have no instinct for horse riding. I understand astrophysics better, and I flunked science."

"That's fine." But from the hard line of his jaw, it clearly wasn't. "I'll round up Molly and we can head for the house."

"What about the missing calf?"

Will scratched his face and looked off to Molly. "I might've not been totally honest on that point."

"Did you not, a mere week ago, promise you'd give me the real Will?"

"Aw, c'mon. If I said we were going for a ride, you would've wanted to turn back after fifteen minutes, so I came up with a good reason to keep going that your big heart couldn't have refused."

"You lied to me."

"It was for a good cause."

"It wasn't. It was for a miserable, selfish cause," Krista said, struggling to her feet. "I hate—no, I loathe—horse riding. It hurts, the horses can't stand me, I'm sweaty, I feel ugly, and I really don't consider it fun if my date is correcting how I sit every few minutes."

He caught her arm. "I'm sorry. We'll try again some other time."

"No, no, no." Krista fumbled with her helmet strap and stripped it off her head. The breeze ran through her hair like a kiss from heaven. "I'm not trying again. I've tried to be a good sport twice. Once for Laura. Once for you. Both times, huge disasters. I realize that lowers my value in your eyes, but there you have it."

He did that long gaze across the pasture again, as if expecting an incoming message from afar. "No, refusing to get on a horse doesn't lower your value."

"But you have to admit this evening didn't roll out the way you'd hoped."

"You're right about that. You need more lessons than I thought."

"You overestimated my ability because you don't even know people who can't ride."

"There's your family."

"They don't count."

"How about this? I'll give Molly a quick run to get some of the spit out of her, and then we'll do what we did at the wedding. You sit and I'll take the reins."

This was humiliating. At the wedding with everyone in their best and everyone watching, it made sense. Now it reeked of failure. And the ride back made for awkward conversation. She'd never been so glad to see a barn.

Never so glad to have her feet on solid ground again. "You do realize that I never plan to get on a horse again." She wasn't joking, either.

He unstrapped the saddle on Molly and draped it on the railing. "I figured that."

"Are we still dating?"

He met her eyes over Molly's rump. "You tell me."

His sideways vote of confidence in them felt like ointment on her sore muscles. She had shown him her talentless side and he still wanted to be with her. She itched to show him another part of her world. "We are, if you're ready for round two with my family."

"I guess if you got on a horse twice, I can meet your family one more time."

"Good. We're going out on the boat this weekend."

Will dipped his head to unbuckle Blackberry's saddle. "You have a boat?" Was it her or did he sound a little choked?

"The family does. Well, us and the bank for the next three years. You up for it?"

"Sure," he said, "sounds like fun." There wasn't a trace of excitement in his voice. Never mind. Nothing was more fun than a day on the lake.

CHAPTER TWELVE

"IT NEVER OCCURRED to you to tell her about your fear of water?" Dana said to Will, as he leaned against the door of her pickup. She was inside the cab, ready to head home with the water tank she'd asked to borrow.

"It did, but the thing is, I'm already in trouble with her family."

"How so?"

He didn't want to count the ways again. "Let's just say that if I refuse, I'll come across as even more of a snob. They wouldn't believe that I only like water if it's coming out of a tap."

"They'll know Saturday."

"I might be able to fake it."

"How do you intend to do that?"

"I sit on a boat, don't I?"

"You mean like Krista had to sit on a horse?"

Will's stomach churned as if he was already on the water.

"You could take lessons," Dana said.

"Yes. But they happen in places where there's deep water."

"You must've drowned in your previous life or something. You've always been scared of water. Janet said bath time when you were a kid nearly broke her. Deal, buddy. After all, Krista got on a horse for you, and we all know she'd rather plug staples in her hand."

"A horse can't kill you."

Dana raised an eyebrow at his shoulder where the horse had kicked, narrowly missing his head.

"Fair enough. Maybe I can figure out a way—"

Dana tensed, her eye on the truck that had just turned in. Keith, back from work early. He moseyed his way up to the house and Dana shifted into drive. "I better go."

Will and Dana hadn't talked about Keith since the wedding, and Keith hadn't filled Will in on his version of events. That in itself spoke of the rawness between them.

Krista would use the opportunity to apply salve to the wound. He preferred to leave it alone, except he'd promised Krista he'd talk to Keith and a good three weeks had already passed. She hadn't prodded him yet. The social media fallout and their own dating disasters were distraction enough. "I take it you two haven't talked since the wedding."

Dana pulled a face. "Plenty about Austin. He texted me about the first word which was good. But if I'd kept my mouth shut at the wedding, he would've called me. Now, he mostly texts. And I try to time seeing Austin when he's not around. Like today." She played with the wheel, clearly wanting to go. "Anyway, I probably deserve it, right? I threw you over and then he does it right back to me."

Keith parked the truck at the house and disappeared inside with bags of groceries. He didn't look their way, even though he must've seen Dana's truck. He could've at least waved. "Not a question of deserving," Will said, "but for the record, this only proves that I'm the smarter brother."

Dana was churning out road dust when Keith reappeared with a box under his arm. The part for the hay binder. Good.

They reached the broken hay binder at the same time. Keith shook out a pair of coveralls. "Dana short on water?"

"Creek's running slow. The wind the other night knocked deadfall further up. Until she gets in there with a chain saw, she plans to haul in water."

Keith gave him an accusing glare. "That's hard work. Slippery, too. Fall with a chain saw and—" He sucked in his breath.

"I offered to help but she has a hired hand through to the end of the month."

"Then what?"

He was talking as if Will was at fault for not managing Dana's life. "How is it either one of our business?"

Keith jerked up the zipper on the coveralls. "Austin's still napping, so I'll get started here."

"You know," Will said, "you can take a break now and again."

"You got the easy life all figured out. You and Dana were talking away."

Enough. Time he had it out with Keith. "And it might've gone on longer except she couldn't wait to hightail it out once you pulled in."

Keith ripped at the box. "I planned to say hello once I got the milk and cream in the fridge, but she'd already left."

"Can you blame her? You blew her off at the wedding."

Keith pulled out the part. "What the…?

This isn't it. I told them.I gave them a picture, wrote it down. And still they get it wrong. I don't have time for this." He shoved it back in the box and made to go.

"Never mind it. You won't make it to town before the store closes, and there'll be another day at least before they get the part in. I'll go in first thing and give them a piece of your mind, okay?"

Will held out his hands for the box and Keith thrust it at him. "Now how about you answer my question before Austin wakes and you have to turn into dad."

Keith sat in the hub of the giant tractor wheel. "He said it, last night. He was walking ahead to his room. He stops, looks back and says, 'Dad.'"

Will felt a beam of pride. "Well now. His second word."

"Third. He also says 'up.'"

"True. Dad, up and Dana."

Keith rubbed his cheek. "Yeah, well, he hasn't said her name in the past while."

"He did today. She stopped by the house to see him."

Keith brightened. "She did?"

"She's visited a few times…when you weren't around."

Keith kicked out his legs, scrubbed his head. "What could I have told her? 'Sure, I've got feelings for you, too. Let's give it a shot because I'm the kind of guy that'll give anything a whirl.'"

Will leaned on the wheel of the tractor, hoping the shade from the tractor would make the conversation less heated.

"So…you do have feelings for her?"

"Yes. Why wouldn't I? I mean, you did."

Not the way he did for Krista. His regard for Dana was logical, but now that he'd a taste of Krista—well, if there was no going forward for them, there was no going back for him, either. "Not the same way, that's clear now. You never let on. When did you figure it out?"

"About two seconds after I suggested she could do better. I guess I realized how much I was giving up."

"Then why didn't you tell her that you'd said a real dumb thing and would she maybe let you reconsider?"

"Because two seconds after that, I also realized that I'd made the right decision. I've got nothing to offer."

"What do you mean? You've got the section of land." Each of the three kids had one, jointly owned with Dave. On his death, the kids took full title. None of them wanted that to happen anytime soon, though. Will had also taken on a second section.

"And she has four in her name. She's not interested in more land. Or bills, and that's all I've got. Nothing but bills, no matter how hard I work. I don't have the time to be with Dana, and even if I did, I can't afford to do anything with her."

"She understands your circumstances, Keith. She has her own means, too. If she chose you, it was because of you. Well, you and Austin."

Keith bowed his head. "She really seems to care for him."

"Loves him like family. And Austin feels the same about her."

"He is a great kid, isn't he?"

"You're doing an incredible job, Keith. That thing with Macey, you're going to look back on it one day and call it a bump on the road. Be happy you got a great kid out of it. But are you going to find some silver lining from turning down Dana?"

Keith sent Will a piercing stare. "A month of dating Krista make you the relationship expert?"

"I'd describe it as a sharp learning curve."

Keith grinned. "Sounds as if she's on one with horses."

"Yeah, that didn't go so well. Which I don't get, Keith. Dana's your complete package. You have feelings for her and you guys agree on everything. Well, except for kids."

"What do you mean? I like kids."

"She wants four."

Keith blinked.

"Anyway, my point is that I've got feelings for Krista, but I admit there's nothing we have in common. She hasn't even given me a clear answer on whether *she* wants kids."

"Not good news, for the heir apparent to the Claverley dynasty."

It wasn't, but neither could he deny that he still wanted her.

"Does she know about your shoulder?"

"Not the whole story."

"And how do you think she's going to react when she finds out?"

He recalled her face when he'd admitted to lying about the missing calf. Wait until she found out about his fear of water, never mind his shoulder. "Not well."

Keith stood. "We're walking disasters."

FROM THE FIRM boards of the dock, Will eyed the Montgomery boat as it undulated from the impact of the boarding passengers. The bit of floatage that separated him from the dark and cool depths of Spirit Lake seemed sturdy enough. It had chairs with arms to grip and seats deep enough so he wouldn't fly out like a plastic bag, as well as life jackets. Bridget was handing some out to her daughters. He spotted a few adult ones. Good, he wouldn't have to embarrass himself by asking if they had life jackets, or come off as challenging their responsibility as boaters.

He might be able to fake his way through this. He was secretly relieved that Mara had begged off. Krista would be hard enough to fool. Mara's professional sharp eye would blister right through his facade.

The girls protested they didn't need life jackets, having passed "level four swimming," four more than he'd ever managed. Bridget snapped them into one, anyway. Wise mother.

"Anyone else want one?" Krista said. But she only looked at him.

He gazed pointedly at the girls puffed out in their jackets over their bathing suits. "Sure," he said. "Good idea. Can never be too safe."

And there, he'd found a clever way to save himself without revealing his total lack of water skills.

He stepped onto the boat, taking a wide stance to absorb the motion. It was barely rocking; his stomach stayed solid. Now, if they could remain tied to the dock…

Jack stood at the helm. "Everyone ready for the best day of their lives?"

A whole day? "I didn't realize it would be for that long," he said to Krista, who sat beside him on the transom seats. She was applying sunscreen onto the exposed parts of her skin, of which there were many.

"We share the boat with another family, so when our turn comes up and the forecast is for sun and clear skies, we take advantage of it. Why? Do you need to be somewhere?"

Yes, anywhere else. "Uh, no."

She took in his jeans, T-shirt, running shoes and baseball cap with the brand of a farm equipment dealership. "You wore your sun protection."

He registered Jack's cargo shorts and sandals. "A bit overdressed, am I?"

She patted his knee. "It's adorable. But the only change room here is in the bow." She assumed that his bag had a swimsuit in it. It had a change of clothes only.

"Um, well, I don't have swimming trunks."

She flipped open the next seat over. "Sure, you do." She held up a brand-spanking-new pair, pickle green with pink flamingos. And some wraparound shades. "Time to saddle up, cowboy."

Fine, he'd dress the part. He took himself up to the hot and airy privacy of the bow. Jack puttered the boat out of the marina as Will wiggled out of his jeans. Jack kicked up the engine a notch. The bow rose up and the towel that Will had discreetly placed across his mid-section slipped off.

"Sorry, man," Jack called, not sounding the least bit apologetic.

Payback for the steak insult. Will never got into a piece of clothing faster. He pulled on his socks and running shoes. He looked like a farmer who'd shopped at a boater's thrift shop.

In the stern of the boat, Bridget was doing safety checks with her daughters.

"Do you enter the water from the back of the boat when it's moving?"

"No."

"Do you enter the water without permission from Jack or me?"

"No."

"Do you enter the water only when there is another adult who has volunteered to supervise you?"

"Yes."

"What are the consequences if you do not follow any of the rules?"

"No stories and no desserts until next time we're out on the lake."

Will thought of a punishment that he'd much prefer. "Wouldn't you ban them from going on the water?"

The Montgomery bunch looked at him as if he'd suggested diving into an empty pool. "We're punishing them, not us," Krista said. "We wouldn't be able to go on the lake, either."

Clear of the shoreline with kayakers, canoeists and dapplers on their inflatables, Jack throttled up even more. Will's stomach lurched with the surge in power. Definitely in deep water now. He slid a look at Krista, who was seated on the bow. With her head tilted back and her arms out wide to receive the wind and the spray, she was in her element. Bridget walked past him to stand beside Jack, her arm looped around his back. He raised his face and they kissed.

For crying out loud, keep your eyes on the ro—lake.

When they'd reached what seemed to Will the point farthest from any shore, where shiny blue spread in all deathly directions, Jack cut the engine. Will's insides sloshed to the same flat calmness as the water.

Krista peeled off her shirt and shorts, kicked off her sandals and splash!—had transformed into a seal. The girls and Bridget followed. All screamed at the cold temperatures but made no move to return to the boat.

"I'll stay in, if you want to join them," Will said quickly to Jack.

"Do you have a boater's license? Only those with one can be alone in a powered boat while it's in the water."

"No, didn't think of that," Will mumbled.

"You can go in," Jack told Will. "I'll stay here and switch out with Bridge in a bit."

"Uh, I'm good."

Jack gave a friendly smile. "You don't know how to swim."

"Not comfortably."

Krista bobbed up beside the boat. "Come in, Will."

Why had he ever thought he could fake this? "Thing is, I'm not very good in the water."

Her blond hair slicked down from an underwater glide, Krista and Jack laughed together. "Kinda figured that out from the speed you put on the lifejacket."

He'd not fooled anybody, especially the one he'd wanted to convince.

"Don't worry, we're in the middle of nowhere," Krista said. "No one here is going to notice if you have a life jacket on. Your reputation is intact."

He wanted his *life* intact. Isabella and Sofia swam and dunked freely in the water. Krista grinned up at him. "It's as easy as riding a horse."

"That's what I'm worried about."

He stood at the back of the boat, toes curled and heart pounding, like an overgrown four-year-old on the edge of a swimming pool.

Jack came up beside him, his back to the girls in the water so only Will heard what he said next. "Can't be the first time you did something that scared you."

"If there was, I can't remember it," Will said as quietly.

"Try this, then. Krista's watching."

Krista with her laughing eyes, inviting him to join her world, her family. But his muscles had seized.

"Push me," he told Jack through a clenched jaw.

"You sure?"

Will gave a quick nod. And just like that, Jack slipped, wobbled and slammed into Will, who toppled into water cold enough to inflict freezer burn.

"Sorry," Jack called from the boat where he'd righted himself.

"No worries," Will said. "You did me a favor, actually."

"You don't have to wear your life jacket," Isabella said, "since you're an adult."

"I want to," Will said. "I… I'm not a great swimmer."

"You should've said something," Krista admonished.

"And wreck the fun for you all?"

"It does make me feel better about flubbing up the horse riding." She dove under water and tweaked his toes, popping up beside him. "A whole lot better."

Will felt like a discarded cork, bobbing around in the lake, trying to stay afloat. "I was born with a fear of water."

Krista twirled otter-like, around him. "I can't fathom that. I've been swimming for as long as I can remember. Mom and Dad were always traveling, and our days seemed to consistently end up at some kind of water—lake, river, ocean. I think it was a cheap way to bathe us. Did I mention they were born hippies?"

She didn't have to. His mother had brought up the subject of Deidre "going off with some guy in a van that looked painted by a kid."

"Like I don't remember learning how to ride a horse," Will said.

"Yep," Krista said. "We're even."

They weren't. Horses and horse riding were his existence. Water was recreation for her. He couldn't imagine being with someone who wasn't comfortable around horses. He'd have to get her back in the saddle.

After lunch, out came the water skis. When would he wake from this sunny nightmare? His shoulder emitted a long moan of protest which Krista seemed to hear. "You don't have to do this, you know."

She was giving him a rock solid out. But he'd also give up a perfect opportunity.

"I do this, and you get back on a horse. Deal?"

Her smile faltered. "I already did my part. You need to catch up to me."

"How many times do I have to ride water before you consider it even?"

She rolled her eyes. "This is stupid. You're risking further injury to your shoulder to impress me, and you promised you wouldn't."

"My shoulder is fine. If it hurts, I'll do it one-handed."

"As if."

He waited.

"Three, okay? Do it three times and we're even."

"You're on. Tell me what to do."

"Bend your knees. No more. Closer to your chest. Not so much." She deliberately echoed his choppy, conflicting instructions from when she was on Molly.

"And when you start coming up, don't stand straight up right away, keep your knees bent."

"Right."

"Say 'go' when you're ready."

"Krista," he said, "I think I've got a leech on my neck. Can you check?"

Revulsion and concern warred on her face as she leaned close. He snatched a kiss. "Sorry,

I was wrong." Jack waited for his signal at the helm. "Go!"

If there was anything he'd learned from bronc riding, it was how to hold on for the money. He rose up and bumped along in the boat's wake. He kept his knees bent, as if sitting in a chair. Still, this was actual waterskiing. As he straightened from his crouch, a wave—and no ordinary wave but a freak tsunami of one—rode underneath his skis and threw him.

His entire waterskiing experience might've lasted for half a minute.

Jack circled around. "You want to get back in the saddle?"

He wanted to get out of the freezing cold lake and get his feet back on solid ground… or at least the semisolid surface of the boat.

But if he didn't keep at it, Krista would never get on top of another horse. She was slicing forward in a powerful front crawl through the water to retrieve the rope. He touched the clasps on his lifejacket. All in place.

"I'm good."

But Krista didn't hand him the rope. "All right, fine. We're even. I can't stand to see your shoulder yanked about." She slapped the water when he opened his mouth. "Get into the boat. It's my turn. Don't even argue."

He didn't.

He flopped into the boat with all the grace of a walrus and watched Krista as she took off on the skis.

She was good, really good. She rode the bumps like a pro and did a full turn.

"Show-off," Bridget grumbled from the seat across from him. She'd stood up straight and hadn't fallen, either. "You had a bad experience in water, Will, or what?"

"Nope. Just don't like the feeling. I argued about it with my mom and she didn't push it. Keith and Laura are good enough swimmers, but not as natural as you guys."

"Krista's the best, hands down," Bridget said. "Don't tell her that, though. She does not need one more thing to lord over us."

"She's rubbing it in because she had a hard go of it last time she was on a horse."

"Noticed the bruises myself," Bridget said neutrally. "Lucky thing you put a helmet on her. She said a hoof clipped her on the side of the head."

Will felt as if the hoof had struck his chest. "She said nothing to me. I have my work cut out now to get her on a horse again."

Bridget leaned closer to Will. "I loathe her ex, as much as any big sister who watches her little sister get hurt. But I will say one thing for her, and it's probably why Phillip is attacking her so viciously. She's not afraid to walk away from a bad situation. And when she said she's not riding ever again, I believe it. You'll have to do more than change her mind. You'll have to change *her*."

He took in the spectacle of Krista, the best-looking person on the lake, and his plan to get her on a horse dissolved. He was trying to change her, to expand her to include his life, but that meant stretching himself in ways he didn't want to, either. So where did that leave them?

Krista had been right all along. They weren't meant to be together. But he couldn't bear the thought of them being apart, either.

CHAPTER THIRTEEN

"HOLD IT THERE," Alyssa said. Krista swore if she had to maintain her pose another second, she'd scream. But she dutifully kept her head angled to Will's shoulder as they gazed adoringly at Austin on Will's arm.

"This might help my image," Will said, "but it's going to make Keith seem like an absentee father."

"My job is to make *you* look good," Alyssa said. "No one's thinking about Keith."

Alyssa certainly understood how to build an image. The "never give up on kids" message had gained traction to the point Phillip's latest picture had reverted to his old cracks about their incompatibility. The dolls rode horses in a merry-go-round. Will-doll was seated properly, and Krista-doll was mounted backward. She was saying, "I think I'm doing something wrong." And the Will-doll thought, "No more than usual."

When Alyssa had showed it to them, Will

had not blown up as before. His expression had gone carefully neutral, almost polite. As if he secretly agreed with Phillip but didn't want to hurt her feelings.

Something had changed in Will since their outing on the lake nearly a week ago. He'd gone quiet. She'd been booked solid the past days, and he'd been cutting hay and baling, on top of working a three-year-old colt, so they'd not had a chance to see one another until now for this brief photo shoot before he headed back out to the field.

Alyssa left. When Krista decided to corner Will about his moodiness, he got a text that made him growl. "Mom and Dad are running behind. They'll be another couple of hours at least." Will had once again pulled the short straw to cover for Keith with Austin until Janet and Dave returned from a bull sale. Meanwhile, Keith's truck had broken down, and he was off on the side of a highway, waiting for a relief truck. He wouldn't be home for hours.

Which meant Will couldn't get out to bale and there was rain forecasted for tomorrow. Apparently, you couldn't bale wet hay or else it would plug the...the something on the baler.

Forget about having a heart-to-heart. Will was too keyed up about the field work.

"Look," Krista said, "how about I take care of Austin? I know the routine. We play, have supper, play, bathe, bed. Janet will probably be home before long. All's good."

"You're sure?" Will appeared the most excited over anything she'd said all week.

Her first experience with children of any kind was five-year-old Sofia eight months ago. They'd forged a lasting bond based on bling and trending hairstyles. Austin couldn't form sentences, distinguish between edibles and poison, and climbed over what he couldn't climb under. But she'd spent time around Austin, watched others care for him. And it was only for two hours. "Very sure."

He practically tossed Austin into her arms before beelining it out to the barnyard.

Austin wiggled from her arms and charged for the living room steps. Krista gasped at the two steps but he flipped to his belly, bumped down and was back on his feet before she could reach him. The monkey was fast.

And reckless. He almost beaned himself on cabinet handles, coffee table corners, wall edges. When he'd crawled onto the kitchen chair twice to use the pepper shaker as a noisemaker, she decided that Austin was better outside. She'd have to run to keep up with him but at least she didn't have to worry about so many toddler traps.

"You certainly have got the Claverley energy, buddy," she said, setting him down in the yard. It was like releasing a fully primed robodog. He immediately set off for the barns. Zero chance she'd let Austin anywhere near an animal.

Where was Clover to ride herd? Probably gone off to escort Will to the field. Krista implemented a Clover technique and got in his space to point him back to the house yard. Austin darted around her and plowed on. "Mutt!" She carried him up to the sandbox behind the house with its assortment of dump trucks and tractors. "There. How about you apprentice here before tackling the big ones?" Except the sight of the trucks and tractors reminded him of the real ones. "Tuck. Tactor." And with the unerring instinct of a migratory bird, he headed once again to the barn.

She had to retrieve him four times, both of their impatience mounting. No wonder Keith looked perpetually on edge. Of course, he could take Austin to the horsies. Every last single Claverley probably galloped with Austin tucked under their arm like a football.

Nope. Kids were not her thing. Not to keep, anyway. And she didn't have a future with Will unless kids were in it. And if there wasn't a future, what was the point of pretending another day?

Because she wanted him. Because, unlike with Phillip, she was too weak to let him go.

"C'mon, monkey, let's go have something to eat." She picked him up and had to hold on tight as he squirmed for release. "What do you want? Strawberries? Ice cream?"

He quieted, listening. Her chatter was more than soothing babble to him. "Peas? Milk?" Wait, did he have allergies? Will hadn't mentioned any, but that didn't mean anything.

She skimmed her contacts. As much as she didn't want to, she settled on Janet. It was her kitchen, after all.

"He doesn't have any allergies," Janet said, "but he is a picky eater. And he refuses to eat anything unless he puts it into his own mouth."

"Why am I not surprised?" Krista said.

"Surprised?"

"At his early display of independence. He's a Claverley, after all."

Janet ignored her and directed her to the roasted potatoes in the fridge, along with the cheese, blueberries—halve them!—strawberries—quarter them! She instructed Krista to only give him a bit on his tray at a time, otherwise he'll wad it all in and choke. "And if you can't manage anything else, there's cereal in the pantry."

She could manage, thank you very much.

She did, too. She managed to clean up every telltale sign of the cereal, and unless Austin pooped them out in perfect circles, she figured she was covered.

Janet texted to say that the bull was finally loaded but they were still two hours away.

No problem, Krista said. She could do the play-bathe-bed routine. After a play made easier by Clover's support, she filled the tub up until Austin's belly was covered. Austin's face began to pucker in distress.

"Oh no, you're not. Water is fun. You're not going to end up like your scaredy-cat uncle." She spied a bottle of bubble bath on the edge of the tub and squirted in a generous dollop, shaking it up with her hand. Bubbles were not a normal experience for Austin, apparently, because his eyes widened at their appearance and for the first time that evening, he launched into giggles.

Finally, a beautiful moment. She reached for her camera phone—there was a sudden splashing—and Austin sunk underneath the water.

His little arms and legs flailed amid the bubbles. Krista grabbed him around the torso and lifted him out. Austin coughed and sputtered, swiped at bubbles over his eyes. She flipped him belly down across her thighs, her lifeguard experience kicking in.

"It's okay, it's okay, it's okay," she murmured, hoping to calm him while inside she was fighting panic. He'd be fine, he was fine, his system was expelling any water, the kid was tough, a Claverley, after all.

His coughing subsided, and Krista reached for a towel, wrapping him up. "There, aren't you a brave boy?"

His lip wobbled and he began to cry. Tears not so much of fright, but anger. "Go!"

A new word. She didn't blame him. She'd ruined his playtime, fed him breakfast cereal straight out of the box and nearly drowned him. His decision was sensible.

She pulled the plug on the bathwater and gathered him into her arms. "Here, we'll leave this scene and get you into jammies, and then we'll take it from there."

Austin snapped. He screamed and kicked her thighs, drummed his fists on whatever part of her he could get at. "Go, go, go!"

"Sorry, buddy, for wrecking your day, but let's get through the next hour together, okay?"

Austin's howls were now full-throated, and she didn't know if his eyes were red from the bubbles or his tears.

Another text from Janet. We've a flat tire. We'll be another hour.

Ugh. She'd give Austin fifteen minutes to calm down, and then she'd call Will. Maybe the sound of his voice would break through to Austin. If that didn't work, then she would beg and plead for him to come in. She'd drive out herself but there was no car seat available.

Fifteen minutes later, with Austin still screaming out his lungs and naked because he didn't want her anywhere near him, her message to Will went to voice mail.

Anger spiked. He knew she was alone with Austin. Why couldn't he pick up his phone? Help her out like she was helping him out? Or was there a reason he couldn't pick up? Statistics about farm accidents flashed through her mind.

No. She had no time to entertain morbid thoughts. Not with Austin aiming to bust her eardrum. Tears wouldn't kill him. Unless—he didn't usually have this soap, so was he having a massive allergic reaction? There would be other symptoms—a rash, difficulty breathing—which he clearly was not having. She checked his head to make sure he hadn't bumped it when he'd gone under. Only sweaty from his performance.

Not having Keith's number, Krista called the only person she knew within reach that might get through to Austin. Dana picked up on the fourth ring.

"As you are probably hearing, I'm with Austin and it's not going well."

"What happened?" Dana's voice was sharp, worried.

Krista filled her in. "I was hoping that you might have a suggestion for how to get him to stop shrieking. I'm sure he's physically fine, but apparently he's inherited the Claverley fear of water."

"Put him on."

At the sound of Dana's voice, Austin's screams fell to body-shuddering heaves. "Dana," he sighed.

Krista overheard Dana talk nonsense about

horses and tractors and strawberries. Austin's shuddering eased off and he relaxed against Krista as Dana's voice flowed into his ears.

Then Krista withdrew the phone. Austin grabbed for it, his face contracting with distress. "Could you possibly talk to him for the next coupla hours?" Krista said, only half-joking.

"Hang on, I'm coming over."

If possible, Austin's cries were even louder during the ten minutes it took for Dana to pull up.

"Dana, Dana, Dana," Austin repeated in excitement and desperation. He flung himself into her embrace and wrapped his own little arms tight around her neck.

"Oh, my guy," Dana whispered and rested her cheek on his damp curls.

Krista's insides twisted. The two clearly loved each other. Yes, Keith hadn't kept Dana from Austin, but neither had he made it easy for them to be together. And sadly, there was nothing Krista could do about it, either. Why wouldn't Keith give him and Dana a chance?

Still wrapped together, Dana moved to the easy chair in the living room. Krista switched to the role of personal assistant, fluttering to them with towel, blankie, diaper, jammies, a sippy cup of cold water. When the two were cozy together, Krista withdrew to the back deck to give them privacy.

Alone, Krista checked her phone. Nothing from Janet or Will. She texted Mara. Babysitting was a nightmare. I'll be home in an hour or two.

Mara replied, Okay. She was probably enjoying the single life of a movie or music accompanied by alcohol. Krista settled into the deck chair, waving away whining mosquitoes, the quiet of the country thundering in her ears.

And where was Will? Out on a tractor somewhere on the Claverley spread, completely unaware of her troubles with his nephew. She couldn't blame him; she'd agreed to this experiment. But it was a failed one. Like her relationship with Will. A month together, and she could already see the cracks yawning between them, wide as a pasture, long as the distance between this ranch and her salon.

I love you, Will, but this is not the life for me.

CHAPTER FOURTEEN

IN THE DESCENDING DARK, Keith drove along the graveled road to the ranch, a few miles from ending his sixteen-hour day of breakdowns, missed delivery times and grumpy customers. He normally used the commute home as a chance to listen to music, blow off steam about work and divorce proceedings, and let plans for him and Austin trickle in. But right now, he was focused only on staying awake long enough to park his truck, whisper good-night to his sleeping boy and enter the same state of consciousness himself.

Half a mile from the Claverley driveway, he saw Dana pull out, the headlights of her truck flashing toward him. Why was she over so late? Needed help with something? And now, like last time, she was leaving again before he could speak to her. No, last time she'd left because he hadn't scrounged up the nerve to come to her. Not happening, tonight.

He slowed to a stop on the road, the universal rural sign that he wanted to speak to the oncoming driver. She drew opposite him and he switched on his cab lights. She didn't, but there was enough power from his to reach her. She looked exhausted, pale even through her tan.

"Hey," he said, "I almost missed you again."

She gave a wan smile. "It's all good. He's settled now."

Keith fumbled to connect the dots. "You were over for Austin?"

"Krista was watching him tonight, and he pitched a tantrum that she couldn't bring him out of."

What a crappy father he was. All along he'd assumed Will or his mother was with Austin, and here Krista had filled in. Austin hardly knew her. No wonder he'd wigged out. He rubbed his face. "I'm sorry, Dana. I— I didn't realize."

"No worries. Dave and Janet only got home themselves, and I helped with the unloading."

"Right. The bull sale. They picked one up, then?"

"Yep. Good shape. But—" She rolled her eyes. "They are actually talking about turning him out with the herd. See what happens."

Keith groaned. "Back to calving in May. Might as well be talking to a wall with them."

Dana gave a small, companionable laugh. She'd always done a lot of that with him, something he realized now that they'd not had a conversation in six weeks. Her right hand passed from the wheel to the gearshift. Ready to drive on.

"Austin's busting out a lot of words now," he said quickly.

She flickered a smile. "I noticed. I heard 'cup' and 'tractor' and 'book.'" Her gaze drifted away to the windshield. "Also heard 'Dana' a few times."

When he hadn't been able to summon up the courage to call her about what had happened at Caris's wedding, he'd composed a text. "You're always welcome over, you know."

She did. She'd just been here, after all. At Krista's invitation, no less. "To see Austin," he clarified.

Except she knew that, too.

She gave a tired smile. "I have visitation rights?"

"I didn't mean it that way. Not exactly." He pushed himself to say more. "Your name wasn't his first word for no reason. You two are close. I don't want to stand in the way of that."

She turned to him, her eyes full. "But you do," she whispered. "You do."

Now he stared through the windshield. Her engine revved up as she shifted into Drive.

"Listen, Dana," he said. "Hold on. That night…what I said…it came out all wrong… I'm sorry."

She looked silently at him. The dim light from his cabin touched the soft slope of her cheek, caught the light red-brown glints in her hair. She was too far away to touch, so he'd somehow have to reach her with his words. Unrehearsed words. The same kind that had got him into this mess the first time.

"Look, Dana. We've known each other since we were kids, and in my mind you've always belonged to Will. When he mentioned that he'd asked you to go out with him, it made perfect sense to me. I never even considered you and me together, until you brought it up. So yeah, you took me by surprise. And my knee-jerk reaction was to shut it all down. But I was wrong."

She shoved the gear back into Park.

"When I thought about it, I started seeing all the advantages. Of how you and Austin love each other, and how I could help you really build up your place so you wouldn't have to hire work out."

Her head dipped. He was losing her again. He spoke faster. "Will says you want four kids, and if you count Austin, we're already up by one. And my divorce won't go on forever, so after going over it in my mind, we actually might work out."

He waited. She lifted her head. Her pale cheeks were flushed. "Let me get this right," she clipped out. "You're saying we should get together for the sake of the farm and kids… as a partnership."

How had he angered her? He was offering her what she'd asked for. "I told you that I thought you could do better. I'm trying to say that I'll work to be what you deserve."

She shook her head. "You still believe I'm settling. Don't you see, settling in my mind would be dating Will. I passed him over because you were the one I wanted. I've had plenty of chances to 'settle' over the past few years, but I held out for you."

Him. Him alone. He could've had this gold. Instead he'd fallen for glitter.

"But now I realize how incredibly stupid I've been," she said. "Because I have standards, Keith. And I want to be with a guy who recognizes his own worth. I want to be with a guy who thinks of himself as highly as I think of him."

She didn't wait for him to come up with words he didn't have. She threw her truck into gear again and drove away into the darkness.

KRISTA DOCKED THE Claverley pickup with its wide hood and high suspension at the gate into the hayfield where Will was baling. At least, she assumed he was somewhere out there. She could only make out row after row of cut hay to where they wavered and then dipped behind a large hill. Had she screwed up Dave's careful instructions? When she'd volunteered to take supper to Will, Dave had pulled out a stubby carpenter pencil and the back of a receipt from a farm supply store and drawn a map, complete with landmarks of a water trough and a rock pile.

He'd also demonstrated how to open the gate. First insert the bottom post and then get behind that fence post and pull the top end of the fence post toward you. He took so long with her that she said, "I think it would've been quicker if you'd taken it out yourself."

He touched his hat. "I doubt it's me he's bent on seeing."

Krista didn't know if Will wanted to see her, either. Especially since she intended to end their relationship. Yes, breaking up in a pasture over supper wasn't classy, given that he'd invited her to come out to catch a little time together. But nothing had changed her mind in the last two days since the babysitting debacle, and she'd learned her lesson from the fallout with Phillip about delaying painful conversations.

And this one would be painful. Her love for the quiet, obstinate, water-phobic rancher had sunk into her very marrow. She didn't want to end things with him, as she had with Phillip. But neither could she see a way forward. And she bet he'd come to the same conclusion. That's why he'd withdrawn from her ever since the day on the lake. That's why he made this meetup so short and so mazelike. He probably hoped she wouldn't show.

And she hoped she was dead wrong.

As soon as she swung from the truck, narrowly missing a plate-size cow patty, she heard what she assumed was the rumbling of Will's tractor. Dave had said that he might be "working the corners" and "would take a bit to come around." Rural language was peppered with these vague descriptors, odd for a people so down-to-earth. "Around about." And the double negative from Dave when Janet had interrupted to ask if he wanted steak or roast tomorrow. *Don't matter none to me, hon.* Credit to him, he'd thrown in a rhyme.

Will's *outfit* pulled into sight. She had never heard that term in relation to equipment before. The nose of the giant green tractor crested the hill, pulling a round machine which she took to be the baler. So, she'd made it to the right place.

She waved but the sun was glaring off the tractor windshield, so she'd no idea if he'd seen her. He passed her, his back to her. Was he ignoring her? He stopped the tractor and dropped a bale from the machine like a chicken laying an egg. Oh. Cool.

He turned off the tractor and crossed the stubbly field to her.

Dusty and dirty, he looked great. As he approached, he held up his hands. "You pack wipes?"

Not the romantic opening she'd expected, but then again this was Will. "On the passenger side of the truck," she said. While he sanitized, she sized up a spot to set up their picnic. What could be more idyllic than a checkered cloth spread out on a field. Except the field was poky and dirty, and the pasture was pockmarked with gopher holes or cow patties.

Will settled the matter. He opened the tailgate and swung the cooler and himself onto it. Of course. He gestured for her to join him.

By the time she crossed to him, he was studying the contents of the cooler. He didn't seem happy. After offering to bring him supper, she'd been seized by a sudden anxiety of what to make for him. Not owning a cookbook herself, she'd flipped through Mara's shelf and then gone online. Mara had assured her that whatever Krista made, Will would love. But what kind of message was she sending by slaving over a meal that she was using as an excuse to break up with him? So she'd gone to the grocery store and picked up a bunch of dishes—fried chicken, potato salad, coleslaw, crabmeat salad, and yogurt topped with granola and berries. On a whim, she'd also grabbed jalapeño olives. All in their plastic take-out containers. But now she saw it through his eyes. A cooler full of random offerings because she had no idea what he liked and didn't care to find out.

Had he figured out her reasoning? She didn't want him to know. Not yet.

Krista hoisted herself onto the tailgate, the cooler between them. "I didn't want to risk you getting sick on my cooking. I'm only good at salads. I figured you'd want more."

He nodded and took out the chicken, potato salad and—the olives. He flipped the lid inside up on his lap, opened the food and tucked in, using the plastic cutlery she'd only remembered when she was halfway out of the store. He tossed a couple of olives in his mouth like popcorn and indicated her empty lap. "You're not eating?"

"No, I—I'm not hungry." She was. Starving. Except it didn't seem right to break it off with him between mouthfuls. "Besides, I forgot to pack extra cutlery. Silly me."

He nudged the olives closer. "Don't need anything for these."

She plucked out one and popped it in, the hot pepper tingling her mouth. "I took a chance on these. I didn't know if you'd like them."

"Like jalapeños, like olives. Never had them together before." He squinted at her. "Not your thing?"

"If I enjoyed swallowing fire, it would be."

"You want a bit of the potato salad to take away the sting? We can share forks."

That seemed far too intimate, considering what she really shouldn't put off saying. She caught him discreetly flexing his right arm.

"Your shoulder's acting up," she said.

"Bit of a kink from turning to watch the baler," he said. "Don't worry, no lifting. That's all she said I shouldn't do."

Krista started. "Who's 'she'?"

Guilt crossed his face, and he dipped his head to the potato salad. "The physiotherapist."

"You said you've been in the field the past week. When did you have time to see her?"

He kept his head down. "It was before then. I can't remember."

Anger prickled in her gut, hotter than any stupid jalapeño. "You deliberately didn't tell me."

"Because you would get all worked up."

"Sorry for caring." She did, too, desperately. This was not going to be easy.

He set down his salad and touched his finger to her bare knee. She shifted away. "Listen, Krista. The physio warned me not to lift too much. That's all, I swear."

"How much is 'too much'?"

"Anything where I start feeling it."

"Will! You were 'feeling it' two days ago when you were carrying Austin. I noticed you wince. How much does he weigh? Thirty pounds? Is that why you tried to get out of babysitting the other night? Because you were worried you might have to lift him and tear your shoulder more?"

"I left because I figured you could handle things for a while. Apparently, I was wrong."

They'd not discussed the events of that night, though she was pretty sure that the Claverleys had probably all taken a vow on the family bible never to leave her alone with Austin or any Claverley minor ever again. Not that there'd likely be another chance after she and Will finished with each other.

She let her anger feed her. Easier to make the break with a white-hot iron.

"Don't try to change the subject. Don't you get that you are risking your ability to lead the life you want by not taking care of yourself right now?"

"I don't need the lecture, Krista. I get it from my physiotherapist and the doctor."

"What does your doctor have to say?"

"Nothing yet. The tests haven't come back yet."

Krista shoved her hands into her hair. This was worse and worse. She stared out across the pasture, while he tore through his potato salad, clearly eager to get back to hatching bales.

"Did you mention the no-lifting prescription to your mother? Or the tests?"

"What does my mother have to do with this?"

"Because I can guarantee that if you had mentioned either of those things to her, she wouldn't let you anywhere near this tractor. You would probably be getting served supper in bed."

"She doesn't exactly pamper me."

"And you don't seem to pamper yourself, at all," she said.

"I am taking it easy," he said. "I already told you that."

"I closed a fence! That took effort from my shoulders. You open and close that fence and probably a dozen others, on top of swinging sledge mauls and toolboxes and saddles and what all, all day long. And you're still planning that celebrity ride!"

He started to smile, that slow, easy Claverley classic that had always made her go weak.

Even now she could feel her stomach clench, but she wasn't giving in this time.

She hopped off the tailgate and began to pace, which wasn't easy when long stalks of grass caught in her flip-flops. "Don't you dare, Will. You mistake my ranting here for someone who cares. Fine, I do care. But not the way you think. I care about your selfish disregard for your health and what it might have meant for our future together."

He stopped chewing. "'Might have meant'?"

His flat voice chilled Krista, but he needed to hear this or—more to the point—she needed to say it. "You go off and commit to something, even when you know it's not in your best interest. Worse, knowing it can damage you. And then you tell me that you want to see if we have a future together. I'll tell you what I see for a future. A life with a man who can't carry our kids in his arms."

His eyes glimmered. "So, you want kids, then?"

"When did I say otherwise?"

"About the same amount of times you said you did. And after what happened the other night—"

"Since you keep bringing up my evening with Austin, let's be honest. Yes, it was difficult taking care of him. I've never babysat a kid so small before. But I was also frustrated because I couldn't get in touch with you. You weren't doing it deliberately, I understood that, but I realized that a life with you would pretty much be a life alone."

He shook his head. "What do you mean? It's a busy time of year for me."

"And it's busy for me, too. And I'm doing it alone, which is my choice and given the nature of my business, the way it'll always be. There's no one to call upon, is there? There's no substitute Krista out there, and that's fine. I didn't name it Krista's Place for nothing."

"You think it'll be different with another guy?"

"Will, this isn't about another guy. It's about you and me."

Will tossed the salad back into the cooler. "Really? Because as big and empty as this place is, it always feels as if we're dealing with your ex."

"I would love nothing better than for him to leave me alone."

"I would love the same thing, but being with you is like hooking onto a net that drags everything with it."

"What's that supposed to mean?"

He took off his baseball cap, scratched his forehead and set his cap back down, his jerky movements conveying his irritation. "It means that everybody comes with stuff. You come with a stalker-ex and a family—"

"What's wrong with my family?"

"Nothing, except they love being on the water, and I'll probably have to go on that boat again—"

"If you are ever invited," Krista said. "How has my family become part of this?"

"Because aren't we talking about our future together, and doesn't that usually include families? Isn't that what's got you so upset—because you'd have to deal with my family?"

"How can I not?"

"Yes, it comes with the territory, but is it really that you can't deal with me? We could've had a nice, quiet meal together, you and me. And believe it or not, ever since you texted, at noon, I could hardly wait for this moment. You and me, talking about our days and making plans because hey, I'm finished this field tonight and could plan time with you."

"And exactly what would we plan to do together? Go to the beach? Take in a rodeo? Hang out with my family? Hang out with yours? I suppose I could give you a pedicure.

That went well. I could talk to you about my day, but I can't share what my customers said or even who they are, and what do you care if I can't decide which line of lotions to carry?"

He drew himself up, hands hanging loosely at his sides. "What exactly are you trying to tell me, Krista?"

"I want you to be honest with me. I want you to genuinely answer this question. Now that we've dated, do you believe you and I have a future together?"

His eyes flickered away, and in that tiny motion, she realized his answer was the same as hers. That this conversation was probably the same one that had played in his mind for a while now and accounted for his quietness around her. He sighed and raised his eyes to hers. "No. We don't."

And there it was. She was right. Time to finish what she'd started. "Then it doesn't matter if we care for each other, and I do care for you, Will, in a way that I haven't cared for anybody." She wouldn't speak of love now, that seemed cruel and pointless, to them both. "In a way that hasn't changed since I was sixteen. And maybe when I was sixteen, we were more compatible than we are now because then I didn't have a different life to give up. But now—"

She broke off. Restarted. "If either of us has to give up who we are to be with the other, then what's the point?"

Will lowered his head and she saw his hands flex. "Bridget warned me that you'd dump me." He raised his head; his eyes burned into hers. "That you'd dump me and not look back. Isn't that what you're doing, Krista? The heart wants what the heart wants, and your heart wants out."

No. She wanted a way in, but both of them knew it was impossible. "Yes," she whispered. "I want out."

"Go, then," he said. "I've got a field to finish."

As she bumped back to the yard in the truck, her insides bumped and rattled along, too. She was coming apart but she had to hold it together until she was once again in the safety of her own home. She parked the truck and hurried across to her car. Janet stood from her flower bed, Austin happily playing in the dirt. She likely wanted a report on Will's progress. Krista yanked her car into reverse. Well, he could tell her.

Oh, he could also tell her what the physio-therapist had said.

Except he wouldn't.

She slammed the car back into Park and marched across the lawn to Janet.

"I won't be showing up here anymore, which I'm sure is a big relief to you. But it might interest you to learn that your bone-head son, the older one, has decided to dis-obey his doctor and destroy his life. You can do something about it, or be like me and turn your back on all that."

Having finally said everythig she intended, Krista spun away and left.

CHAPTER FIFTEEN

WILL INTENDED TO load up on cereal, toss back his pills and take his coffee down to the barn to work with the horses. But he arrived in the ranch kitchen as his mother poured the dregs of the pot into her cup.

"I'll make another pot," she said.

But he was already tucking in a new filter. Though, given his state of mind, he might chew the ground beans straight from the bag. He switched on the coffeepot and leaned against the counter.

In his high chair by the table, Austin shoveled scrambled egg into his mouth.

"When did he start using a spoon instead of dropping it?"

"After watching his grandfather operate the front end loader, no doubt."

Will reached into the cupboard for the cereal box.

"That's Krista food," his mother said. "I'll

make you scrambled eggs, too. Hash browns are warm in the oven."

"Krista food?"

His mother got cracking. "She fed it to Austin when she was taking care of him. Pieces were stuck to his bib."

Krista wasn't his anymore, but Will felt a shot of defensiveness. "She fed him. Along with bathing him."

"I'm not complaining. Austin is not her responsibility." She was whipping the eggs into a froth. "Krista stopped by before she left last night."

If possible, the pain in his shoulder ratcheted to torture levels.

"Why didn't you tell her about what the doctor had said?" She poured the eggs into the hot pan with a great sizzle.

"It was no secret. She already knew."

"She knew you had a weak shoulder. But you deliberately hid from her how bad it was. And I bet you've hid the worst of it from your father and me, too." He couldn't meet her eyes and she grunted, whisking the crap out of the eggs.

He sighed. "Point is, I didn't want her to see how bad my shoulder might be." Will opened the oven to take out the hash browns and load them onto his plate. "It's all right for a guy to have an injury that heals, but something chronic and permanent, something that prevents him from carrying on with life, that's completely different."

His mom ladled out his scrambled eggs. "So you withheld the truth to impress a girl. And how did that work out?"

She had him. "I'm eating." He made a bee-line for the table. He flicked egg from his nephew's hair and replaced it with a kiss. "Tell me what you've got planned today, buddy."

"Whatever you two decide. I'm helping your dad with the horses. You're on Austin duty."

Austin and Will looked worriedly at each other. "When's Keith back?"

"Three, hopefully. There's roast beef in the fridge to make us sandwiches. We'll be up at noon."

"Mom, I'm not going back to the way things were," he said. "Remember? Sitting around either in a hospital or here, watching shows in the middle of the day like a senior. Except at least a senior can say they've done something in life. Don't you remember? All I could be trusted to do was hold Austin when he was sleeping, which a bed could've done just as well."

His mother dropped the frying pan into the sink with a clatter. "Face facts, Will. You're heading straight back to sitting around again, and this time, if you don't, there might not be any point to you getting out of the chair."

"I'm sure I'll find a way to stumble on," he said, "for what it's worth."

His mother drew herself up. "Are you saying this place isn't worth it?"

He wasn't sure what he was saying. He only knew that twenty-four hours ago he had plans, plans for one-on-one time with Krista, plans to tell her his intentions to buy out Keith and Laura, plans to share his dreams and see if she'd like to be part of them. To keep trying despite logic shaking its head. Now they'd been scrapped. "I guess part of my plans had to do with settling down, and I guess that's not going to happen."

"Maybe your plan should be," she said, "to come up with some fancy talking to get Krista back."

"We agreed to end it."

"You two haven't been together for two months. Even your brother's disastrous relationship lasted longer."

Maybe long enough. Krista had been an indulgence, a life experience that he normally wouldn't expose himself to. They'd not carried things far enough for there to be the complication of an unexpected pregnancy. He glanced over at Austin. Not that he would've minded. Krista wouldn't have abandoned their baby. She would be part of his life in one form or another for the rest of their lives.

He wished things had become more complicated with Krista.

"I guess we were smarter about its chances of success." Except he must've woken twenty times last night, each time the loss of Krista pounding through him like the pain through his shoulder. Right now, he wasn't sure which pain was worse. He tossed back his pills. One of those agonies he could lessen. "C'mon, I thought you'd be relieved it's over between me and Krista."

His mom poured coffee into two thermos mugs. "She's grown on me. She's been good to Laura. And she's the first girl you've gone out with who actually seems to care about your well-being as much as I do."

From rock to hard place. From Krista to shoulder. His mother was relentless. "I intend to rest over the next few days."

"You're only resting because there's a break in the field work. I can operate a baler as well as you."

"But you shouldn't have to, Mom. That's my job."

"We run a farm," she said. "It's everyone's job."

Disappointment and frustration flared up. "Four generations of Claverleys, and it all comes to an end with me. Too busted up to carry on the name."

"The name? Is that what this is all about? You ended things with Krista because of a name?" His mom pointed at herself. "Oster-huis. That's my maiden name. That's half of what you are. The best any Claverley can ever be is half of one. The other half is made by women with a different name, a different up-bringing, a different way of thinking. There hasn't been a Claverley man who hasn't had to accept those differences. You're no excep-tion. Stew on that while you change the diaper of the next generation of Claverleys."

KRISTA SCOOTED ON her wheeled stool from Mara to Bridget, pulling along her mobile pedicure station. Booked so tightly now, she was rethinking her one-on-one model. The trick was to deliver quality to both customers, so neither felt neglected and she didn't appear rushed. If she could work out the bugs with her sisters, she'd be good to go.

But relaxed sisters on their Thursday night out made for chatty sisters, and the subject tonight was once again her.

"Are you sure there's no chance of reconciliation?" Bridget said, wriggling in her chair. "There's something stabby in the back. It's not as comfortable as your first one."

"But I lucked out on the other one. Do you know how much they cost new?"

Bridget gave her a look, the same one she'd given Sofia when the girl had complained her carrot sticks were on the wrong side of her plate. "Three months ago you would've been over the moon to be so busy you needed a second chair. You got what you wanted. Stop finding problems."

Her big sister had a point. Her dream business was a roaring success, thanks in no small part to her stint as Will's fake girlfriend. But it had come at the cost of their relationship.

"You're right," Krista confessed. "I should be happy."

"But you're not," Mara said, dabbling her

toes in the warm water, "which brings us back to Bridget's question."

"Nothing has changed. It's the same answer I gave Mara the night I broke up with Will."

"Things might've changed in four days."

"They haven't, they won't. What color did you decide on, Mara?"

"White with yellow daisy decals."

Krista suspected Mara's choice was intended to lengthen their time to grill her. Bridget, too, picked a shade that would require three coats.

"Could we have a change of topic, please?"

"Sure," Bridget said, "how's the Troll?"

Her name for Phillip. He apparently had not learned that she and Will had broken up as his memes persisted. She dried her hands on a towel and showed her sisters his latest creation. Krista-doll was puckered up, waiting for Will-doll to kiss her. The quip: The longest ten seconds is not riding on a horse.

"Krista-doll also blogged a recipe on how to make cow patties," she added.

Her sisters made grossed-out faces. Bridget moaned as the rods in her chair kneaded her lower back. "How's your counter-campaign going to work now that you and Will aren't together?"

Not together. Another relationship she'd ended. She should've felt relief or satisfaction that she'd done the right thing. Except...she missed him. She missed sending him texts and waiting for his lame, short replies. She missed not making plans with him. Worse, she couldn't stop worrying about his injury. "It's not going to," she said. "I'm sure Alyssa can carry on with Will."

"People will notice," Mara mused. "Most of the comments on the Celebrity Ride page are about how cute you two are together."

"If they only knew the truth," Krista said, setting Mara's foot on her lap and applying the file.

Mara jerked. "Leave a little skin."

"Sorry." Krista cupped her hand around her sister's toes to restore the relaxed vibe she'd clearly botched. She'd better siphon away her negative energy over Will before her real clients arrived. "You've seen us together. We have nothing in common. We'd make each other miserable. Real Will would turn into Will-doll."

"Doesn't mean you two didn't enjoy being with each other," Bridget said, her words slurred from the kneading effect of the chair.

"Easy for you to say, Bridge. You and Jack

function like one person. Eat together, work together, talk together, parent together. Will and I don't have a thing in common. By the way, Phillip and I also looked good together."

Her phone sang. "Alyssa. I'll let it go to voice mail."

Then Alyssa sent a text. OMG. Call me about the Will situation.

"And it's official," Krista said, lowering Mara's feet into the bath. "Alyssa knows we've broken up. Exactly what she wanted. Should hit the social media fan soon."

"Read it," Bridget said. "What does it say?"

"I don't read texts when I'm with clients," Krista said, "and that's what we're pretending you are."

"Pretend it's an emergency text."

Krista couldn't deny her curiosity—and dread. Better to absorb Alyssa's snide commentary here and now with her sisters than with a client. I heard from Laura about you and Will. Could we work something out? Then in a new text, as if she needed a moment to compose herself: I am wondering if you two would be willing to continue the social media front until after the celebrity ride is over. Maybe by then Phillip will have backed off, too. I have not talked to Will yet about it. I want to hear from you first.

"That sounds civil," Bridget said.

"It sounds that way because she will do anything to make sure the celebrity ride happens," Krista snapped and lifted out Bridget's feet quickly, water whooshing about. Not very relaxing. *Get a grip.* "Not that I blame her. She's poured her heart into this cause. The money could save the lives of kids or at least make their days easier, so my little heartache doesn't matter. I get that. It's the way she goes about it. She said she hasn't, but I bet she already talked to Will. Knowing him, he would've said that if I agree, he'll go along with it."

"I don't get it, Krista," Bridget said. "That sounds reasonable. Why are you annoyed at him, for letting the choice be up to you?"

"Because he believes that there's no point being honest if it means someone's feelings get hurt. He's leaving me to do the dirty work. And dirty work—" she nailed Bridget with the secret anger she'd held since her breakup conversation with Will "—is apparently what I do in relationships."

She and Bridget had a stare-down that

ended with her interfering sister shrugging her shoulders. "Prove me wrong."

Which meant she and Will would have to prolong their relationship by faking it for a few more weeks. Full circle. Except… Krista squirted lotion in her hand in preparation to massage Bridget's feet. "I don't want him to do the ride. It'll ruin his shoulder, if his stupidity already hasn't. I can't stand being with someone who deliberately risks his health. And worse, he lied to me. He deliberately didn't tell me the whole truth. And he knows how I feel about honesty and liars. I can't trust him."

"Or," Mara said slowly, "he's the kind of guy not to burden others with his troubles."

"I was his girlfriend. He's on the hunt for a wife. What kind of wife wants a guy who doesn't tell her the truth?"

"Krista, you two were dating for what? Six weeks, maybe?" Bridget said. "And you guys were doing it biweekly? I'm not sure he violated some sacred trust. He has a tendency to keep his troubles to himself, is all." She nodded at Krista's hands. "Any of that meant for me?"

She'd rubbed the lotion into her hands instead of Bridget's feet. Self-massage. She normally treated her hands daily before her first appointment, a routine she'd dropped this work week. Ignoring her hands, the source of her "talent." She stretched out her fingers.

"That's the thing, I could've really helped him. These hands could've taken away some of his pain. I could've learned how to massage the area or helped him with his exercises or anything. He only let me help once, and that was because I caught him in the act of icing his shoulder. The rest of the time he tried to convert me into somebody I could never be in a million years."

"Are we the ones you should be telling this to?" Mara asked.

Krista squirted out more lotion and this time applied it to Bridget's feet. "It doesn't matter. Once his shoulder heals, what then? There's not much call for spas out on the farm. And horses, the ranch, that's his passion."

"If it heals," Mara said.

Krista froze. Her fear voiced in Mara's quiet, irrefutable tones. No. If her touch really was her gift to the world, then— *Sorry, Will. No more hands-off.*

Krista picked up her phone. "I got your message," Krista said, as soon as Alyssa picked up. "Sure, if Will agrees, I can continue with the act until after the celebrity ride. But I was wondering if we should push a new angle."

"Oh?"

"Yes, I was thinking we should play up Will's shoulder injury. Build in the human drama of him risking himself by riding with an ongoing injury."

"I'm not sure Will would like that."

"We don't have to go into all the details. Mention he's doing therapy. Maybe a picture of him and me in the physiotherapist's waiting room, or doing an exercise."

"I could ask—"

"Alyssa, it's a condition of me doing this."

She sighed. "Okay, let me know how it works out."

Krista shook her head. "Nope. You want this. You deal with the ornery celebrity." Krista hung up before Alyssa could protest.

"There. I proved you wrong, Bridget. Don't you dare smirk."

But it was no use. For the rest of the session with her sister-clients, she had to put up with their sly suggestions for other social media poses she and Will could submit to.

Seated beside Will in the waiting room, Krista opened her phone at the trill of an incoming text. "Ah good. My two o'clock confirmed she can switch to Thursday instead."

"You didn't have to come, you know." He meant it, would've preferred it. He would have said so except he was acutely aware of Alyssa sitting directly across from him. For the occasion, she'd brought a handheld camera and was recording.

She smiled up at him as if he was her whole world. "I wouldn't want to be anywhere else." A nice line—too bad Alyssa had written it.

She had written lines for him, too, but that hadn't gone well at the rodeo, so he decided to wing it here, as well. Besides, it would shake Krista out of her rut, knock some honesty out of her. "You might not want to be here, depending on what the doctor says."

The visit with the specialist was real. The X-rays and imaging results were in, and the doctor would not be faking the delivery of the results.

Krista slipped her hand over his. "We'll get through this." A borrowed line but taking his hand wasn't.

He looked down at the curl of her hold over

his, her gentle warmth seeping into him. He missed her touch on him. In the weeks they'd dated, he'd grown used to the glide of her fingers, the peppering of her quick kisses, the deliberate brush of her side against his. He'd come to crave it. She'd not done it for money or because a camera was rolling or because it was part of their arrangement, but because she'd wanted to. Now they were back to faking it.

Only now that he'd had a taste of the "real" Krista, it was hard to separate the two. Her soft voice was pitched exactly like when she'd agreed not to give up on them after Phillip had started his campaign. Will made it "impossibly hard" she'd told him. Not impossible, as it turned out. He carefully squeezed her hand before releasing it.

"Thanks, Krista. That means more than you'll ever know."

"Cut!" Alyssa said. "Great, I can work with that."

Alyssa seemed to have gotten over him quickly enough. Gotten over her trouble with Krista, too. The two of them had orchestrated this "injured-Will" angle on their own. He could've refused, except it meant he could be close to Krista. He was that pathetic. But that was Krista's pull. She made him breathe easier, took the duty out of living and made it a thing of pride and possibility. He only seemed to be a source of aggravation for her. Somebody she had to deal with for a higher cause.

The receptionist came out. "Will?"

Will stood, Krista tight beside him. His fingers twitched and then he let himself indulge. He took her hand.

"Wait!" Alyssa said, reaching for her camera. "Could you do that again?"

They reenacted his dependency on Krista, which was getting increasingly easier to do. They walked, hands entwined, down the corridor, Alyssa ahead shooting, walking backward into the consulting room.

"You aren't going to film the actual delivery of the news, are you?" Krista said.

"That's what we agreed on," Alyssa said. "Right, Will?"

He *had* agreed, but faced now with the examination table and its white stream of paper, the doctor's stark desk with its computer and the windowless, white walls, he didn't want to be here, much less have hundreds, maybe thousands view his reaction to the results.

But to back out was to show himself to be as weak as his shoulder. A coward.

Krista hadn't let go of his hand, even though this bit of drama wasn't going public. "Maybe this is a little too raw for our viewers. They could be informed of the upshot. Will can do a little update afterward. We can even have the doctor explain to the viewers what's going on."

Alyssa turned to Will. "What do you think?"

Both sets of eyes swung to him, each wanting a different answer, but it was the one beside him with the blue eyes, the one he'd slow-danced with and even now held his hand, that he spoke to. "I like Krista's idea."

The doctor knocked and entered, surprise registering at the crowded room. Alyssa moved to leave, holding the door open for Krista.

Krista hesitated, and that was enough for him. "You could stay, if you want," he said, not quite able to meet her eyes.

"If you don't mind," she said, every bit as casually as him.

"Are you willing to make a statement about Will's condition afterward?" Alyssa said to the doctor.

"Statement? I doubt it. Why would I ever do that?" He looked Alyssa up and down, his steely gaze fastening on her camera. His doctor scared Will a little. He wasn't much older than him but he carried the authority of a surgeon general. Alyssa waggled her fingers. "No worries. I'll arrange it with the front desk."

The doctor glared at the door after she left and then turned to Will. "This is my place of business, isn't it?" He frowned at Krista.

"This is Krista Montgomery," Will said. "She's—a friend."

"More than a friend," Krista said.

"We can be honest with him, I think," Will said.

"Well, then," she said and withdrew her hand from his. The empty space felt like a cold draft.

The doctor glanced between them and retreated to his file. "Right, this is where we're at."

A year of surgeries had taught Will some of the terms that the doctor let fly, but there were new ones, as well. Ones that pointed to exactly how narrow his options were becoming. He'd overdone it with the rodeo and the farm work. Krista was scraping her lip with her teeth, her face scrunched with worry. She seemed to have forgotten she didn't need to fake it.

"Are you recommending surgery?" she asked.

"I don't want to go that route yet," the doctor said. "The thing is, it'll be a wait, anyway, and there's lots that can be done that's preventative."

"Should his arm be in a sling?"

"There is that, especially while he's watching videos or around the campfire or sitting on the deck."

"And what is the maximum weight he should lift?"

"I'm right here," Will informed her.

"Good, then you shouldn't have to be reminded what to do."

"I've got a list you can get from the front desk," he said, "of dos and don'ts." He looked sharply at Will. "Now be honest, how are you managing with the pain?"

Even now, his shoulder felt on fire. "It's sore most of the time," he admitted.

Krista stood. "I'm going to leave because I've seen the X-rays and there's no way that's the truth, Will. You never seem to tell the truth when you're with me. At least be honest with your doctor."

"I double every bedtime dosage so I can sleep for a few hours," he said quickly. "So,

I'm managing it, but I could do with some different kind of help."

"That sounds about right for what the X-rays show," his doctor said and tapped his mouth with his fist.

Head bent, Will noticed Krista's toes, pink like wild roses. They were curled and as he watched, they slowly relaxed. She resumed her seat and he breathed again.

She *must* still have feelings for him, because in this room, she didn't have to fake a thing. She'd admitted she cared for him when she broke things off, but he figured she'd said that to soften the blow. Gone was her anger because he hadn't been honest about his shoulder. She could only be upset now because the doctor had nothing good to say. He opened his hand on his knee, palm upward. She sighed and laid hers on his. He quickly clamped his fingers around her hand. There, something real. The doctor was inputting Will's prescription. "Careful you take this as directed because they are strong enough to knock out a horse."

"Speaking of which," Krista said, "in your opinion, should Will in his present condition be participating in the bareback ride planned for three weeks from now?"

"I wouldn't recommend he do anything that risks further injury to his shoulder," the doctor said.

Krista looked in triumph at Will.

"Having said that," the doctor said, "I'd also have to recommend he avoid stairs because that would increase his risk of further injury, too."

"So you are suggesting that he take reasonable risks? Will, are you listening?"

He had been listening. To his doctor, to his physiotherapist, his mother, Alyssa—and Krista. Listening because they all cared about his health, and who was he to override that? He'd stayed quiet and that had caused confusion and distrust among those he loved. Time to come clean and say what he'd only come to accept in these last few days when he'd lost the one person he wanted most by his side.

"This is the thing, Krista. This ride is about more than me keeping my word, and it's more than about the kids. Both mean a lot to me, and I'd do it for either one of those reasons. But I'm doing it because it'll be my last ride. I'll never get on a bronc again. I don't want my last ride to be one where I ended up injured. Defeated. I want one more chance to do it right. I want one more chance where I can make myself proud."

Krista chewed her lip and stared down at her pink toes. He jiggled their held hands. "Because the heart wants, right?"

She flashed him an annoyed look.

His doctor handed Will the prescription. "Good luck." It wasn't the most reassuring thing for a doctor to say to his patient.

They were halfway out the door when the doctor said, "So what do I tell the camera?"

Will considered how much of his medical condition was fair game. "Hold nothing back."

"After all," Krista added, "Will isn't."

Will wanted to believe that beneath the irritation and irony, there was the tiniest thread of faith in his determination to leave the arena on his own two feet and his head high.

CHAPTER SIXTEEN

As Krista was about to close for the day, Alyssa came in. She breathed deeply and flopped onto Krista's sofa. No appointment, no invitation. She held up her phone.

"I'm taking out your ex."

It was yet another meme. The dolls sat on the fence. Krista-doll said, "I could give those kids a speed spa. That's all they need." Will-doll's thought balloon read, "About as useful as this ride of mine."

Krista handed back the phone as she took a seat beside Alyssa. It was nasty but— "Hey, Alyssa. It's just a joke. Maybe you shouldn't take it so seriously." Krista deliberately used Alyssa's exact words from their earlier blowup with Laura before her wedding. The incident that had fractured Alyssa's friendship with Laura. The two were talking again, though Laura had confided that it was only because Alyssa was respecting Krista.

Alyssa's head bobbed sideways, like a dashboard toy, absorbing Krista's poke. "I hear you," she said softly, and then her voice rose again, "but this—this is more than personal. It's about children. It's…cruel."

It was.

"I'm sure you'd love for this guy to get taken down, too," Alyssa said.

"Maybe for the sake of others, but he's now more like a rock in the shoe for me," Krista said. She had enough clients now, repeat clients who knew her for who she was. If her conflict with Phillip came up, the reaction was sympathy or a comparable story of their own.

"A rock I intend to grind into powder," Alyssa said. "What dirt do you have on him?"

Back in the winter, Krista had come up with all kinds of malicious scenarios to crush Phillip. But nothing was more satisfying than the sweet revenge of success. "I'm not sure that's the route to take. It's important that he's convinced it was his idea to stop so he can keep face."

"This ex must've been totally head over heels with you. He's obsessed." She sighed sharply. "You really are trouble. The worst kind because you don't ever mean to be."

Was Alyssa handing her a compliment?

Krista proceeded with caution. "You sound like Bridget when she had to pick me up from the principal's office after I got punched in the face from a fight I was trying to break up."

"A fight over you, remember?"

"Yeah," Krista said. "Those days are over."

Alyssa held up the screen of her phone with the dolls. "Really? They're still fighting."

"Phillip but not Will."

"Put them in the same arena and see what happens."

"Not with Will's shoulder the way it is," Krista said. "That is one fight I would definitely put an end to."

Alyssa set down her phone and turned to Krista until their knees grazed. "You really do love him, don't you?"

Krista tried to laugh it off but her breath caught in her throat and she made a strangled noise. "All those guys fighting over me at school? And the only one I really wanted was the guy who flat out rejected me." She nodded at Alyssa's look of surprise. "Yep. Will Claverley. I've been stuck on him for a long time."

"The fish that got away?"

This time Krista could laugh. "You clearly

have not seen him in water. He's more like a rock. A terrified rock."

"I heard about that. Everybody was amazed he got in there for you."

"Yeah, well, in the end, I guess he shouldn't have bothered."

Alyssa sucked in her breath, the kind that signaled she was about to blow up. "Krista, you know I was angry when you and Will got together. Here was a guy I hoped could put up with my…explosions. I'm aware that I can be—intense. I so want things to go right that I end up making a mess of them. I ruined my friendship with Laura because I wanted her wedding to be absolutely perfect." Alyssa twisted her mouth. "I blamed you for abandoning our partnership when you probably left because I was so insufferable."

Krista had no idea Alyssa had such a low opinion of herself. "Honestly, you didn't need me. You could handle the business on your own, and you've proved it."

"But it's made me a nervous, high-strung wreck. You had a way of bringing me down. I thought Will could help me chill a bit. And I wanted to make him feel good about himself again. Show him his fans, give him a pep talk when he was low. But then I started taping you two together and I realized—" Alyssa sucked in another breath "—I realized how good you two were together because you weren't perfect for each other, and neither of you seemed to care."

But they *had* cared, and that was the problem. "Appearances can deceive," Krista said quietly.

"Or," Alyssa said with equal quietness, "they can show what the people in the picture can't see for themselves."

She was wrong, but on the brink of resurrecting their friendship there was nothing to be gained by arguing the point. "Thank you, Alyssa. Is this us patching things up?"

"It's me admitting that my own worst enemy was never you." Alyssa's head shot up and she snatched up her phone. "Worst enemy! I got it. How about this? The numbers from the video of the doctor visit are high— by the way, you would not believe the stupid hoops that doctor put me through before he'd allow me to record him. He's the most infuriating, insufferable, conceited man I've ever met."

"I don't know," Krista said, "he seemed genuinely concerned about Will."

"Oh, I'm sure he has a heart—somewhere,"

Alyssa said. "Probably keeps it buried in a closet and brings it out to scare kids on Halloween. Anyway, views are up but now I'm getting comments and emails that people are worried for Will. I've even had a lawyer from one of the sponsors contact me about liability waivers should Will get reinjured on his ride."

"Are you saying that this has backfired?"

"No, but maybe we should address their concern. I was thinking that you could speak for every mom and girlfriend out there who doesn't want to see their guy hurt."

Their guy. Will wasn't her guy. But the world believed he was, and she'd agreed to play along in this game where the fake and the real had become one. "What's the plan?"

HOURS LATER, KRISTA leaned against a real fence with a real Will beside her, while Silver had her head over the railing between them.

Alyssa was a ways off, fiddling with her camera, adjusting for the evening light, which at the rate she was working would soon disappear entirely.

Silver snuffled in the direction of the pocket on Krista's hoodie. "You found me out, girl." Krista withdrew a baggie of apple slices and offered one to her, steeling herself not to flinch at Silver's giant mouth.

"You cut up an apple for her? She has teeth," Will said.

"But then she'd crunch through it, leave and then where would we be without our prop?"

"Point taken." Will tugged at the neck pad of his sling.

"That sling a prop, too?" Krista said.

"I'll have you know that I've been wearing it every time my butt's parked in a chair. You ever try eating with your opposite hand? Austin and I are quite the pair at supper."

"That I'd like to see."

"Not if I can help it."

"Somebody," Krista informed Silver as she fed her another apple slice, "is grumpy that he has to take care of himself."

"The problem is that I'm not allowed to take care of anything other than myself. I'm on lockdown. Dad saddled up my horse today. He hasn't done that since I was six. I might as well play with Austin in the sandbox."

"Quit feeling sorry for yourself," Krista snapped. "If you were a horse, you'd be shot."

Silver jerked her head. "Not you," Krista cooed. "Who would dare hurt you with those big brown eyes and long eyelashes? And your pretty, pretty hair?" Krista ran her fingers through Silver's forelock and Silver lowered her head.

"Why did she do that?" Krista said.

"Because she likes it," Will said. He sounded even more irritated.

"What I said or what I did?"

Will looked at her as if she was jerking him around. "Both."

"Finally, I can pay her back for all the trouble I caused her," she said, rubbing Silver behind the ears.

"Don't worry, we won't shoot you for it," he said.

She'd never seen Will this grumpy. Alyssa had mounted the camera now, so filming might actually start this century. Meanwhile, she'd have to deal with Will. "C'mon, I didn't mean you should be shot. All I'm saying is that a lot of people would be glad to put up their feet for a while."

"That's not the point," Will said. "If I was sure that six weeks of rest—or six months!— would solve all my health issues, I'd hate doing it but I would. It's the uncertainty. Or the realization you might have to give up on your plans and dreams, and that people bound to you will have to change theirs as well because of you. I can't stand that, and let me tell you, the second I sit that starts running through my head."

The raw pain in his voice stabbed Krista. What would she do if she couldn't operate her spa anymore? If she had to let go of the life she'd created for herself? She instinctively reached out to him, her fingertips on the coarse canvas of his sling. "You will never be useless, Will Claverley. You'll become a one-armed rancher and carry on. And everyone you love and who loves you will be right there with you."

His voice dropped a fraction. "Everyone?"

His hazel eyes latched on to hers, and she couldn't pull away. He was asking her if she loved him, and she did. Not the girl-crush infatuation but the hard kind of love. The kind of love that recognized she would do anything to keep him well and happy, even if that meant there was no place for her in his life.

"Yes," she said firmly, "everyone."

Something leaped in his eyes, something that she'd not seen since the rodeo when he'd asked if he could date her for real. When they agreed to try despite all the differences between them.

"Cut!"

They whirled to Alyssa, who was beaming. "Perfect! I got it all. This should show everybody that no matter what happens, he'll rise stronger than before. The one-armed cowboy thing was brilliant, Krista. I got a good close-up on Will's reaction. That'll connect with the kids."

Krista opened her mouth to protest that she hadn't realized the camera was rolling, that her lines were not planned, but then she caught Will's eye. The special something in his eye had vanished. A hard, wary look had crept in.

Along with Alyssa, he believed that she'd said it all for the camera. They were wrong. Loving him had never been the problem. Living with him was. But if she denied it, then he'd clutch to the futile hope that they could work things out. Better to stick to the hard kind of love. After all, she already had a reputation for walking away.

"I'm glad you liked it," she said to Alyssa. "I thought it came off pretty natural, too."

Will jerked away from the fence. "Since I'm no longer needed here, I'll be off."

He strode off, leaving Alyssa to stare between the two of them. "What did I miss?"

Krista rubbed Silver's cheek. "You caught it all."

No CANCELLATION OF the celebrity ride this time around. The skies had been wide and blue all day long. Mid-August heat plastered Will's jeans to his thighs as he waited outside a vendor truck for his fries and burgers. People had pressed themselves under beach umbrellas, overhangs or thin skirts of shade from horse trailers and viewing stands, happy to wait out the break between events with popsicles or cold beer under a tent.

The evening mutton-busting event was announced over the speakers, and people began to mosey to the arena. His ride would be up in a couple of hours. He'd already given his speech during the afternoon show to rustle up excitement. A bare-bones, Krista-less one.

She wasn't here yet. A wedding party had her booked solid into the early afternoon, a wedding he'd be at right now if not for the rescheduled celebrity ride. One his entire family would've been at too, except that his mom and dad had chosen to come to watch him ride. Laura and Ryan would go. Keith had better show up, too, because Dana would be there.

His brother still had a shot at happiness.

He remembered the glide of Krista's face away from him, the break of her blue eyes from his, her casual answer to Alyssa. *Natural*. Three weeks on and the word stuck in his throat. He'd fallen for her little speech about being there for him. But it had all been for Alyssa's camera. He'd refused to take any more video with Krista, and Alyssa had not argued the point. Maybe Krista had requested the same thing, who knows. They'd not communicated since that evening, relying on Alyssa as a go-between. Yet he still checked for messages from her half a dozen times a day, hopeless as it was. No painkillers for a broken heart.

The burger vendor called his number and Will picked up his order. Then he made his way to where his dad sat alone at a set of bleachers at the rear of the arena set up for entrants and their crew. Out in the arena, sheep and kids were lining up for the mutton-bustin' races.

"I can still feel the greasy crunch of that sheep wool in my hands," Will said, handing a loaded burger over to his dad. "And the smell. Like when Austin puked up grass."

His dad spoke through a mouthful of burger. "I remember Keith trying to convince the organizer he was four so he could race against you."

"Then when he was four, he beat me."

His dad frowned. "I don't remember that, but I s'pose he could've. He can hold the saddle every bit as good as you."

"I know, but I'd never tell him that."

About to take another bite, his dad pulled the burger back, gusted out his breath. "I don't know that I ever told him, either. I should've. Might have made him rethink his choices."

"You talking about Macey?"

His dad shrugged, his attention on the little cowboys and cowgirls in their helmets as they sidled up to their woolly mounts. "That, and the whole ranch thing. You and Keith, you're both suited to take over, but it's always gone to the oldest kid. Up to now that's always worked. Other sons had their plans to move on."

His dad seemed to be suggesting a partnership. "I don't mind ranching with him, Dad. We just don't have the same ideas, is all."

"Only way for that to work is if one of you ended up unhappy, and now with both of you in that state, it's not pretty." Around a mouthful of burger, he added, "I kind of hope he patches things up with Dana."

His father was far more observant than Will had ever supposed. "You know about them?"

"Have for years. At least, her part."

"She told you?"

"Saw it for myself. She'd lift her head like a colt whenever he came close. Those two always kept an eye on the other."

"You're smarter than me. Could've knocked me over with a toothpick when she admitted it to me. Krista figured it out and talked Dana into telling Keith about how she felt. He declined her offer."

"Know that, too. From your mother." His dad wiped his mouth. "Hard to watch your kids fall. In and out of the arena."

That was his dad's way of declaring his love. Will had to swallow a couple of times to get the chunk of burger past the lump in his throat. When he did, he said what children said more and more to their parents as they grew up, whether it was true or not. "The kid in the arena tonight will be fine, Dad. And the kid out, he has another chance tonight at the wedding."

"He's going?"

While the announcer and the clown bantered about the upcoming high-stakes sheep race, Will texted Keith to ask.

Soon as I get Austin into more than a diaper, I'm headed out the door.

Keep at it. Dana will be there. Dad wants you to finalize a Claverley-Stanziuk merger.

Great.

Have fun.

You too. Don't show off.

Will sent Keith a grinning emoji because Keith hated emojis.

"What did he say?" his dad said, neatly folding his wrapper into tiny squares he'd later deposit into a garbage can. His dad didn't like messy garbage.

"He's going," Will said.

"Good. One down."

What did he mean by that? A buzzer rang out and the first heat in the mutton race took off. Three-quarters of the kids dropped off their sheep like shook flies, but two hung on until the halfway mark and then it was down to one boy. Will could see the gritted strain on the boy's face as he held onto the side of the sheep to cross the finish line.

"He earned his pay on that one," his dad said. "You could learn a thing or two from him when it comes to Krista."

His mom had been talking to him. "Dad. We gave it a shot, but you've got to admit we're from two different worlds. We might care for each other but that doesn't help with the day-to-day." Lines straight from Krista's playbook, but true.

His dad watched as the clown passed the boy his mutton-bustin' trophy. The kid looked more interested in the coupon for free ice cream. "Caring's better than the opposite."

"It's not like it is with you and Mom. You two do everything together. And she loves the country life. Krista's—not Mom."

His dad tipped back his cowboy hat and stared at Will as if he was talking in a foreign language.

He pointed to the boy. "That was what I had to be with your mother."

It was Will's turn to stare.

"I had to hang on for all it was worth to cross the finish line with her."

His father was dead serious. "First time I asked her to come out to the ranch, she stayed seventeen minutes. That was how long it took before she was dive-bombed by a barn swallow, stepped behind a horse as it let go from the back end and tripped over a pail full of milk. She said the place was out to get her, and I was thinking that myself, to be honest. She took it as a sign."

"But you didn't."

"I did. I took it as a sign that she was the one meant for me."

"How did you figure that?"

"Claverley tradition," his dad said, as they watched all the other kids receive their trophies plus a popsicle. Every kid got a trophy regardless of performance, but every kid knew that only one got bragging rights. "Not a single Claverley right from my great-grandfather down married a so-called suitable woman. The first one married the younger sister of a duchess."

"I thought that the story was made-up. The one about how when he met her she was on a horse. With a gun. Standing over a dead bear."

"That part might have been a stretch, but she was related to a duchess. So you can imagine an Alberta ranch was a bit of reduction in lifestyle from English aristocracy."

"I knew she came from England but—" Will shook his head.

"And then my grandfather married a ballerina."

"I assumed by 'dancer' people meant country or something." So much for knowing the Claverley legacy.

"Nope, a ballerina. But it gave her a good sense of balance and she took to horse riding easy enough. Rode better than him, he said. Stood on a horse bareback."

"But Grandmom was a rancher's daughter," Will said.

"*Born* on a ranch. But remember there were nine kids and those were hard times. She was sent to live with her aunt and uncle in Calgary when she was three. Her wedding gift to the place was a piano. I remember in the summer, milking and listening to the piano drifting down the hill, my dad singing along. Those two were their own concert."

"So…how did you get Mom to like the ranch?"

"I'm not sure it was any one thing. She agreed to come out again, and the second time wasn't so bad, not that it could've been worse. And after that I made sure that I always had a plan for something we could do together when she came out."

"I tried horseback riding with Krista, and I tried being part of her life but you know how I am with water."

"All I'm saying," his dad said, "is every

last single Claverley has picked an unsuitable woman for their wife and every last time it's worked out."

"Except for Keith," Will said.

"Keith is the second born, and the second born have the guts to make their fortune off the ranch. There's a whole tradition about them choosing country girls, if you'd like to hear that."

His dad's phone pinged. "But it won't be today. Apparently your mom has finished visiting everyone with a tongue and is ready for me back up in the stands."

"You go. I'll have to gear up soon enough," Will said.

"You ready for Tosser again?"

The bronc that had busted his shoulder. Will had welcomed the opportunity to ride him one last time. "Question is if Tosser's ready for me."

His dad didn't laugh but looked to Will's right shoulder. "You have the best last ride, son."

There was caution and pride in those simple words. Will swallowed. "I will. And what you said about holding on until the finish line… I'll keep that in mind."

His dad stood, casting a line of shade

across Will. "You do that. There's never been a Claverley on this ranch that's taken the easy way out. Just remember that crossing the finish line might only require meeting her halfway."

As he moved off, a text came through. Krista. Stuck in traffic. Hope to make it in time. Don't fall.

Her first contact with him in three weeks. An unfiltered private message for his eyes only. *Don't fall.*

He wouldn't. The world could believe that he was doing it for the kids. And he was. Krista might think he was doing it for himself. And he was. But only he knew—and maybe his dad—that in the end he would hang on for Krista and their future together.

I won't, he texted back. Got too much riding on it.

CHAPTER SEVENTEEN

"COULD I BORROW this handsome young man?"

Keith looked up from where he was wiping wedding cake off Austin's mug and paws. It was Caris, Dana's sister.

"Sure," he said, "so long as Austin's okay with it."

Ever since Krista had babysat him, Austin had become choosier about his caregivers. Not that Keith blamed Krista. She'd at least been there for his son.

And Dana.

He'd spotted her at several points of the wedding, but hadn't gotten within talking distance. Partly because Austin was a handful. Partly because whenever he got close, she disappeared into the crowd. As if on purpose.

After the ceremony, Keith had brought Austin back to the ranch for what turned out to be a three-hour nap. Keith himself had slept for two of those hours, and had woken feeling like a new human being. Like someone ready for a fresh start.

Caris held out her hand to Austin. "Hey there. Would you like to come see Dana before the dance starts?"

Austin hopped off his chair, took Caris's hand and allowed her to escort him through the milling crowd of dresses and dress pants to his favorite lady. Geez, why hadn't he thought of that?

Dana stood with a loud, laughing group. Keith recognized them all. Farmers and ranchers in the district. He imagined that the conversation circulated around cattle prices and hay bale counts and how much rain they'd all gotten. He could keep up with them.

He rose at the same time that Dana caught sight of Caris approaching with Austin. Dana's smile faded and she sidled away. Austin hadn't seen her but Caris had, and she called out Dana's name. Dana kept moving, even though she must've heard.

She shouldn't be avoiding both him *and* Austin. That wasn't fair. To any of them.

He made sure Caris could stay with Austin then headed to find Dana. He waylaid her coming out of the washroom. She must've touched up her makeup because her lips were extra glossy. She had on the same short dress from Laura's wedding, a shade of bluish green or greenish blue that he'd decided was his favorite color.

"Hey," he said.

"Hey," she said and hesitated. Someone passing by bumped her from behind, causing her to take a step toward him, one he quickly matched with one of his own. She glanced at the entrance to the men's washroom. "I won't keep you. Have a nice evening."

He touched her elbow. "Could we talk?"

She frowned, a refusal already forming on her shiny lips.

"Five minutes. That's all I ask."

They ended up by her truck in the field that had been converted into a one-night parking lot. It was a pretty spot. The dance reception was at an old renovated barn on the neighbor's ranch. Dana immediately set her gaze on the horse corrals. Probably noting number and kind, like he was. "Look," he said, "I accept that things are…uncertain between us, but what you're doing to Austin isn't right, either."

Dana spun to him. "What exactly am I doing to Austin?"

"I saw you hurry away from him back

there. I get that you might want to distance yourself from us, but there's got to be another solution besides running away from him."

"Idiot," she said. "I'm not running away from him. I'm running from you."

"I'd never stop you from seeing him. For both your sakes."

"Aren't you listening? I can't have Austin without you, and since I cannot have you, then neither Austin nor I can have each other. Don't you understand how much it hurt to walk away from your boy? I love him, Keith. I love him as if he's my own."

He'd said the wrong thing, messed up again. "He loves you, too," he mumbled.

"For now," she said, "but he will find someone else. He's got the old Claverley charm."

"I think it skipped a generation," he joked by way of a small apology.

She didn't return his smile.

"You led your five minutes by telling me about Austin. You should've sold yourself, Keith Claverley. Took me in your arms, told me I was pretty, brought me a glass of wine… kissed me. Something that said I was yours and you were mine. And now your time's up. Please leave so I can calm down enough to go inside and enjoy myself again."

She crossed her arms and glared at him. Words fluttered up and he snuffed them all, fearing that it would only worsen matters. He walked away, the crunch of the gravel under his boots like the grinding in his gut.

He might as well take Austin home and they could have a quiet night. There was still enough light for them to peel off their good clothes and go outside. Or watch a movie and gorge on junk food.

The band was striking up. Guests were drifting back to their tables in preparation for the first dances. He couldn't stand another wedding, another bunch of slow-dancing couples. He found Caris easily enough, but Austin wasn't in sight. "Hey, Caris. We're going to head out. Where's Austin?"

"Oh, Laura took him. He was starting to fuss. She mentioned getting him some food."

No Laura or Austin at the food table. He was taking another survey of the room when Laura grabbed his arm. "I can't find Austin. I turned my back—and he was gone."

Keith forced down instant panic. "Where did you last see him?"

She pointed to the platter of watermelon farther down the table. "We're checking everywhere. Ryan has people looking, too."

"He's got to be around here somewhere," Keith said. "He can't have disappeared." He went over to the band and asked them to make an announcement.

Keith held his breath, praying for someone to pipe up that he was right here all along. But only a worried murmur rippled through the crowd. The bride herself was checking under her draped table which prompted all the guests to peek under theirs. Austin's name was repeated and called in the foyer, everyone sharing Keith's fear. No. Not fear, concern. No need for fear.

It was clear Austin wasn't inside the barn. The hunt spread into the parking lot, and well-dressed guests knelt and squatted to check under vehicles. Mechanical chirping arose as vehicles were opened, searched and closed with soft thuds again. "No. Nope. Nothing."

Where had Austin's two tiny legs taken him? He ran to Dana's truck. She was nowhere around, and he peeked inside and under, in case Austin might've recognized her truck. Nothing.

Stabbed with a sudden horrifying instinct, he looked to the corrals. There was Dana running flat out in bare feet to Austin who was toddling straight to the corrals. The horses were prancing and skittish, clearly not used to kids and strangers.

Keith shouted Austin's name, hoping that the sound of his voice would make his boy stop or at least slow enough for Dana to catch up. He didn't hear or didn't listen.

Keith did the only thing he could and ran after them, too. Dana reached the graveled lane that ran alongside the corrals just after Austin crossed it and picked up speed at the sight of the pacing horses. She didn't stop even as she crossed the hard pebbles. As Austin began to squirm through the railings, she scooped him up.

Keith stopped, dropped his shaking hands to his knees. He prayed his thanks, even though he didn't attend church. But he recognized a miracle when he saw one. He spotted Dana's high heels where she must've flung them and he picked them up. Behind him there were whoops and clapping. He waved and the guests drifted back to the hall.

When he reached Dana and Austin, she was still holding him tightly, their faces tucked into each other's necks. He stood close and let them be. There was nothing to be said.

Austin lifted his face. "Dad." He patted Dana's shoulder. "My Dana."

Dana looked up at Keith, full of joy and anguish. He brought his hand to his son's back and carefully, carefully his other hand to Dana's neck. Her gaze didn't waver, flared with hope. His thumb stroked her cheek, and she leaned into the caress.

"Don't let me talk, Dana," he whispered. "I'll screw it up and I kinda want this moment to last forever."

Her arms still tight around their Austin, Dana touched her lips to his and made it last.

KRISTA SQUEEZED HER car between two pickups at the far end of the overflow parking lot at the rodeo. Will had organized a VIP parking spot for her closer to the action, but she wasn't sure how to get there and right now she was all about speed. Will's ride was scheduled to start in six minutes and counting.

She texted him, for what it was worth. Alyssa or one of the handlers probably had his phone, as he would already be down by the chutes. She texted Alyssa, too, and her one-answer reply was Hurry.

As if she wasn't. As if she hadn't been all day.

She'd packed a sweet outfit for the inevitable after-event pictures, but there was no time to grab it. She shoved her phone into the back pocket of her denim shorts and ran. At least her running shoes were suitable.

She gained the stands at the opposite end of the chutes as the usual rodeo princesses carrying flags galloped past and exited. Krista scanned the crowd for Alyssa or Will's parents, but it was hopeless among the few thousand gathered. Her eye caught a screen with a slideshow featuring Will. His picture and name, a quote from him about how every kid deserved to get up after they fall, and his ride where he'd been bucked off.

Krista had not seen the ride before. She stood, riveted to the screen. The horse bucking madly, Will leaning to the outrider for the dismount, the twist, and then Will flying through the air to land crumpled on the ground. And the riderless horse not stopping, kicking at Will. Krista's heart pounded as if it was real, as if she didn't know that Will would survive and be around for her to touch and hold.

This was the paralyzing fear that Janet had experienced. A fear borne from love. But a fear that had corroded Krista's love for him. She'd spent their brief relationship worried sick for him. And it wouldn't end until he finished this ride. Maybe then she could get beyond her fear, and find something else, something more that rose above their differences.

If he lived through this ride.

A girl with a Ride for the Kids button waved a pack of tickets. "Get your tickets. Win gift cards, saddles. Grand prize is a purebred mare from the Claverley Stables. One for ten. Two for fifteen." Krista shook her head. She'd already donated the man she loved to this ride.

The rodeo announcer came on. "And now the moment we've all been waiting for—"

And dreading.

"Will Claverley's Ride for the Kids. If you haven't bought your ticket, you have a few minutes left. Tickets must be purchased prior to the end of the ride, and folks, the ride only lasts ten seconds."

The girl was swarmed, as the announcer began to detail Will's rodeo history. He'd been disqualified from his first ride in the junior rodeo because he'd lied about his age, inflating it by a year in order to meet the minimum requirement.

Everyone laughed while Krista seethed. It was a miracle he hadn't been injured sooner. Was he going to catch up on his quota of injuries on this last ride? Break a leg, bust ribs, snap his spine.

Because that could happen. Drawn like a slasher movie fan to scenes of horror, she looked again at the screen to see the horse lash out at Will crumpled in the dirt. The same horse that Alyssa had arranged for him to ride tonight.

The rodeo announcer's voice continued. "Will agreed to have this video run, even though for some it's tough to watch. He wanted everyone and especially the kids to see that we all fall and each of us can find a way to get back in the saddle."

"Or not," Krista muttered. "You could stay out of the saddle and live another day, you arrogant twit."

Two buckle bunnies shot her dirty looks and moved closer to the chutes. Through the railings, she could make out Will in his trademark blue checkered shirt and the horse. That horse.

Alyssa had nearly squealed with excitement when the same bronc was booked for Will. And the announcer played it up. "Will is taking on his old rival, Tosser. And let me tell you, Tosser's attitude hasn't sweetened over time."

As if on cue, the horse banged inside the enclosure, and the gate shuddered.

"Please step away from the railing." A burly security officer spoke to Krista and she released her grip on the fence. Just as well, she'd seen enough.

She closed her eyes and pictured Will easing himself into the saddle. It would only be seconds now. The handlers leaned over to do a final check.

All eyes were on Will now. Waiting for his nod.

Krista felt more than heard the gate release. Her eyes flew open.

The horse came out, all four feet lifting off. Will made it worse, raking the horse's sides with blunted spurs, and Tosser whipped and twisted. Will rode the swings, head all the way back against the horse's haunches. Tosser broke into a series of fast donkey kicks.

"Please, please, please," Krista begged Tosser, Will, time itself.

The buzzer blared and Will had stuck the ride. The horse didn't seem to care. He kept right on bucking and the outriders crowded close to loosen the girth strap on Tosser and for Will to transfer over.

It was in that transfer that things went

wrong. Tosser rammed against the outrider's horse and it stumbled sideways. Will fell, the hooves of two horses all about him.

Krista didn't remember climbing the fence. She would've cleared it, except that the same security officer grabbed her ankle. But she had the momentum and tumbled into the arena.

She slammed to the ground, winded. She couldn't move. She saw a second outrider cutting Tosser away from Will, both horses on a dead gallop for her. The outrider's horse started to brake, hooves high, but Tosser's wild eyes latched on to hers—

Krista held up her hands in a desperate effort to save herself.

FOR FIVE NIGHTS NOW, Will had woken from the nightmare of Tosser charging at Krista, a replay of a cold hard fact.

The bronc had earned his owners a good living from his dedication to nailing anyone who came into contact with him, and that had been exactly his intention at the sight of Krista lying in his way. But because Krista had raised her hands, his front hoof had barely clipped the palm of her right hand. X-rays showed two broken metacarpals. She would have a full recovery.

Now almost a week later, he hoped their relationship would have one, too. He considered it a small victory that Krista had agreed to come out to the ranch for a family barbecue. Every last single Claverley in attendance glided over the fact he and Krista were technically no longer a couple. Perhaps they were too distracted, Krista included, by how Dana and Keith very much were.

He bumped shoulders with his tomboy best friend when they were alone in the kitchen. "Good job getting little brother to see the light of day."

"I heard that," Keith said, rounding the corner. "Remember I crossed home plate before you, big brother."

Well, tonight, he'd try to hit this one out of the park. He slipped away to the barn to start the process. When he returned, everyone had spread away from the outdoor dining table to the deck chairs.

"There you are," his mother said on the swing set with his dad. Everyone was paired up: Laura and Ryan, Dana and Keith, his parents. Krista was wedged in with Austin on one of the same chairs he'd hauled to the gazebo for her speed spa.

"Let me cut his hair," Krista said, combing Austin's curls with the fingers of her good hand.

"You've only got the use of one hand," Dana pointed out.

"I'll have it back in a month. How about then?"

Dana bit her lip. Keith put a hand on her knee. "I'm sorry, Krista. But we can't rush into this."

Dana managed to both scowl and smile at Keith's teasing.

"I've got some hair you can play with," Will said and stopped. "Okay, I heard that as soon as it came out. I'd like to show you something, Krista."

Krista dropped a kiss on Austin's curls. "I better go before Will jams his foot any farther into his mouth."

Once clear of the house, Will took Krista's uninjured left hand and guided her to the barns. She stopped, her running shoes skidding to a brake on the grass. "You promised me I wouldn't have to ride. Right in the emergency waiting room, you promised."

"And you won't," he said. "Not tonight, not ever if you don't want to. But I think you'll enjoy this."

"You're not going off riding either, are you?"

"Not tonight, but I've been riding since the rodeo, yeah."

"I meant in another rodeo."

"Those days are over. Officially retired."

"No matter if Alyssa—or anybody for that matter—comes to you with another request for a charity ride?"

"Yes, we're done. After seeing you in that rodeo arena, I know the taste of heart-in-mouth. I won't put either of us through the wringer again."

Her blue eyes shone, and he slid his arm around her waist, pulled her close, leaned in for—

Her phone chimed and she gave it a peek. "Phillip."

Trust the jerk to cut into his evening alone with Krista.

"I'll deal with him some other time," she said.

Another time Will might not be around to help her through it. He released his hold on her waist. "Take it."

Krista tapped her phone. "Hey, Phillip. You're on speaker, so Will can hear you, too."

"Hey," he said, and added, "okay."

Krista said nothing, and Will didn't care to make it easy for the guy who'd spent the last couple of months interfering in their lives. Phillip cleared his throat. "I was calling to say that I saw the video of you down at the rodeo."

Who hadn't? Alyssa's camera had been rolling. It showed his confused expression as he'd quickly rebounded to his feet after the fall and wondered why the crowd wasn't applauding. Then he'd seen Krista, flat on the ground, and Tosser charging. He didn't remember running but the video proved it. It had tracked his run across the arena, him kneeling at her side, calling her name, while Tosser was finally herded through the gate.

The camera didn't catch her answer but he'd remember it until the day he died. She'd blinked up at him, her face twisted in pain, and said, "Are you okay?"

He'd managed a choked "Yeah" before the paramedics swept in. The video had gone viral—a quarter million views in five days and still curving upward. Some comments had whole lines of heart emojis. And diamond rings. And requests for a follow-up wedding video.

"In our earlier conversation," Phillip continued, "I said it would be me who'd decide when you and I were finished."

What an arrogant piece of—

"I remember that," Krista said, shooting Will a cautionary look.

"Well, after watching that video, I'm saying it's over now."

As if it wasn't already. Will fought the urge to rip the phone from Krista and lay into him. Krista seemed to sense his intent and angled the phone away. "By 'over,' do you mean you're going to stop with the dolls and any other trolling?"

"Have you seen anything since the rodeo?"

"I haven't, but that doesn't quite answer my question."

"It's over."

"Good to hear." She paused. "You take care, Phillip."

"Yeah, you too. Hey, Will. You still there?"

He'd always be with Krista. "Yep."

"Just wanted to say...don't let her take any long-distance trips without you."

Krista had risked a charging horse to get to him. "She can travel to the moon. She'll always come back to me."

After disconnecting the call, Krista poked

his chest. "You think you got me all figured out."

For the next part of their evening, he hoped so. He brought her around to the side of the barn where he'd put cross ties on Silver. Krista's hand jerked in his.

"If there's no riding, why do I see a mounting block beside her?"

"Because it has all kinds of uses." He handed her a currycomb. "Like for brushing her back."

Krista tapped the hard bristles with the fingers of her casted hand. "You want me to brush down Silver?"

"Mom rode her hard today and she only got a roll in the pasture afterward. So, yeah. A horse deserves a brush down after their rides."

"Every time?"

"Before the saddle goes on, for sure. To check for burrs or cuts or bite marks. After you ride the horse, it's also good practice."

Krista regarded Silver. She picked off a fleck on the horse's withers. "All right, what do I do?"

He took up another currycomb for Silver's other side and gave her pointers as they worked together. Not that he really had to.

Krista had the touch. Silver's muscles relaxed; her neck lost its archness; her head went down. She made a rumbly snort. As close as a horse ever comes to purring.

The mare had never done that for him. And rarely for Janet.

Krista traced the fingers of her broken hand along Silver's spine. The horse quivered in response. "I could do this all day. This is totally therapeutic. For me."

Should he push it? "If you're up to it, there's another part to the grooming."

He crossed behind Silver to come up beside Krista. "Do you want to try giving Silver a pedicure?"

Krista's eyes widened.

"You don't have to if you don't want to," he said. "I get that. But I'm also sure that Silver doesn't have an aggressive bone in her body. And even if she did, you have melted them all."

She smiled. Touched his jaw with the fingers that had just run along Silver. He nearly let go with a quiver himself.

"You know I always wanted to meet you halfway on ranch life," Krista said softly. "I'd given up but this…this I could do. No. This I *want* to do. You and me, being together like we are now, talking, working together. I could really, really get into this. So yeah, let's do this."

He demonstrated the "pedicure" on Silver's back left hoof, carving out the dirt from her shoe, pointing out the tender triangle to avoid.

Krista positioned herself at the second hoof and gave Silver the command Will had taught her. Silver's hoof came up easily and Krista caught it in her good hand and tucked it between her knees. Seconds later, the hoof was on the ground once more, clean.

Will grinned, ready to finish up. She straightened. "Next," she whispered. She did the last two as easily as the first. He passed her a rubbing cloth to wipe her hands with, and when she returned it, he slipped his arms loosely around her waist. No more putting it off. "You know," he said softly as if speaking to an edgy horse, "a good groomer is pretty important to have around a horse. If you have the right touch with a horse, she's yours."

Krista lifted off his hat, and ran her fingers through his hair. She might as well have caressed him from head to toe for the sensation that crackled through him. "That only apply to horses?"

"You know the answer to that." He kissed

her, long and slow, her body molding against his. Yep, he, too, might have some talent for softening up a person. The only one he cared to, anyway.

"I don't care if you never touch a horse again, or if you don't want to bring me another supper in the field. You can spend all your days at your spa, doing what you do best. As long as at the end of the day, you're with me. I love you," he whispered. "And I intend to marry you."

"I love you, too, but—" she pursed her lips and gave him the same mischievous look from the day he'd first walked into her spa "—I'm dealing with my fear of horses. What about yours and water?"

"If you marry me, I'll leave it in your hands."

"Deal." And she closed it in a way that had him near to purring.

EPILOGUE

"THAT GIRL WAS born under a lucky star to get this kind of weather in October," Janet whispered to Dave as they took their place in the first row of seats at the Spirit Lake pier.

"And to marry Will to boot," Dave said.

His wife sighed sharply. "All three in one year!"

"At least Keith and Dana saved you the trouble of a wedding." Keith had called them up one Saturday morning last month to say that he and Dana were having a few friends and family over to her place and would they like to come?

He and Janet had arrived to a surprise wedding. There on the porch with everyone in sweaters or jeans, Keith and Dana were married before a justice of the peace. And it was back to combining the next day.

Today, Dana had taken a seat at the far end, so she could scram with Austin in case he acted up. She was talking quietly with Alyssa and Caris seated behind her. Across the aisle, Krista's family was lined up. Deidre leaned forward and waved. Janet waved in response.

"She's probably happy that if she couldn't be a Claverley," Janet said through her smile, "at least her daughter will be."

Dave turned in surprise to his wife. She rolled her eyes. "As if I didn't know she'd come on to you."

He scrolled back through their thirty-six years together to the courtship. "So that's why you suddenly stopped putting me off?"

"I wasn't putting you off. I was seriously considering you, and I couldn't get over how entirely unsuitable she was. She was always flitting off."

"I dunno," Dave said, suppressing a smile. "You know about Claverleys and unsuitable women."

"Yes, but if you were to have an unsuitable woman, I decided it was going to be me."

He took her hand. "I've never regretted your decision."

The look she returned might've landed him a kiss, except that their eldest son, in the company of Keith, Brock and Laura's Ryan, filed in. Beside him, Janet gave a tiny gasp. The same gasp as when she pored over the photo album after a couple glasses of wine. He didn't mind her getting emotional. It kept the attention off him when he had to swallow hard.

Then, the bridal party and the guests rose as one. There was no music, only the slap of water and the occasional cry of seagulls. Laura and Krista's sisters came down first and then Krista herself on the arm of Jack, her cousin.

She was a bright, lively thing, all right. Just what Will needed. She waggled her fingers at him and Janet, and Dave grinned. "It'll be good to have her around more often now," he said to Janet.

"She'll be able to practice her auntie skills on Austin," she whispered back.

"There'll be time for that."

"The next is coming in seven or so months."

Wha…? He stared at his little daughter. Soon a mother. "All this because you kicked over a bucket of milk."

Janet patted his arm. "Shush."

THE WEDDING CEREMONY went along much like all the others Dana had attended this summer, including her own. She and Keith had aimed for spontaneity, simplicity…and speed. He and Austin had taken up residence that night in her home, and she'd woken the next morning married and a mother.

She tightened her arms around the soft sturdiness of her son. Her son. Austin gave a huffed squeak, and Keith slid them a questioning look. As Will and Krista were pronounced married, their eyes met, and she mouthed what for years she'd denied herself: *I love you*. He smiled and blushed, like a bride.

Like a typical bride, anyway. Not like Krista. She and Will were stripping.

Dana turned to Janet and Dave, who seemed as confused as her. Guests laughed, hooted. Camera phones came out like umbrellas in a downpour.

Krista's dress fell away to reveal a tiny one-piece swimsuit at the same time that Will, already in bare feet, shimmied out of his pants. He wore a pair of black swimming shorts. Together, they turned away from the audience.

The black lettering on Krista's backside and the white lettering stenciled on Will's shorts read Just Married.

KRISTA AND WILL, holding hands, walked to the edge of the pier. "You are fine," Krista whispered, "with not wearing a life jacket?"

"I'm good. We've practiced. Besides, my wife's within arm's length."

"Ready?" Krista whispered, hardly believing that the man, the life she'd always wanted was hers from this day forward.

Will peeked down into the dark, cold waters. He'd surface. With Krista beside him, he always would. "I am."

And together, hand in hand, they took the plunge.

* * * * *

Get 4 FREE REWARDS!

We'll send you 2 FREE Books plus 2 FREE Mystery Gifts.

Love Inspired Suspense books showcase how courage and optimism unite in stories of faith and love in the face of danger.

FREE Value Over **$20**

HARLEQUIN SELECTS COLLECTION

19 FREE BOOKS IN ALL!

From Robyn Carr to RaeAnne Thayne to Linda Lael Miller and Sherryl Woods we promise (actually, GUARANTEE!) each author in the Harlequin Selects collection has seen their name on the *New York Times* or *USA TODAY* bestseller lists!

#379 CAUGHT BY THE COWBOY DAD
The Mountain Monroes • by Melinda Curtis

Holden Monroe and Bea Carlisle are hoping a road trip will give them time alone for a second chance—but it's a special Old West town they happen upon that helps them rediscover their spark!

#380 THE TEXAN'S SECRET SON
Truly Texas • by Kit Hawthorne

Single mom Nina Walker is shocked to see Marcos Ramirez again. Especially since her ex-husband has no idea he's a father to a son! Will the Texas rancher forgive her and finally claim his family?

#381 A FOURTH OF JULY PROPOSAL
Cupid's Crossing • by Kim Findlay

Former bad boy Ryker Slade came home to sell his father's house, then he'll leave. Instead he finds a connection with the pastor's daughter, Rachel Lowther. But Rachel also plans to leave town—unless Ryker gives her a reason to stay...

#382 THE MAN FROM MONTANA
Hearts of Big Sky • by Julianna Morris

Tessa Alderman has questions about her twin sister's death in a white water rafting accident, at the same time she's drawn to the man who may have the answers...Clay Carson.